The Banks of the
RIVER THILLAI

The Banks of the River Thillai

Published by The Conrad Press Ltd. in the United Kingdom 2021

Tel: +44(0)1227 472 874
www.theconradpress.com
info@theconradpress.com

ISBN 978-1-914913-17-4

Copyright © Rajes Bala, 2021

The moral right of Rajes Bala to be identified as author of this work has been asserted in accordance with the Copyright, Designs and Patents Act 1988.

All rights reserved.

Printed and bound in Great Britain by Clays Ltd, Elcograf S.p.A

Typesetting and Cover Design by The Book Typesetters
www.thebooktypesetters.com

The Conrad Press logo was designed by Maria Priestley.

The Banks of the
RIVER THILLAI

Rajes Bala

Characters

Gowri, Saratha, Buvana: three cousins

Nadesan:	Gowri's father, Mailar's brother
Kasipathy (Kasi):	Buvana and Poorani's father, Indira's husband
Mailupody (Mailar):	Saratha and Sangars's father, Sathiya's husband
Sathya:	Saratha and Sangar's mother
Ragu:	Saratha and Sangar's brother.
Poorani:	Buvana's sister
Shiva:	Saratha's beloved
Indira:	Buvana's mother
Grandma:	mother of Kasi and Gowri's mother
Palipody:	Grandma's brother
Theivi:	Palipody's wife
Ramanathan:	teacher
Parames:	Ramanathan's wife
Nathan:	Ramanathan's brother
Kamala:	a distant cousin, Ragu's beloved
Rajah:	Gowri's suitor
Nagayam:	Rajah's father

Acknowledgements

I would like to thank (the late) Mr. S. Balasubramaniam, Professor S. Sivasegaram and Mr. M. Naminathan, who gave support and encouragement during the writing of this novel. I would also like to thank Professor K. Siritharan and lawyer Mr. D. Rengan for publishing my novel in Tamil. My thanks to (the late) Mr. V. Varathakumar for helping to translate it from Tamil. I thank my dear friends, Ms. Savithri Hensman (first editing) and my grateful thanks to Ms. Susie Helme for the final editing. I thank my dear friend Ms. Stephnie d'Orey for her support. My special thanks to my boys, Nirmalan, Arunan and Seran who are the rocks who stand firm with me in my life with so much support and gave me the inspiration to continue my writing.

This novel is dedicated to my dear people of Kolavil, who enabled me to think differently, to break free from tradition and from the past.

My sincere thanks to the London Arts Council for providing a grant to translate my novel.

My thanks to Mr Siraj Mashoor, (Akkaraippattu) for allowing me to use two of his photos for the front cover.

Chapter 1

DECEMBER 1957

owri felt restless when she heard happy voices and noises coming from her uncle's house. She wished she could go over and join in their merriment, but she had to finish her housework first. Almost all the women in the family circle were already there. Some were working, others were not, but all sounded full of joy because her cousin – Mailupody's eldest daughter – had reached puberty that day.

Mailupody, the elder brother of Gowri's father Nadesan, had a naturally powerful voice, accustomed to commanding others. It was a mark of how special the occasion was to him that his voice was a little louder than usual.

It seemed as though he was trying to tell the whole world the good news, as well as bossing everyone in the house around. 'No wonder he's happy,' Gowri thought. Saratha, according to tradition, had become a woman.

Gowri had woken up in the morning to the whooping, repeated thrice, through which the women were signalling the happy event to the village. The message was, 'Listen, all of you, our daughter Saratha is no longer a little girl'. The news had created a jolly atmosphere. To a Hindu family like theirs, a young girl reaching puberty was a special occasion, to be celebrated with friends and relations. Uncle Mailar (as Mailupody was usually known) had already planned that his daughter's womanhood would be celebrated more magnificently than that of anyone else in the village, since he was the village head.

Mailupody owned more land than anyone else in the village. He was always looking for a chance to display his wealth and status. How could he throw away this opportunity? 'Today, Auntie Sathya will be very happy, too,' Gowri thought. Uncle Mailar's wife Sathya was a beautiful woman from another village. She always did what her husband told her. Her uncle and aunt had always been proud of Saratha's elegance and beauty. She was the best-looking girl in the village.

There were five stages in the life of a woman, Gowri had learnt from her Grandma. The first stage is infancy, lasting only until the age of five. Her cousin Saratha had now left the second stage, girlhood, behind.

Gowri's parents had left for the paddy field very early that morning, before Saratha's news was announced. Her grandmother had gone to Uncle Mailar's house at once. She had not yet returned. Almost all the housework was left to Gowri, and she had plenty to do. Grinding chillies, husking rice, chopping firewood – all had to be finished before she could join the celebration at her cousin's house.

The sky had been dull since dawn; there had been no sunshine. It was December. The monsoon was approaching.

When Gowri looked upwards, she could tell from the way the clouds moved that the rains were coming soon. Sometimes they would continue for days. River Thillai would break its barriers and start to flow towards the village, causing damage. Mud huts would be destroyed, paddy fields swamped with mud.

She could see the river from her house. It seemed swollen. Debris from the hills and jungle, tea estates and distant villages floated past. Flowers of many colours, branches from trees lay stranded on the banks. Any day now, the river could break from its course, flood the fields and cut off communication with neighbouring villages. This frightened the villagers, most of whom had only a few days' food stored.

Grandma hated the heavy rains. She would often talk about how the Gal Oya dam, the biggest in Ceylon, according to her, would overflow and destroy the villages around it. 'These modern men are trying to hold everything in check by building barriers and dams, but when Nature's on the rampage nothing can stop it. What will happen when the heavy rains come and the river flows over the top of the dam or it falls down?' She would answer her own questions; she might be confused about many things but not about that.

'Hey, Gowri, have you husked the rice yet?' Grandma called from Saratha's house. Gowri hurried to finish the work. She placed the sack on the earthen floor, to prevent the grains from getting mixed up with the sand, and pounded the rice.

Because there was no sun to dry the rice, it was moist; breaking the husks off the grains seemed almost impossible. If Gowri did not husk the rice thoroughly, she would have to listen to one of her grandmother's complaints. Grandma would keep up a never-ending flow of words; even in her sleep she would mumble about something.

Gowri stopped pounding for a while when she saw her cousin Ragu, Saratha's brother, and some other young men approaching along the narrow lane. Perhaps they were looking for a healthy, young areca nut tree to cut a branch for

Saratha's ceremony.

Gowri turned when she heard the cackle of an old man next to her. It was Grandma's brother Palipody, who had only a few stained teeth left and numerous wrinkles on his face. His laughter sounded like empty tins being rattled by a child. She knew that he might crack a joke. The old man was outrageous. After a few cups of pungent liquor bought from the town or brewed in illicit stills, he would tell vulgar jokes. If anyone tried to reprove him, he would become even cruder.

The old man sat on the broken trunk of a coconut tree, laughing for no apparent reason. His *verti*, a large rectangle of cloth wrapped several times around his waist, was bunched up; he wore nothing underneath to conceal his private parts. Ragu arrived with his friends.

'Hey, what are you all doing?' old Palipody asked one of the young men who arrived with Ragu. 'Trying to pluck some good unspoiled branches for your girlfriends, eh?' The young men did not reply, but stopped near the well, where sturdy areca nut trees grew plentifully.

Some of the youths gazed in dismay at the slippery bark, wet from the rain which had fallen the previous day. If they had been from the caste whose task it was to tend palms, they would have had little difficulty in clambering up nimbly. But who could ascend with speed and grace?

The old man began to sing:

People can hear the happy song,
ringing out from far away,
for a man's been waiting for a girl
who's become a woman today.

12

The young men laughed.

One of them, Rajah, tucked the cotton kilt-like *lungi* about his thighs. He began to climb the tree to cut off a branch laden with areca-nuts for today's ceremony. It was the tradition that it was a girl's future husband who fetched the branch that would be placed over the brass water-pot as a good omen in her house on the day she reached puberty; her family had usually selected her prospective bridegroom before she became an adolescent. Gowri remembered that, every time someone had teased the local girls about their future partners, Rajah's name had been linked with her own.

'Wait and see, Saratha, I'll tell you who cut off the branch for you today,' Gowri promised herself silently.

Another of Gowri's cousins, Buvana, had reached puberty the previous month. She had been the butt of jokes by Saratha and others, who had hinted broadly that Ragu was connected with Buvana in villagers' gossip.

Gowri was almost old as Saratha and Buvana. Soon she, too, would have her first period. What would happen to her then?

According to local custom, young women were not allowed to go to school after they reach their puberty. A few, who were progressive and had money, stayed at the boarding school in the town to continue their studies. But Gowri's family, though forward-thinking, was not prosperous enough to send their adolescent daughter to this school.

She had dreamed of growing up to be like her teacher, Punitha, but their family clung to the old ways, especially Grandma, who was against education for girls. Saratha, Gowri and Buvana were her granddaughters. Last month she had stopped Buvana from going to school. Now she would tell Uncle Mailar to stop Saratha from going. Then what would happen to Gowri?

The prospect of a future without education, without any chance of emulating Punitha, saddened Gowri. Her misery, and the fine red dust which flew from the chillies she was grinding, made her cough and cry.

If her dreams had to stop when she reached puberty, she would rather not become a woman. She became a little annoyed at Saratha's timing. Why could she not have waited until the first term of the new year to start her periods? It would have been more difficult for Grandma to stop them then. It was now December. Gowri felt as if her cousin had let her down.

Gowri poured the chilli powder from the wooden mortar. The voices and sounds near the well told her that the young men were not succeeding in getting the branch they wanted. When she raised her head, she saw the local clothes-washer, *dhobi* Nagan, taking bright silk sarees from his pile of clean clothes to festoon the house where the happy event was taking place.

She reminded herself that she had to hurry. Firewood had to be chopped before she went to Uncle Mailar's house. 'Be careful with the rice, don't break it into pieces!' Grandma yelled.

Gowri could see Grandma was approaching and smiling at Palipody.

'Well, now we've only got to wait for Gowri's big day,' the old man said to his sister. 'Then, all three of your granddaughters will have to stay safe indoors until you find some young men for them to get hitched up with.' He made his usual tin-like noise as he giggled.

'What are you laughing at? What's so funny?' Gowri did not hide her distaste for his remarks. He would grin for no reason, laugh at anything. She could not remember the last time she saw him sober. Somehow, he would find something to drink to keep him happy. *Arrack* was distilled from the fermented milk of the coconuts which grew abundantly nearby. Perhaps Uncle Mailar had given Palipody some and it had gone to his head, so that he could not keep his nearly toothless mouth shut.

'What is the matter with you?' Grandma demanded. 'Why are you so cross? All he said is that girls have to stay at home when they become women.'

Gowri wished she did not have to listen to or look at them. She stated firmly, 'We are going to carry on going to school.' Grandma and her brother Palipody laughed loudly, derisively. Underneath that dull, drizzling sky the loud laughter seemed out of place.

Gowri knew that Grandma had no respect for women who studied or went out to work. The world in which she had grown up had been strict and limited. None of her friends had sought fulfilment beyond their own fences after they reached puberty. Young women of her generation had to wait until they were married for the freedom to venture out of their homes. This was the tradition which she had been brought up to accept unquestioningly, and which Grandma had imposed on Buvana when she reached puberty.

Now, Grandma was concerned with seeking the advice of astrologers on the girls' future and their prospective

15

husbands. How could she understand Gowri's ambition of going to college and aspiring to a different kind of life? No wonder she guffawed!

The old man and Grandma resumed their conversation, but it was interrupted by the noisy banter of the young men. Gowri noticed their cousin Shiva was among them, his face flushed. She knew the reason but could tell nobody. However, it was not easy to keep a secret in the village. How long would it be, she wondered, before people noticed Shiva's bicycle passing back and forth along the lane near Saratha's house with no obvious purpose?

Almost all the parents in the village were worried to distraction about finding 'proper' husbands for their daughters; reputable young men from respectable family backgrounds who had good jobs. Who had time to be bothered about young women's education?

'You are cleaning that rice carefully, aren't you, Gowri?' She looked up. Shiva stood by her, a bright smile on his face. His handsome looks would go well with Saratha's beauty. Although he lived a few lanes away, he studied in Batticaloa town, returning to the village only at weekends and holidays. She felt too awkward to look at him or talk to him.

'Hey, you!' Old Palipody gripped Shiva's shirt and told him, 'It's up to you to cut the branch for your cousin's ceremony. You're the right one to marry her.'

The young man was dragged towards the tree by the old man and other young men. Shiva gazed up at the towering trunk, and around it at the onlookers watching expectantly. 'Oh, no, it's too slippery,' he said, clearly reluctant to make the attempt.

The old man laughed, then changed his expression to one of severity. 'Look here, my lad,' he barked, 'this is our tradition, if you want to marry the girl, it has to be you who provides the branch of areca-nuts for the ceremony.'

'Well...' Shiva mused, but did not finish his sentence.

'Young man,' Palipody said, 'if you aren't capable of doing your duty, then strangers may start coming from outside our village to take our women away.' The others laughed at Shiva.

Suddenly, he tucked up his *lungi* and began to climb. It was funny to watch though Gowri pretended not to notice. Ragu joined in the crowd's merriment at the efforts of Shiva, who kept struggling up and then slipping down. 'Think about the young woman who is going to be happy to hear that you cut the branch for the ceremony,' the old man advised; 'then you will have the strength to do it.' Maybe he was right. Shiva reached the top and lopped off a fresh, healthy branch. Pleased, Grandma took it, congratulating Shiva on his courage in climbing the slippery areca palm.

Chapter 2

The sky was so dark that it seemed as if the rains were about to start at any moment. Gowri wanted to run over to Saratha's house to see her. She could not imagine her cousin staying indoors from that day onwards. The three girls were similar in age; Saratha was about nine months older than Gowri and about six months older than Buvana. They had been constant companions; the village lanes, banks of the River Thillai and paddy fields had been their playground.

Their village, Kolavil, was one of the most beautiful villages in the Batticaloa region on the east coast of Ceylon. The village was situated about thirty miles from the provincial capital Batticaloa. Much of the nation's food was grown in these fertile rice fields, irrigated by numerous streams and rivers. Kolavil was flanked by the River Thillai which flowed from the hilly up-country, through varying landscapes and past several villages, then embracing Kolavil before emptying itself into the Bay of Bengal.

The village was small and upheld traditional values to an extreme. Some beliefs had probably changed little since settlers reportedly arrived in the East from the Kalinga region of north-west India about 259 BC, even before Buddhism came to Ceylon. Emperor Asoka was reputed to have sent them to Ceylon as political exiles after winning a battle with the king of Kalinga. People from Kolavil had certain religious rituals unlike those of any other Tamil areas in Ceylon. Some involved witchcraft and black magic.

All were Hindus and worshipped many gods and goddesses, and would perform rituals all year around to placate them so that the villagers would be blessed with health and the necessities of life. They did not understand the industrial world outside. Heavy machinery, electricity, cars, and the cinema were unfamiliar. Many were uneducated. Some were prosperous, enough to send their children away to study in the towns and cities. But most were content to produce plenty of children to help them in the paddy fields. Although the village social structure was matriarchal, education was rarely thought about or discussed; and that of girls was not regarded as a suitable topic for conversation. Girls were destined to get married, have children and help their husbands on the land.

In many ways the three cousins were not exceptional. They had enjoyed village life thoroughly. As young girls they played in the fields, swum in the rivers, wandered through woods and danced around the trees and ponds as the cinema stars did in Tamil films.

There was no cinema in the village, but sometimes in summer a mobile film projection unit would arrive at nearby Akkaraipattu town, and the girls would go with Uncle Mailar or Ragu. It was a big treat.

Gowri liked this cousin of hers, Ragu, the one expected to become Buvana's bridegroom, very much. In the village, the children of two brothers or two sisters were seen as cousin sisters or brothers. The children of a sister and brother were allowed to marry but not the children of two sisters or two brothers.

Gowri's father Nadesan and Ragu's father Uncle Mailar

were brothers so, for Gowri, Ragu was a cousin brother, and she adored him. They had so much in common. They enjoyed reading books, as Gowri's father had a big library with thousands of books brought from India. Ragu, five years older than Gowri, was at college in Batticaloa town. When he came home for the holidays, she enjoyed talking to him about a variety of things which she read in newspapers or magazines. He would also bring books and magazines, and would sometimes take the girls to the cinema, usually to religious films, as Grandma would not allow them to go to other sorts.

Sometimes he had taken them to watch films about monsters, ghosts and demons. When the girls were small, these seemed very real to them and they had nightmares for weeks. Grandma would be cross with Ragu for taking the girls to watch inappropriate films. The kids in Kolavil were brought up to believe in the efficacy of witchcraft, demons and supernatural power, so, for them, such films could be overwhelming.

Gowri had many sleepless nights after visits to the cinema. But nothing would bother Saratha. She wasn't afraid of ghosts and demons. And anyway, she preferred romantic films which she would watch attentively, copying the style of the actresses in talking (seductively), walking (sexily), singing (fairly well), and dancing (beautifully). She had large brown eyes, delicate lips and an elegant figure. She was aware of her beauty and how to make use of it, and would speak in sweet tones to please Grandma if this helped her to get what she wanted.

Saratha would imitate the glamorous heroine of the latest

romance she had watched. She would take a silk saree belonging to Auntie Indira, Buvana's mother, wrap it around her and dance. Gowri and Buvana would be persuaded to accompany the leading actress in her singing and dancing.

The girls would perform among the ponds and bushes near their homes. Sometimes Grandma would arrive in search of them. Then the plot would take a new turn. The old woman hated the cinema and often complained that the actors and actresses were corrupting young minds. She vigorously loathed provocative songs and dances. In fact, what appeared in films was far from explicit, but she would always talk as if they contained the most shocking scenes. She did not approve of adolescent girls going out at all, particularly to the woods, as she believed the girls would be attacked by malevolent spirits. She would encourage them to go to temples and demand that they do *poojas* (praying, showing reverence) at home. They were not generally allowed out alone except to go to school, and were accompanied by their parents even to temples and hospital.

At the thought of having to leave school, Gowri felt thoroughly dejected. She wished that she were like Vasantha, who lived a few lanes away, or Gowri's cousin Kamala – born to parents whose daughters were allowed to carry on with their studies in Batticaloa town.

Grandma would never accept the idea. But what about her aunt, Saratha's mother? Would she view the matter differently? After all, she did not come from this village but from Thirukovil, where women could study and go to work.

When Auntie was a young girl, Uncle Mailar had seen her at the Thirukovil temple and immediately fallen in love with her. Within a few weeks he had asked his parents to go and propose marriage on his behalf. Less than a month later he married her and brought her home. The whole village went to see the beautiful bride from Thirukovil. Aunty Sathya was still beautiful, and Saratha bore a closer resemblance to her than to Uncle Mailar.

Saratha's physical beauty was not accompanied with any great mental ability. She was a mediocre student, not particularly interested in any subject, and she did not like her teachers unless they complimented her on her lovely outfits and expensive jewellery. She had a sharp tongue, and would speak cuttingly to people whom she disliked. But anyone on whom she turned her charm found it hard to resist. She tended to be drawn to those she could manipulate. She could persuade Gowri and Buvana to do anything she wished, such as pinching Auntie Indira's best sarees for their games.

She would be their leader in rebellious forays to the old man's mango tree to steal fruit, and in daubing chicks with watercolours so that the mother hen would go frantic with confusion at the sight of her young ones in multi-colour. Sometimes she would borrow her brother's trousers and shirts to dress cats and dogs. The poor animals would grunt and moan at the difficulty of walking in human costumes.

Saratha did not like Grandma's strictness or old Palipody's jokes, and she would tell them so to their faces. Grandma often complained that it was because Saratha's mother came from another village that her daughter did not respect local customs, traditions and beliefs.

Uncle Mailar was proud of her wit and beauty, but her lack of studiousness occasionally made him unhappy.

'If my daughter is clever, I'll send her to Colombo to learn to become a doctor,' he would sometimes say. But Saratha was not interested in studying. To her, school was a place where she could show off her new dresses and talk about cinema stars and the latest fashions.

Would she stay indoors from now on? Gowri could not bring herself to imagine the free bird caged forever. She wondered what Auntie Sathya would say. Sometimes she would make remarks such as, 'Why should she have to go to school? When she becomes a woman, there'll be no shortages of princes who'll grab at the chance of marrying her.'

'Indeed,' Gowri mused silently. 'Does Auntie Sathya know that Prince Shiva is taking an interest in her little princess?'

Unless someone made a firm decision to back the girls up in their wish to stay at school, Gowri decided, they would have little chance. What about Ragu? Would he support his sister Saratha in going to school? He always encouraged Gowri to study. He would lavish praise on her whenever he heard of the academic progress she was making.

If Gowri could have a chat with Ragu, he might persuade his parents to let Saratha to stay on. Then Buvana would definitely follow suit. Getting Uncle Kasipathy and Auntie Indira to agree would not be very hard. They had a reputation in the village as innovators. For instance, Auntie Indira had bought a Singer sewing machine to make dresses, and Uncle Kasi was trying to buy a tractor.

The major obstacle was Grandma. Gowri did not expect to be able to persuade her to understand about women and education. Grandma was a very tall woman of over seventy, though nobody would have been able to guess that she was that old. Her stature and imposing appearance won respect from others. She was like the skilfully-crafted mahogany wardrobe at Gowri's home.

Grandma's eyes were large and piercing, although her vision was now impaired. She walked with the steady rhythm of a well-trained soldier. She would speak clearly and forcefully, illustrating what she said with myths and folk tales. She would ask questions, then answer them in the same breath. She did not like it when girls went out or argued with their elders, and had always nagged her granddaughters to stick to traditional values.

Gowri stashed her firewood away from the drizzle, trying to put the thought of Grandma from her mind.

Taking the damp part of her saree, which was covering her hair from the drizzle, from her head, Grandma looked at Gowri. 'What is the matter?' she inquired.

Gowri did not want to argue. There was no point in expecting to have a reasonable conversation. It was like anticipating that one could be understood by a block of wood or shape a slab of a stone with one's bare hands.

'Why do you have such a long face?' Grandma approached her granddaughter.

Gowri looked up at her. The weather was dull, the sun could not be seen, but Grandma could see the girl's eyes sparkling with confidence. The old woman suddenly saw herself in her granddaughter, strong and determined. She knew of Gowri's ambition to be a teacher.

'Listen, my dear granddaughter,' Grandma began, just as the rain began to make spots on the sandy soil, 'We women shouldn't expect too much out of life. We're here to stay at home, learn to cook, have children and serve the family. It's no good talking about going school and all that business. I never stepped outside the fence when I was your age. All this loose talk is unwomanly and will bring nothing but disgrace to the family.'

Gowri tried to light the fire, but most of the wood was too damp to use, and there was more smoke than heat. She derived some satisfaction from her Grandma's fit of coughing due to the smoke. Her figure was blurred in the haze.

'I can't get used to the way young women nowadays go against their upbringing and think they can do anything they like,' she stated through the smoke. Gowri ignored Grandma's comments, but she would not stop talking. 'When a girl reaches puberty,' she continued, 'the one and only thing for her to do is to get married and have children. That's the beauty of womanhood.' Gowri had heard this many times, so she continued to pay no attention.

The rain became heavier. Chickens and dogs scurried to shelter from the downpour. Palipody stumbled along drunkenly, still singing in the rain.

'Does he think he's a poet or something?' Gowri asked herself. He was Grandma's brother, and both were enthusiastic singers of folk-songs and reciters of poems, of which they had a plentiful store in their memories. When Gowri thought about it, she did not know how to argue with her Grandma at all. Ragu and her father were quite different: they were usually willing to listen to both sides of a case.

'Hey, girl, the water's boiling! Clean some rice and get on with the cooking.' The old woman's orders came through the smoke, like the voice of demon from the darkness. 'It' s not just the water, Grandma, my mind is boiling with anger and frustration, too,' Gowri thought, but said nothing. 'Good Lord, what would I do if I had to stay home all day? Learn how to sew from Auntie Indira and how to cook from Saratha's mother, or carry on having verbal battles with Grandma?'

She could not come to terms with having to abandon that dream of being like her teacher, Punitha. Gowri's thoughts flashed back over the past few years and, while she was washing the rice, she wandered mentally along the paths where her memory took her. Joy filled her when she remembered Punitha Teacher. Gowri daydreamed of the day when the new teacher had arrived, and of the opening of the village school.

Chapter 3

For many years there had been an old style single-sex school in the village, at which Grandma often spoke. There, young men had been taught by the local 'wise man' about Hindu myths, herbal medicine and a little about casting spells, benign and malevolent.

Grandma was a very good storyteller. She would recount a wide variety of tales. Most were from the epics *Mahabharatha* and *Ramayana* or were about ghosts, demons, monsters, prehistoric creatures and flying magic horses which would take a handsome prince to the beautiful woman he loved. Then she would tell stories about their village, ancestors and various superstitions. Some were terrifying.

Her grandchildren would sit on her knees, her lap and all around her in the evenings or in the bright moonlight. She would prop herself against one of the mango or palm trees, and the shadows sometimes seemed to illustrate the horror stories.

Now and then she would tell of the white men who had come on horses, robbed the temple of its jewels and destroyed it. The stories of these men who had done so much harm in the past to her village made Grandma cry at times.

She would occasionally speak of the first world war, but her clearest memories were of the second, which had ended only fourteen years before. The village was only a mile away from the Bay of Bengal, and the children saw large ships every day. She would recall how similar ships had been sunk by the

Japanese during the war. There had been an 'underwater ship', she said, which had been bombed by a 'flying ship'. Most of the white men aboard had died, but a few had been saved by the villagers. Items of furniture from the wreck could still be seen in the village, evidence that this event had really occurred. Uncle Mailar's house had an iron bed taken from this bombed ship.

After the bloody war, according to her, the white men had gone home and given freedom to Ceylon, leaving the Ceylonese to manage their own affairs. She would happily describe the first election after independence. She said that people from the capital city, Colombo, had come in large cars to ask the villagers to vote for them. In return, the villagers had demanded that the candidates from affluent urban areas should build them a new school.

At that time boys who could afford to have a bicycle or could afford the bus fare would go to school in Akkarippattu town, while those who were prosperous enough to pay boarding fees would send their children to one of the big colleges in faraway cities and towns. The ones who were most affected by the lack of a village school were the girls who wished to study but who could not, since there was nowhere nearby for them to go, and their parents did not have the means to educate them privately.

Auntie Indira was the only woman in the village who had reached O-level standard, as she had lived in Trincomalee, and left there during the war after marrying Kasi from Kolavil. When she talked about the value of education, she would be met by Grandma's sharp-tongued criticism.

Uncle Kasi was quite different from most of the other men

in the village. After Ceylon gained independence from the British, he had started a campaign to build a village school, which he won by continually arguing with the authorities in Batticaloa, who were mainly from the Jaffna region in the north of Ceylon. At the time of the campaign, Uncle Kasipathy was a prominent member of the Kolavil community who went to Colombo to meet the appropriate ministers and civil servants. The second world war and getting independence made some villagers think differently and seek the betterment of their village.

Gowri's father Nadesan had been in India during the mid-1930s and taken part in the Gandhian non-violent resistance when he was in his early twenties. He had come back full of new ideas for a new nation and allied with Uncle Kasi in bringing change to the village.

Despite Mailar's disapproval, he had sold most of the land he inherited to go to India. To his brother's further annoyance, Nadesan returned with nothing but portraits of Gandhi, Nehru and other prominent leaders of Indian Congress Party, and a simple costume made from home-spun cotton cloth.

In the early 1950s Gowri's father and Uncle Kasi had set up the first library in the village. For the first time in their lives, the villagers had begun to find out about the outside world – including the Chinese revolution, socialist Russia and, of course, the coronation of Queen Elizabeth the second – by reading daily newspapers.

Uncle Mailar had felt threatened by all these changes. His power and position were being eroded by newcomers. who were becoming important figures in the local community. As the English saying goes, 'If you can't beat them, join them.' So Mailar had decided to join his brother and Kasi in organising the building of a new school.

After a long struggle, it had opened. Dignitaries had come all the way from Colombo for the opening ceremony. The villagers had spent days preparing food and decorations. Bushes and turfs of grass had been cleared away, most of the houses and huts whitewashed. Money had been collected so that a feast could be given to the ministers and others. Three large goats had been purchased from Muslim traders from Akkaraippattu town, vegetables and bananas brought by bullock cart all the way from Thirukovil and Pothuvil.

The women had gathered together and prepared the food with jolly songs and poems, as they were accustomed to do on festive occasions. The men had decorated the entrance of the village and put up a big 'Welcome' sign.

Children had been given new clothes and imitation jewellery. Gowri, Saratha and Buvana had each been given a fine Indian silk skirt by Uncle Mailar. It was made from beautiful material which, according to Auntie Sathya, had come from a faraway place in India called Kanchipram near Madras.

Saratha characteristically had wiggled her bottom in appreciation of the fine texture of the fabric. Buvana and Gowri were proud to have skirts of pure silk. Wearing them, they danced joyfully around the orange, mango, lemon and coconut trees in the moonlight, out of Grandma's sight.

As the head man and the richest and most eminent person in the village, Uncle Mailar had been appointed to the chair of the welcome committee. He was clad in a white silk *verti* boarded with gold thread and a silk white shirt – the national costume – and an elaborately decorated turban, which Nagan, the *dhobi* who washed his clothes, helped him to put on. His long hair and his moustache oiled by the family barber, he had made a lot of noise to ensure that no one forgot his importance.

When the day of the ceremony arrived, the villagers stood in a line along the sandy road, which had been cleaned time and time again during the night to remove any trace of the dung of wandering cattle. Mailar, a large jewel encased in gold on his ear and a costly chain around his neck, greeted the minister with a garland; white jasmine flowers had been plucked from nearly every garden to make this.

He had been excited to welcome the VIPs. It had been an excellent opportunity to show off his wealth and status.

He would often confide in his *dhobi* Nagan, when he was under the influence of potent *rodi,* a type of *arrack* distilled illicitly in the village, that he was sad when the white people left Ceylon. 'How on earth are the natives going to manage the administration of this country?' he would lament. 'Up to now the Sinhalese and Tamils have got along okay. Just wait and see what will happen.'

Gowri's father Nadesan, who had little in common with his brother, would retort, 'Whatever problems we're going to face, those are our business. Why should we let the white men control us? Would you let your household be run by someone else?'

Kasi would always take an opposite point of view to that of Mailar, whom he described as an arse-licker.

Mailar took great trouble to win the favour of officials who arrived in the village, especially doctors, who were mainly from Jaffna. He was not empty-handed when he came to pay his respects. To ensure that he would receive good treatment from the doctors, he would hire a bullock cart or porters to bring them presents. These would comprise sacks of rice, fruit and vegetables, as well as honey and money.

After independence, some people refused to give 'presents' to officials. 'We're free now,' they would say. 'We are entitled to free medical treatment. Why should we pay for what's ours by right?' But Uncle Mailar continued to pay bribes. His 'corruption' led to numerous arguments with Uncle Kasi and Dad, but Uncle Mailar would not change his ways. He was the *podi* (landlord) of the village, after all.

In the land reform after independence, poor villagers had each received three acres of land to produce the crops they wanted. Uncle Mailar suddenly had to face up to the challenge of competing with several petty landlords.

He particularly hated a distant relative of his – Rajah's father, Nayagam – who bought small plots of land from villagers who could not make use of them without basic economic support. Nevertheless, Uncle Mailar continued to behave regally in the village. He had bought new clothes for everyone for the school opening and given generously to the cost of the feast for VIPs. He had spent lots of money to hire musicians from other villages to play on the occasion and asked the Tamil teachers to teach the children songs of welcome.

Gowri's older cousin had sung beautifully for the VIPs, while adult women had offered them a traditional welcome. The visitors, mostly from Colombo, had never before seen a village like Kolavil. They could hardly believe that a way of life scarcely different from that of the eighteenth century could still exist in Ceylon.

They had eaten spicy goat curry and rice well mixed with fried vegetables, drunk bottle after bottle of *arrack* and became thoroughly sozzled before the speech. After cutting the ribbon, the principal VIP started to speak about the importance of school and education. He was so drunk that the poor villagers could make little sense of what he was trying to convey, but they gathered he was explaining how the school would bring progress to the village. Parents should encourage young men and women to go to school and study, he had said.

Grandma had not liked this at all. 'Men and women together?' She had made faces at the drunken VIP. 'We do not bring up our girls to be loose women,' she had commented, but her voice had not carried as far as the ears of the important visitors.

Soon afterwards, classes had started at the school, but only for children up to the eighth standard. Everyone who wished to study further had to travel to the nearest town. Nobody had yet bothered to challenge the authorities to provide secondary education, since those who wanted it used what resources they had to acquire it. But Gowri, Buvana and Saratha could not dream of travelling outside the village because of Grandma's opposition.

A few girls, distantly related to Gowri, had gone to a Christian girls' school in Batticaloa town. 'Whatever happens in the world, I will never allow my granddaughters to go to a Catholic school,' Grandma had vowed.

She did not like Christians, she would say. But this had nothing to do with any religious ideology. There was a church, St Mary's, in the nearby town. It was run by an American priest, who tried to convert villagers to Christianity by offering small favours like places for their children in the town school or help in getting jobs in government departments.

Father Thomas wore a long white gown with trousers inside and a lengthy chain with a golden cross. He ate bread, drank wine and used toilet paper. Grandma could hardly believe that anyone could live in such a manner. 'Cleaning his bottom with paper!' she would exclaim incredulously. 'Why can't he use water from the well like other people? And drinking wine! How could a holy man do such a thing?' In her limited knowledge, holy men were close to God and so should observe the highest standards of conduct, including total abstinence from alcohol.

Father Thomas could not convert a single person from Kolavil. As he travelled past on his way to the jungle, where he would try to persuade the nomadic forest-dwellers to adopt the Christian faith, Grandma would talk with disgust about his work. 'Why can't those white men leave us alone?' she would grumble. 'We don't go to their country drinking *rodi* and make people change their religion.'

The priest tried to break through the caste system, another thing which Grandma did not like. 'They don't treat us as equals, why should they tell us what to do with our beliefs?' she would shout.

Though it was only two miles away, she would not allow her granddaughters to go to school in the town. Young men would hang around the shops making fun of girls on their way there. Some local boys went to the school, but walking there every day was an ordeal. In the rainy season they practically had to swim, due to flooding by the River Thillai. In summer, the sun would heat the tarry surface of the road, which would become scorching hot. Grandma would not let her precious granddaughters suffer like that.

Chapter 4

'**W**ell,' Gowri reflected, 'it is not really fair to blame Grandma for the way of life in this stupid village. How many parents are truly keen on their children's education? Most take their children out of school to help them in the fields.'

Sometimes there would only be a handful of pupils in the classrooms. The teachers would gossip or chew betel leaves and areca palm nuts most of the time when the pupils were away in the fields, especially during the harvest season, when hardly any children would stay in school. Gowri remembered the old headmaster, female teacher and *pundhithar* (a pundit learned in literary Tamil) who had staffed the school when it was opened.

Gowri could not remember the female teacher's name, but her face was unforgettable. She was old and had many protruding teeth, which made her speech difficult to understand. She often appeared ill and would sometimes give lessons to the pupils in a very careless manner. One day she stopped coming. Gowri never found out whether she had retired or been asked to leave.

If the headmaster was expecting a visit from the inspector of schools, he would tell the Tamil teacher to go and catch the pupils who were not at school, who could normally be found in the fields or play areas of the villages or at the top of a very tall trees. The teacher would roam the village gripping a large cane, his mouth full of areca palm nuts and betel leaves. He always wore an immaculate white *verti* pulled up to his thighs, so that he could walk fast. The village was full of big and small ponds and old trees. Some trees were many centuries old; their branches spread over nearly an acre. The banyan trees had many holes in which rabbits and other little animals would hide. Sometimes small children would hide from the Tamil teacher, too.

He usually went to the children's houses first to find out why they were not at school. His research would not always produce useful knowledge. He could find hardly any of the students at home. Their parents would provide all kind of excuses to explain their loved one's absence.

The Tamil teacher, whose name was Sinnathamby, would then take himself to the overgrown fields and ponds, as well as wooded glades. When he poked his cane into the holes in trees, rabbits and squirrels would scurry out in a rage. Sometimes he would angrily call youngsters who had climbed up to the high branches. Instead of coming down, they might urinate or defecate to demonstrate that they definitely did not intend to study. He would stand, soaked with urine, cursing them in highly grammatical Tamil.

He would take off his worn-out slippers to wade into ponds just in case children were hiding there; hollow stalks could be used to breathe by those below the surface of the water. Often, he would be bitten by a water snake or some other creature he had disturbed.

When he went to the houses, he would face not only hostile parents but also wandering dogs, which hated men in bright costumes with a cane in their hands. The dogs would bark and chase him, an expression of vigour on their faces.

Sometimes they would seize his white *verti* in their teeth, leaving him half naked.

When he could not stand the dogs any longer, he would inform the municipal environmental health department about the vicious strays in Kolavil. Council workers would arrive in a large van to round up the strays. But the dogs, which had plenty of experience in evading the authorities, would disappear in no time. Occasionally, the council workers would catch household pets, which were sometimes named after politicians or film stars.

One day the village had rioted against the environmental health workers after they had captured a dog called Sivaji, a shopkeeper's watchdog, which was named after a famous Tamil actor. The Tamil teacher was blamed for the incident and verbally abused by many villagers for capturing Sivaji.

Once he had captured a notorious truant, Sankaran, at a fish pond. The teacher had brought him away and given him a bath to wash off the mud. But within a few hours the boy had escaped from school, and his mother, Parvathi, stormed up to the school to demand an explanation for the ill treatment her son had received.

She had arrived at the school gate and called the Tamil teacher over for a 'chat'. He had not dared to come out and face her but had watched through a gap in the window and listened to her language, which would never have been awarded a certificate of merit.

In a voice which could be heard for miles, Parvathi had queried the right of teachers to cause chaos in such a peaceful and tranquil Kolavil village and force children to go to school. She had talked not just with her mouth, her facial expression had changed rapidly, her hands making all kinds of gestures, as she scolded the teachers. As usual her saree did not fully cover her huge breasts, which shook in rhythm with her words. To the Tamil teacher, she was as fearsome as the Goddess Kali.

Whenever Parvathi came to the gate of the school, a sizeable audience would gather for the free show. The teacher would often say that he would resign rather than stay to be abused by Parvathi, bitten by mad dogs and water snakes, soaked by urine from naughty boys and, most of all, waste his time in the village lanes. But as far as Gowri could remember, he had been slow to leave. He had staged a few old-fashioned plays of a high quality, winning a good reputation for the school.

After he had left, new teachers had come. One of these was Punitha. The three girls were taken aback; they had not known that such a beautiful woman could exist. They knew little of what lay outside the village. For the most part their world was Kolavil, only a mile long and a mile wide and with just five hundred inhabitants, situated amid green paddy fields and surrounded by the River Thillai to the east and south, the town of Akkaraippattu to the north and ponds and more fields to the west.

The girls had been to the market at Akkaraippattu, the famous Murugan temple at Thirukovil and the nearby hospital when they were ill. They had looked the new teacher up and down, expressions of naivety on their faces, and asked her, 'Where did you come from?'

She replied, with a beautiful smile, 'I am from Kallady.'

'Kallady?' the three had chorused in unison. It was a

suburb of Batticaloa town. They had heard of the mythical fish there which came from the sea at the full moon, of the sandy beach, miles long with plenty of cashew trees and of the bridge, one of the most famous in Ceylon. The girls always wanted to go to Batticaloa and to see numerous sights, including a train – they had never seen one of these in their lives.

The teacher had told them all about the town, the beach, the singing mermaid, the Kallady bridge and of course the railway station. She also promised that, if they ever had the chance to attend a regional cultural festival at Batticaloa, she would take them there. Punitha had taught them a beautiful dance to perform at a cultural event. Until then they had only been able to imitate film stars in secret, dancing among the bushes, around the ponds and trees.

The girls enjoyed learning to dance properly from Punitha. When the pupils staged a programme for the parents, the three had won congratulations from the villagers. The audience had been incredulous that such talent could exist among the girls and boys of the village.

Grandma had worried that the girls would fall ill because envious people might cast the 'evil eye' on them. She had asked her brother Palipody to perform rituals for the girls to protect them from evil. He had been no more sober than usual as he mumbled sacred *mantras*, spreading holy ash over the girls' eyelids and the rest of their faces. After that, they had gone around with a headache for days. Dad had made caustic remarks about the old man's 'mumbo-jumbo'.

The girls would never stop hanging around their favourite teacher, Punitha. When they were alone, they would imitate

40

her. Saratha would put on one of Auntie Indira's sarees to try to look like her.

The teacher wore bright, beautiful sarees. She walked elegantly, and her smile was reminiscent of the soft golden sunlight at dawn. Her figure was like that of one of the statues the girls saw in Indian magazines. They would discuss her, comparing her with the film stars they had watched in the mobile cinema. Saratha could walk and talk like Punitha, and with her cousins would pretend to teach; mango, banana and papaya trees were their pupils. Then the girls would laugh at their own act.

'When we grow up, we'll wear sarees the way Punitha Teacher does,' they would promise each other. Their imitation of Punitha was not wholly convincing; their youthful figures lacked busts. Sometimes they would stuff mangos, small young coconuts or large lemons up their blouses, lifting up their chests to keep their make-believe breasts in place, and walk softly to find out what it looked and felt like. Then they would fall on the sand and laugh uproariously at their invention, or receive a thrashing from their Grandma's broomstick if she caught them pretending that they had breasts.

Grandma hated woman who wore bras. The only woman in the village at that time who wore one was Punitha. Grandma was frightened to see the girls imitating the teacher, whom she regarded as brazen. 'Women shouldn't wear clothes which provoke men and turn their thoughts away from what's wise and proper,' the old woman would comment. But what she said about Punitha in no way lessened the girls' adoration of their teacher.

During the holidays they had been impatient to see her again. But one day they received a shock. The news had arrived that Punitha could not come any longer.

They had asked the headmaster why, but his reply was evasive. Who would tell them why?

There was one person who knew all the latest gossip about the village; Sundaram, a fellow-pupil of theirs, who was full of information about every subject. They had asked him about Punitha's sudden disappearance. His teeth were so rotten and badly stained that it was hard to believe he chewed any food with them. He had smiled at the girls. None of the girls liked his smile or his decaying teeth but they had been eager to know what had happened to their favourite teacher. He said that she had been sexually harassed by the inspector of schools. She protested at his behaviour. As a result, she had been transferred to another place.

Sexually harassed? None of the girls had any knowledge of sex, let alone understood the concept of harassment. All they knew about relationships between men and women was what they had seen in Tamil films, in which fully-clad lovers would sing and chase each other around lakes, pools, trees and bushes. The cousins asked him for more details.

Sundaram had promised to get more information and come back to them. The girls bribed him for further information with juicy sweet mangos and some savoury snacks.

Gowri had tried to figure out what all this was about. Saratha had overheard, from gossip between her mother and her friends in her house, that the inspector had 'behaved badly' towards Punitha. Behaved badly towards to a woman!

Gowri had recalled an incident at school a few years before when she had learnt what 'behaving badly' meant.

Most of the students used an open field for a toilet, as not many in the village had a proper lavatory. The poor people would go near a river bank or behind the bushes to relieve themselves. During the rainy season the water supply would get mixed with sewage due to flooding. Then children would get bad stomach upsets because of the threadworms which thrived in these conditions.

To treat those infected, the sanitary inspector would arrive, accompanied by a medical team equipped with 'listening wires' (stethoscopes), with plenty of colourful portraits of threadworms, tapeworms and all kind of other worms which caused trouble due to lack of hygiene.

One day the school had a visit from the health team with posters of worms, a listening wire and Antipar – a medicine to eliminate the enemy in their stomachs. The team gave medicine to the children and waited for them to produce samples of excrement and urine to be analysed, to find out which species of worms were present.

In some cases, the health workers would have to examine children's stomachs to ascertain the shapes and sizes of the worms in order to establish their patterns of growth. Apparently one of the team 'behaved badly' towards one of the girls by turning his attention from her worm-filled stomach and fondling her small breast.

The news had spread throughout the village within an hour. The child's father and some of the other villagers had reacted by turning up with sickles to attack the medical staff who had so shamefully treated an innocent ten-year-old who

43

had come to them to be treated for threadworm. That incident had made Gowri very angry with men who 'behaved badly' with girls.

The three girls had talked of what the schools inspector might have done, filling in the details with their colourful imaginations. They had decided to attack the inspector if he ever revisited the village school. The girls had asked Sundaram, with his rotten teeth and odd smile, to help them to do something to the inspector.

'Do what?' the boy asked, still grinning.

'Do what?' Saratha had become very angry with him. 'You must throw stones at that bad man who has kept Punitha Teacher away from us, that's what.'

Sundaram had stopped smiling. 'Throw stones to injure the inspector?' he had queried.

'Yes!' the girls had chorused, Saratha the most loudly.

'Well...' He had been highly reluctant to participate in the planned ambush.

Saratha had been cross with the boy for his cowardice. She had told him how he could hide in the overgrown bushes around the temple of Ganesh.

There were many stories connected with that temple. The overgrown bushes were abundant, not like the wild plants and trees which sprang up on the fertile soil near the river; they had been brought by Hindu villagers from other areas. They were special plants with mystical powers.

There was a terrifying myth that a seven-headed snake lived in one of the trees at the temple; it had the power to bite and kill people who were violent and vicious. Sundaram told the girls that he refused to hide among the bushes; he did not relish the prospect of encountering a seven-headed cobra in the course of fulfilling his classmates' ambush plan.

Saratha had been deeply discontented at the lack of action against the inspector. She had told her cousins that she might take the broom that was used to clean the school and hit him if he ever returned. But when he had come back to carry out an inspection as usual, nothing of the kind had happened. Her voice had stuck in her throat when he had asked her to repeat her nine and ten times tables.

Although Saratha appeared impenetrably dense in the classroom, in social and family activities Gowri and Buvana admired her enthusiasm and lively interest. She had a talent for picking up information from old women who had nothing to do but gossip in the afternoon in the shade of the jak tree, while they played traditional games with sea-shells or picked nits out of one another's hair.

Saratha would arrive with water, betel leaves or areca nuts for the grown-ups during their non-stop gossip sessions. She would come back and report the details to the other two in interesting ways. The snippets she had picked up from the adults would be retold tastefully, rather as a naked figure becomes a beautiful woman when it is adorned with a silk saree.

Gowri and Buvana treated Saratha as the leader of their gang, though they would never admit this to her. No matter what problem they were facing – whether it was to do with Grandma, school or their great-uncle Palipody reciting vulgar poems to them – it was she who worked out how to deal with it. Now she had reached puberty, she would stop being active outside her house. Who, Gowri wondered, would support her in her plan to continue her education?

Chapter 5

Still washing the rice, Gowri's thoughts were interrupted when she heard Uncle Mailar's raucous laughter. Old Palipody will be happy for another few days, she mused silently. Thunder roared and lightning flashed in the sky; the wind howled.

Gowri saw Ragu heading towards to the well to have a wash. 'Gowri, aren't you going to join the others in our house?' He smiled at her with brotherly love.

'Well...' She hesitated.

'What's the matter?' He tilted the pail to draw water.

'What's the point of going there? Grandma and old Palipody will talk about nothing but how to fix up the girl with a husband.'

'So?' He did not know why she was so upset. After all, it was hardly an unfamiliar subject in the house. Palipody and Grandma could spend hours talking about nothing but the matrimonial prospects of her granddaughters and grandsons.

Ragu was a handsome young man with a peaceful and kind expression. He often smiled. He was the opposite of his sister Saratha. She was an extrovert, whereas he was more reserved and introverted. Whenever he came home during the holidays, he would spend more time at Gowri's house than his own. He glanced his cousin questioningly.

She sat in front of the charcoal cooker watching the simmering rice and their dog Amuthavalli. The name for the dog was given by the Tamil teacher, Sinnathamby. *Amutha valli* was a term for a sweet nature and beautiful woman, and the dog had given birth to more puppies than any other bitch in the village. Amuthavalli, who was pregnant and tired, lay asleep by the fire. She would wag her tail when Gowri, her favourite human in the household, returned from school in the afternoon. Gowri thought the dog understood her better than did Grandma, the oldest and wisest woman in Kolavil.

Any minute, Gowri's parents would soon be returning from the paddy field. She hurried to finish the cooking.

Ragu was one of the most important people in her life. He would bring famous novels which debated woman's role in society, morality and issues affecting woman which had never previously been discussed openly in Tamil literature. One of these was *Thorn in the Heart* by Dr. Varatharasan. This novel was about a woman who had an affair after her marriage and conceived a child who grew up and fell in love with his mothers' boyfriend's daughter, so she was forced to tell the truth to the world. The novel was written in a way that evoked deep sympathy for the mother, who had suffered so much guilt because she slept with her boyfriend after she was married.

Such works by Tamil writers were rare. Sometimes Gowri would discuss modern novels with Ragu. Saratha, however, spent most of her spare time reading film scripts, singing songs from the cinema and sometimes acting the part of the heroine with Gowri and Buvana as her co-stars. Ragu was not particularly interested in his sister's way of life and her high-pitched songs filled with romantic illusions. He would usually laugh when he heard Saratha singing, but he did not dare to interfere, for she had a tongue which could cut through anything and anyone, as sharp as the tusk of one the wild boars which would sometimes wander out of the jungle near Kolavil. Ragu stroked Amuthavalli's coat tenderly, as he would have liked to stroke Gowri, and asked the reason for her sad face.

She guessed what he was thinking, but she wondered if he would ever understand her. Or did he believe, as other villagers did, that the destiny of girls was nothing more than getting married, having children and caring for their families? There was nothing wrong with having a family, Gowri felt, but it should not be imposed on everyone. The rice was well cooked, and she put the lid on the pot.

'*Anna*' (brother), she called softly. The weather was getting worse, the raindrops bigger and the wind louder.

'Yes?' He wrapped a towel around his naked shoulder to shelter himself from the cold wind.

'Will Auntie let Saratha stay at school?'

'What?' His voice expressed his doubt.

'Well, Grandma and others are trying to make out that we'll all have to stay at home after...'

'Saratha is thick,' Ragu tried to laugh.

'She's not going to become clever by staying at home till she's married, is she?' Gowri remarked.

'That's true, but I don't think Saratha herself is at all enthusiastic about school.'

'Yes, but what else can she do? She'll learn all the latest love songs from Tamil cinema by heart and deafen us all. Why don't you ask your parents to let her continue at school?'

He looked pensive, but said nothing.

'Please, talk to them; they'll listen to you,' she begged him.

48

He gazed at her affectionately and said, 'I realise you're keen to carry on studying. I'll see if I can talk to my parents about Saratha.'

'If Saratha stays at school, Auntie Indira will let Buvana go, too. Then we'll all be going to school, and Grandma won't be able to stop us.'

He looked at the sky, which was beginning to empty itself in the same way that Gowri had poured out her heart, and walked towards his house. More people had arrived, and the noise had increased. Gowri was desperate to go over and talk to Saratha.

By now, Aunty Sathya's family had arrived from Thirukovil. Uncle Mailar did not like them at all. He was not keen on anyone richer, more famous, or better-educated than he was. He could not tolerate the idea that anyone could be superior to him in any way. Gowri could hear his voice getting louder. She did not like him much. The entrance to the yard was decorated with banana trees with fruit on them so as to bless the girl who had become a woman today with fertility and prosperity. Inside the hall was decorated with bright sarees, coconut and mango leaves and various flowers from many houses. A brass pot of water with flowers, herbs, petals, perfume, oil and turmeric to purify Saratha had been placed at the front of the building. These purification rituals indicated that her childhood would be washed away and a new era of womanhood would commence.

The house was full of people of both sexes and all ages. On one side were giggling girls; on the other side, under the orange tree, were many young men from the village including Shiva, Rajah and Ragu.

The old men had already drunk themselves silly, the old women were busy organising the bathing ceremony which was to take place. After the first bath to follow puberty, Saratha would have to wait for seven, nine or eleven days before she had another very grand bathing ceremony, in accordance with custom. That would be an important occasion. An astrologer would have prepared a horoscope predicting her future on the basis of the time and date she reached puberty.

A selected group of women would be going to consult the astrologer in a few days. It would generally consist of an old woman – no doubt Grandma, in this instance – and a couple of aunts. Gowri presumed that Aunt Indira would be one of them, as talk of a proposal for Ragu to marry Buvana was in the air.

Aunt Indira poured the first pot of water tinted with turmeric and the second with jasmine flowers. Then others followed. The women's whoops mingled with Uncle Mailar's delirious drone, which went on like a gramophone.

After the bathing ceremony, Saratha was adorned with a beautiful new golden-threaded silk Bangalore saree and blouse, and jewels already presented by her relatives. Naturally beautiful, she now looked splendidly elegant. 'No wonder Shiva was wandering up and down the gravel path with his ancient bike,' Gowri thought after admiring Saratha's beauty in this new setting.

Until yesterday, she had been a girl with freedom to roam around the village, like one of the flamingos which gathered on the banks of the River Thillai. She had led her cousins in all kinds of adventures, danced gracefully and battled with their outraged Grandma. Now she would have to learn to behave like an adult. She would not be allowed even to go outside her fence. Gowri could not imagine Saratha – who had so much more pluck and determination than she herself could ever display – as a caged bird. How would she cope with being confined from then onwards?

Saratha smiled happily as soon as she saw Gowri come into the room. Her mother was busy yapping away about her daughter's good looks and the delightful presents she had received.

'Hey, where have you been all day?' Saratha clipped Gowri's ears playfully, radiant with joy and beauty.

Buvana's little sister Poorani was there to keep Saratha company, as tradition dictated. Buvana was very shy and quiet, but Poorani was the complete opposite; she was a chatty and extroverted ten-year-old. She was eating a plain rice and vegetable curry in the corner of the room. She had taken a bath with Saratha, so the young girl was shivering in the wind coming through the window. Her presence reminded Gowri of Buvana.

Why had Buvana not come? Gowri wondered.

'So where have you been hiding today?' Saratha giggled happily.

'I have been busy. Since the Raven (the girls' nickname for Grandma) has spent all day dancing around your house, and Amma and Appa have gone to the field. I ended up doing all the housework,' Gowri explained.

'Gowri, did they get the areca branch near your place?' Saratha asked excitedly. Gowri suddenly realised the reason for her cousin's agitation. She was indirectly asking who had

51

picked the branch. 'Should I answer directly?' Gowri asked herself.

She looked at the pot in Saratha's room, with a coconut placed over it ceremonially decorated with areca branches. Gowri said, 'There were a lot of boys with your brother.'

The frustration in Saratha's face was obvious; she could barely wait to know the answer. 'Old Uncle Palipody said...' Saratha fumbled for words. It was the first time in her life that Gowri had seen Saratha lost for words. Her eyes were popping out with curiosity.

She could not even mention Shiva's name. Gowri tried to keep her own expression unaltered. Saratha shook Gowri's shoulder and asked, 'Did he – did he cut the branch?'

'He', indeed! When had Shiva become 'he'? Gowri wondered. She smiled at Saratha.

'Why are you grinning?' Saratha exploded like a firework. Poorani was still busy eating her food.

'Hey, Saratha, hurry up and finish your meal,' Gowri said. 'We have to put the turmeric paste on you.'

'The old man said he'd talked to you, too.' Saratha was still trying to extract information about Shiva from Gowri.

'How can a young man like that talk to people like us?' Shiva was studying at the college in Batticaloa. 'We are the village idiots.' Gowri kept her face sad.

'He comes from this village, too, he's not a city gent,' Saratha insisted.

'Yes, but he's studying in town. That makes all the difference.' Saratha hated to be thought of as a village girl. She did not want to be identified with local peasants.

Gowri had begun to plan how she could get Saratha to

change her view of education.

'If we could go to school and study,' Gowri continued, 'he'd be able to hold proper conversations with us. Otherwise, he might say hello to us out of politeness, but he couldn't get truly friendly with us.'

Saratha's face reflected her confusion. All her dreams of Shiva were fading with Gowri's words about schooling. Education had been the last subject on her mind.

Gowri would never have believed that the name 'Shiva' could have so much magic power over Saratha. She stared at Gowri and asked, 'What are you talking about? They will never let us continue our studies at the other school.'

'Why should we go to the other school? We could stay on at the one in our own village. If all three of us decided to go, nobody would be able to stop us, and that would become one of the reasons for allowing higher education in our school,' Gowri replied.

Saratha sank to the floor with the weight of so much thinking. Gowri watched her and knew that Saratha's mind was battling with two things. One was her love for Shiva, the other was her dislike of studying. To get the one which she liked very much, she would have to face the other. Gowri hoped that her plan would work.

Grandma came in with turmeric paste; Aunt Indira and her daughter Buvana followed her.

'Here you are, Buvana. Apply the paste to your cousin. Be gentle and thorough. Your touch must persuade the family to accept you as an in-law,' the old woman laughed, addressing her son's daughter. She looked at the three girls proudly and told Gowri, 'You'll soon become a woman like these two, then we'll have to find husbands for the lot of you.'

'No, you won't!' Gowri protested. It was easier for her to answer back in front of others. 'Tell her, Auntie, why should we stay at home when we could go to school? Go on, Auntie, tell her we should carry on going to school,' she said firmly.

Saratha looked confused, disbelieving, but Gowri would not retreat. 'Hey, Saratha, tell them we're staying on at school.'

'Yes...yes – we – we'll stay on,' Saratha mumbled. Her face was ghostly pale. What Gowri was saying was altogether too much for Saratha to take in at the moment.

Poor Buvana had never been as quick a thinker as her cousins, but she had been placed in a situation in which she had no choice but to side with them.

Grandma was furious with the girls. 'Did you hear them? We're doing our best to protect these young ladies from gossip, but what are they trying to do? Parade in the streets like whores!'

Gowri dared not to look straight into her eyes, knowing the fire spilling from her. Gowri knew that worshippers sometimes vowed that, if they recovered from illness or some other calamity, they would carry blazing fire pots around the temple. That heat would be intense as the flames consumed the contents of each pot – sandalwood, jasmine, other plants – signifying the purification of the believer's soul from sin. She had no intention of doing the fire walk now.

Chapter 6

The rain did not stop.

After having a good meal and something to drink at Mailar's house, Gowri's parents and Grandma came home late. The wind, lightning, thunder and downpour created an intimidating atmosphere. On the verandah, Grandma burnt herbal margosa tree leaves to keep mosquitoes away. At the other end, the dog Amuthavalli, which had had her puppies, could not sleep. Birds perched on nearby trees were trying to find somewhere to settle as branches were torn off by the heavy wind.

Just after midnight, as the noise of the wind was becoming worse, there were shouts and screams: the village was flooding. As Grandma had been predicting for the past few weeks, the dam in Gal Oya had burst, and water was spreading throughout the surrounding villages and fields, including Kolavil. Where would people go? The village was largely surrounded by the River Thillai, and the river was already beginning to drown it. Where would people go?

It was dark, with the noise of thunder and heavy rain, and everywhere could be heard the voices of people screaming for help. The atmosphere was frightening. Trees and branches were falling. Humans and animals were running towards the highest places for safety. Palipody and his ageing wife, Theivi, dragged themselves through the mud and fallen branches towards Gowri's house, built on some of the highest land in the locality.

Theivi was shattered by shock. Almost everything she had was in her little house. Once upon a time they had been among the richest landowners in the village, but Palipody had used up most of his wealth on alcohol, and they had become increasingly poor. They had ended up with a mud hut, nothing but a pair of cows, a few chickens and goats and some clothes. Today, she had been unable to save much except for a few garments and her drunken old husband. She wept for the cattle, goats and poultry which had been swept away. Palipody was still tipsy after last night's feast at Saratha's house.

When daylight broke, the villagers could see the damage caused by the flood. The scene was like a battlefield. Very rare types of trees which were centuries old, and with various stories attached to them, had fallen, as had homes and other buildings. Many houses had been flooded. Household furniture, pots and pans had been carried far away by the rapid water. Animals had also been trying to avoid the rising water but had been affected. 'Mighty Varna (the rain god) and Bagavan Vaayu (the god of wind) declared war on us!' some older villagers cried.

What had become of the school? Tears filled Gowri's eyes as she ran towards to it. With the water still rising, she could not reach it. The temple near the school was badly damaged. 'What has happened to the god Ganesh who is supposed to protect all of us?' she thought.

People were praying to Ganesh to help them. But the poor god, who had occupied the small thatched temple for so long, had nobody to help him. His statue was now stuck in the cracked trunk of a fallen tree. Another tree had toppled onto the school, smashing the roof and with it Gowri's dream, which she had only gained the confidence to put into words the previous night, of carrying on her education with her cousins.

'What the bloody hell are you doing here?' Grandma screamed furiously at Gowri.

'Grandma, look... look at the school!' Gowri cried like a child, even though many young men were around, including Rajah, Shiva and her cousin Ragu.

'Stop it, you stupid girl! People are drowning, and all you care about are your silly school and your silly dreams.' Grandma dragged Gowri home, away from the flood. Gowri cried all the way; she could not care who was watching. Her aspirations had been shattered with the thunder, destroyed by the flood.

'What is the matter?' her mother asked, when she saw her daughter crying.

'What is the matter, indeed! Crops, livestock and houses are lying in ruins, but she is crying because the school is damaged. What is the matter with your damned girl? Who does she think she is? Studying and all. Is she going to London to see the queen or something?' Grandma roared like a tigress.

'Oh, let her be, she's only small,' Mum tried to mediate.

'Small? Small, indeed! Don't be daft, she'll be a woman today or tomorrow. What will happen if she gets her period while she's wandering about the streets? Does she care about tradition? Does she give a toss for our customs?' Grandma's wrath was severe; arguing with her would do no good. She had held her beliefs for the greater part of a century. There was no point in arguing with her from a mere twelve years' experience of life.

Gowri went away to borrow some garlic to make herbal water for old Theivi. Palipody had never bothered much about his ageing wife. He was out with the young men, who were helping the other villagers to cope with the flood.

There was little anybody could do regarding the flood. The devastation was greater than anyone could have imagined. Every year the villagers expected some flooding from River Thillai, resulting in minor damage, but nothing on this scale. The village had been self-sufficient in food and other essential goods. Now, there was a shortage of coconuts, rice, firewood and other necessities. Kolavil was completely cut off from Akkaraippattu, the closest town, where people usually went to trade.

The landlord Mailar put his stock of rice on sale to his hard-up neighbours and offered generous loans at high interest rates. 'What a man! He would trade his own dead body if he could make money out of it,' Grandma mumbled.

The young men in the village found they had plenty of hard work to do in helping people through the crisis. Shiva was kept busy, as were his friends. Though they had been educated in the towns, there was much manual work for them – removing fallen trees and branches, for instance. Saratha was happy to watch Shiva, although the circumstances were not right for romance. She loved to see him with her brother Ragu. They both studied in Batticaloa, in different places, since Shiva was at a college run by the church, but Grandma would not allow Ragu to go a Christian college. So, the youths had little opportunity to mix when they were in town.

Gowri was depressed after the flooding of the school. In the past she had enjoyed the heavy rains and moderate flooding. The girls used to dance in the rain and squelch barefoot in the mud. She had never come across a flood like this.

'What's the matter?' asked Ragu when he saw her looking so miserable.

'Nothing,' she replied curtly.

'Why was Grandma shouting at you when you went to see the school?' He knew that girls were not allowed to go out if they were approaching puberty because of the belief that if a girl had her first period outside her home it would bring bad luck to her uncle and to her future husband.

'School, school,' she sniffed as she scraped a coconut with a scraper. 'Poor girls like us shouldn't think about school, should we? Who knows, maybe God is punishing us by destroying the temple because we upset Grandma by telling her what we intended to do.' She cried like a child.

'Don't talk mumbo-jumbo, Gowri.' He tried to persuade her to relax.

'Honestly, I think the gods don't want us to go to school.' She had to find someone to blame to make sense of the calamity.

'Far from it, the gods are going to help you.' He smiled confidently.

'How?' She stopped scraping the coconut and stared at him.

'Well, the MP's going to visit the village to see the damage. We're going to ask him to rebuild the school and at the same time get permission to have O-levels there. This'll mean that girls won't have to travel far to do their exams.'

'Really?' She must tell the others, she thought.

Already, as she could tell, there was a great deal of confusion. Mailar was the one giving loans to the villagers, while at the same time helping them to fill in forms to get compensation from the government for the flood damage. Meanwhile, Nayagam, Rajah's father, was spreading the word that Mailar was trying to exploit people who had been severely affected.

Mailar and Nayagam had been enemies for a long time. As Grandma had explained, Mailar was the traditional landowner in the village, whereas Nayagam had been a poor man whose family had worked on Mailar's land during the second world war. When Nayagam was young, he had gone away to seek his fortune in Trincomalee town, which was an important harbour for the British navy at that time. A few years later he had returned with a huge sum of money. Nobody knew how he had earned it. There was a lot of talk in the village about Nayagam's wealth, but nobody dared to discuss the subject openly, for people relied on borrowing from him during the ploughing season.

Mailar hated new things, new rivals. He thought he was the best. His social status had suffered badly when his brother Nadesan returned from India after losing all his money, and his brother in-law Lingam had tried to develop opportunities for the villagers to study, for instance, by opening the library. The flood had given him the chance to act like a king taking care of his subjects. But he was upset by the scandal being spread that he was exploiting the situation.

Gowri knew that divisions among the villagers could

damage any initiative that might benefit them. Getting resources for Kolavil would be hard. She hated it when grown-ups played games with young people's future. The tiny minority of villagers who were knowledgeable had to organise in order achieve anything. They had no Tamil MP or influential figure to help them. The majority of residents of the area were Muslims, and elected Muslim MPs, while the ministers were Sinhalese. There were a few prominent citizens from Jaffna but most of these were like the inspector of schools, a harasser of women and who doesn't believe the girls need education.

She felt deeply frustrated by the whole situation. She was so despondent that she could not even shout at the god Ganesh, whom she held responsible for the disaster, or at Grandma for cursing her wish to study. She did not want to believe in gods or miracles at all. Meanwhile, Saratha spoke, thought and had visions of Shiva almost incessantly. Whom else but Gowri could she talk to about him?

A few days later the flood receded from the village, leaving heavy scars. No place remained intact. Most of the paddy fields had been destroyed. People who had lived in them had come into the village in order to survive. This meant that there were more children at school than ever before. The young men put up thatched huts to serve as temporary extra schoolrooms. Most of the new pupils had little concern for studying. They were hungry and came to school so that they could get free milk and bread.

Now and again, the government helicopter would drop food parcels containing flour and powdered milk. This caused diarrhoea and vomiting, since the flour was full of maggots.

Uncle Kasi cursed the so-called help of the others, which sent unwanted, rotten food to people who were already suffering after a natural disaster.

'What a joke,' Dad had said, complaining that villagers who had received aid had rapidly become ill as a result.

'We in poor countries have no choice but to accept these lousy gifts,' grumbled Uncle Kasipathy.

'Don't blame the white people. Our folk didn't know how to cook the food properly.' Mailar came to the defence of white supremacy as usual.

The chaos continued for a while. The school needed more teachers to cope with the influx of new students from the surrounding area. The MP came to visit the village after the turmoil had died down, and promised to look into other local problems as well as the request for the development of the school. Soon another teacher was welcomed. He was from Kalmunai and transferred from a Tamil-language school in one of the tea estates in the hilly terrain of central Ceylon.

He was married to a teacher from the northern province of Jaffna. Some of the girls stared at her as Gowri and others had stared at Punitha long ago. The new teacher's name was Ramanathan. His wife had not liked the estate school. The Tamils there were not like the long-established Tamil communities in the north and West of Ceylon but were descended from labourers who had been brought from south India during the nineteenth century by the British to grow coffee, then tea.

These working-class plantation-dwellers had been kept in isolation from their neighbours, given very little pay for their work, and made to live in highly unsuitable conditions by the

British administrators. They had begun to organise politically but had been stripped of their right to vote upon independence. The children of the estate workers had little prospect of jobs other than growing, pruning and plucking tea bushes, or of a life outside the long, windowless buildings where the workers dwelt, one family to a room.

It was because of Parames, his wife, that Ramanathan had come to this village. It was just eight miles away from his home town in Kalmunai. News about him reached Gowri's house through her great-uncle Palipody, who regularly visited Kalmunai to buy *arrack* at the tavern. The teacher seemed very friendly and helpful to the villagers. He joined the volunteers who were helping to clear the flood-damaged places. The new school started in the makeshift hut, but many young people went to the next town because of all the damage and chaos at the village school. Gowri started to cry when she heard that some girls related to her were at the town school, too. But Grandma would not listen to her arguments about going to school.

The major ceremony to celebrate Saratha's womanhood had yet to be performed, having been postponed because of the flood and ensuing problems. Now Uncle Mailar was busy preparing to stage the next act of the drama which would display his popularity.

One of their aunts from Thirukovil joined other women who were going to visit the astrologer to ask him to predict what lay in store for Saratha. Saratha's mother Aunt Sathya prayed that her daughter would have a prosperous future.

Saratha had been the first girl to be born in her immediate family. The time she reached puberty and the position of the stars and zodiac at that moment would play an important part in determining what was to happen in her future. Grandma was much more worried about this than anyone else. She had been brought up to believe in – and shape her life according to – myths and superstitions.

Saratha had gotten her first period on a Friday, which meant that, according to Grandma, she would find her own partner without her parents' permission. 'Don't I know it?' Gowri smiled to herself when she heard the old woman talking to her mother about how astrology would affect her destiny.

Grandma continued to talk about the traditional beliefs. Friday was one day when no mother would want her daughter to have her first period, because, no matter how carefully the parents protected her, she would find her own partner or run away to her lover. How Saratha could run anywhere with Mailar guarding her like a monster, from a house with a seven-foot fence, was beyond Gowri's imagination.

Grandma went on to explain to the aunt from Thirukovil that 'if the girl had her first period on a Saturday, that would also not be good, since that would bring hardship and lack of prosperity. Sunday would be auspicious, but would lead to an unremarkable life. Monday would be excellent – a woman would never look at a man other than her husband. Tuesday would bring misfortune and widowhood, while Wednesday would bring luck and lots of sons. If on Thursday, the girl was not be trusted – her affairs would lead to bloodshed.'

After listening to all this 'mumbo-jumbo', as Ragu would have described it, Gowri wondered on which day Grandma herself had reached puberty.

Chapter 7

The new teachers, Ramanathan and his wife Parames, came to visit Mailar's family. They asked what the girls were going to do after Saratha's ceremony. Gowri considered bringing up the subject of education to find out what the new teachers' opinions were. Her cousins and she had not much time to talk to the couple. She did not expect that they would like the village much. It was very primitive, without electricity, a bus service or other modern facilities. Most teachers came from other parts of the province and did not stay in Kolavil. They would take the bus up to Akkaraippatu and walk to Kolavil from there, the same way after school in the afternoon in the scorching sun, while most of the villagers were taking a nap under the trees in their houses or a wonderful woody area on the edge of the village that had the oldest and tallest trees. Ramanathan and his wife were the first teachers to decide to live locally.

There were no lights after dark except in the temple and shops. Choruses of frogs in numerous ponds would croak lullabies at night, while foxes would howl in the jungle just a few miles away. But, whatever the weather and regardless of the prosperity and welfare of the village, the recitation of folk poems could be heard after nightfall. Every now and then, the music of the flutes and drums, carved by hand, would fill the air.

Gowri thought about the new teachers. Would the recent arrivals adapt to this place?

When the teacher Parames came to the house, Saratha looked as beautiful as ever. At the same time, the women who had been to consult the astrologer returned with cheerful smiles on their faces. What had the astrologer told them? Had he predicted that Saratha would marry Shiva? Saratha almost chewed off Gowri's ears in her excitement. 'Go on, Grandma, tell us what the astrologer said. Is Saratha going to get a university degree or something?' Gowri joked provocatively.

As they expected, Grandma seethed with wrath and asked the teacher not to listen to such nonsense. 'Tell her, teacher, we're village women. Why should we need education?'

Parames looked at the girls. She could see from their expression that they were interested in going to school. Meanwhile, her husband Ramanathan had arrived with the young men and had heard what had been said. He sat down on the mat, took the shawl from his neck, wiped the sweat from his forehead and said clearly, 'We're going to rebuild the school, Grandma.'

She did not reply.

'What will we do until then?' Gowri put the question with no hesitation.

'What everyone else will have to do – go into town until the school is ready to start O-level classes.'

Gowri loved the sound of it. She was surprised to find that these words increased her determination so much.

'What are you saying, sir? We have a tradition which we should obey and respect. We don't let girls out of the house after they reach puberty.' Grandma was almost in tears.

'You can't live in the past, Grandma. Haven't you heard that the Indian prime minister's sister Vijayalakshmi is going to the United Nations? Don't you know how many women are fighting for their rights?' He sipped tea and smiled at her.

Gowri's mother, Buvana's mother Indira, Saratha's mother Sathya and the aunt from Thirukovil listened to him. 'Why should they waste their lives grinding chillies to powder and pounding rice to flour? Why can't they develop their talents, do something else?' he asked forthrightly.

'Such as what?' Grandma shouted furiously. 'Is anything more important than being a good wife and mother?'

'Yes.' He looked at her.

'What?' she screamed.

'Being herself is more important than living for others.' He held his anger back behind a broad smile. Mailar brought a tray of betel leaves and areca nuts and other ingredients to go with betel-leaf chewing.

'What do you reckon?' the teacher asked. Mailar smiled stupidly and did not answer. 'You see, a man like you who has been a bastion of traditional values should be at the forefront of the movement for progress. Let the girls study, let the world get better and wiser.'

Mailar became more nervous. He had never liked the new order coming to the village or any other change.

'For us to be able to study, we all had to do something unfamiliar, make a journey,' Parames reminded him softly.

'Ah well, we have to do what the rest of the world's doing. We can't avoid change, can we?'

'I don't know what's happening to these girls. I don't want them to go out.' Grandma brought the conversation to an end.

Later Gowri told Saratha quietly, 'The new schoolmaster seems a nice man.'

Poor Buvana was confused as usual and asked, 'So, we're going into town to study?'

Gowri got cross with her 'slow-motion' cousin and replied, 'Yes, you clot, we're going to school, provided Saratha doesn't start a song and dance about love and marriage.'

After the visitors had left, the adults got to gather to talk about the astrologer's predictions. Gowri was getting impatient, too. What had been predicted?

The grown-ups' voices were too low for the girls to overhear everything being discussed, but they gathered that the astrologer had made some remarks about the man Saratha was to marry. He would be handsome, well-educated and live in the north of their area, and, according to the stars, she would be less than eighteen when the wedding happened.

'Nobody had to tell us that,' Gowri thought. 'Saratha will marry any minute now and produce hundreds of babies in no time.' But Gowri warned Saratha that Shiva was just one of numerous young men who could fit the description; if she wanted to be sure of winning his heart she had to go to school.

The biggest and final ceremony for Saratha was about to begin. Saratha's relatives on her mother's side from Thirukovil came in a massive procession with various kind of sweets and presents accompanied by drummers and dancers. Mailar had organised a feast for the whole village. It was commonly known that offering food to poor people was an act that would bring blessings from the gods, but his concern was for showing off his wealth, which was why he had invited everyone. Old Palipody had been sozzled with drink for days. His wife was staying at Gowri's; she was not at all well.

Gowri's mother was expecting another child. As far back as Gowri remember, her mother had been carrying, giving birth to or suckling a baby practically all the time. She suffered greatly when she was pregnant. She was often nauseous and would eat yoghurt, mango or some unusual food which she craved. She was often tired, and would rest underneath the jak tree in the afternoon.

Now that she was pregnant again, she was feeling sick. She vomited loudly. Every time she did so, the dog raised her eyes and moaned in sympathy. Even the hen with sixteen chicks seemed to weep at the sound of the vomiting.

Grandma made fancy snacks for her pregnant daughter. The old woman was very proud that Mum was carrying her sixth child and hoped her daughter would have four more to earn the title 'perfect mother'. Gowri sometimes wondered about the traditional notion of perfect motherhood. Mum seldom had the time and energy to play or do anything constructive with her children.

Gowri went to see Saratha, whose talk was all about Shiva.

Saratha would do anything, go anywhere in the world for him. She would worry continually whether her clothes were stylish enough for his taste. While Gowri was there, the grown-ups arrived. Mum suggested as she ate yoghurt, 'When you consider the astrologer's remarks, it seems as if Rajah is going to marry Saratha.'

Suddenly Grandma got irritable and said, 'Why Rajah? Saratha has plenty of suitors on her mother's side who could marry her.'

'What's wrong with Rajah?' Mum stopped eating yoghurt for a while to raise the question.

'Because he's more closely related to Gowri than Saratha.'
It was customary to marry someone from a related clan.
Gowri and Rajah were related a few generations back, as
Grandma's father had married into Rajah's family. In those
days, it was almost unheard of for someone to marry outside
the village as Saratha's father had done.

This gave Gowri a shock. 'Oh yes, you old cow, you've got
everything planned for me!' she wanted to yell. She had no
intention of being married off to Rajah or anyone else for a
long time to come.

Aunt Indira smiled at Gowri. Grandma asked Indira, 'Are
you going to let Buvana go to school?'

'Why not? They're only kids. Let them enjoy their
childhood.'

The conversation broke off as the music for the ceremony
began. There were people everywhere, including some new
faces whom Gowri had not seen before. Ragu was there with
his friends from college, who had come especially for the
ceremony.

Ragu had not been back to college since the flood. Mailar
had kept him back to help with work in the fields, saying,
'What will you gain by going to college? Maybe a clerical job
in town. How much will you earn from that? It's better to
spend your energy on Mother Earth and let her look after
you.'

But Gowri prayed for her cousin brother to return to his
studies. She wanted him to do well academically, and she
hoped he could persuade his parents to let the girls to go
school like Kamala, their distant cousin who was studying in
Batticaloa. Kamala was a pleasant girl with a lovely smile. She

was chatting with Ragu; they seemed to enjoy each other's company. Kamala did not care a toss what Grandma thought of her. She was moving around and talking with everyone whom she knew.

Gowri liked Kamala, although she lived in Thirukovil and did not often visit. Gowri wanted to talk to her about the problems around schooling. Gowri also wanted to mention that Ragu might not go to college any more, but there was no opportunity to discuss such things. The house was full of people who were eating, drinking, and talking all at once.

A group of women were grinding turmeric to a paste and adding perfume to the liquid. One part of the puberty ceremony was when the girls would pour yellow turmeric water on the boys whom they fancied. It was a myth in the village that, if a boy was splashed by a girl at a special ceremony such as this, he might be her future bridegroom. Saratha wanted water thrown on Shiva and asked Gowri to do it for her as Saratha wouldn't be allowed to be mingle with others that day.

The hall was full of elderly people from the village. The old girls like Grandma were enjoying themselves by throwing water on old men. It was a jolly event; everyone got wet, and there was much laughter. Old Palipody joined the young men in chasing girls to splash water on them in revenge. The ceremony went smoothly. Saratha received various presents from her relatives. She seemed stunningly beautiful and happy in her red silk saree and a gold-threaded blouse. She was bedecked with jewellery, some of it heavy and out of fashion.

Her eyes wandered through the crowd, following Shiva.

She did not care less who noticed it. Grandma was having a wonderful time tossing water on young men. She asked Buvana and her sister and Poorani to throw water at Ragu. Buvana hid, embarrassed, but Kamala was not in the least bit hesitant. She filled a huge bucket with yellow water for Ragu.

Gowri joined the chaos. She had nobody in particular to make wet, but she drenched Palipody thoroughly by accident, as he was unsteady on his feet and collided with Gowri's water bucket. She filled the bucket again and looked around for Saratha's target Shiva. She saw Rajah and felt shy and hesitant. She had never really thought about him, but her Grandma's conversation that afternoon had made her realise that whatever she did today might lead to gossip and speculation in the family about her and Rajah. She dreaded any talk linking her name with that of a young man. It might destroy her ambition to continue her schooling.

She was poised reluctantly to throw water on Shiva with Saratha behind her, screaming at her. Kamala hurried to toss water at Ragu. Gowri began to swing the bucket towards Shiva. Meanwhile, Ragu and Shiva made a hasty escape. To the amusement of all the onlookers, both girls poured water over a young man whom they had never met before.

He looked shocked and bemused at getting wet and being laughed at. He raised his damped eyes, his expression puzzled, and looked at the girls, smiling. Now he was wearing an outfit yellowed with turmeric and perfume.

There were guffaws all around. Kamala was disappointed at missing Ragu. Gowri felt sorry for the young man, wondering who he was. His piercing eyes made her turn her face away.

Aunt Indira whispered to the teacher Parames, 'Who is that handsome boy?'

'Oh, that's my husband's brother Nathan.'

Grandma stopped laughing when she saw the unknown young man standing with a soaked yellow outfit in front of the crowd. She turned and looked at the girls who had poured turmeric water on him. Gowri and Kamala stood there for a few second watching Grandma's reaction. She did not say a word, but Gowri could see the change in Grandma's face; for a few seconds there was a fearful expression in grandma's eyes, then it was gone.

Does Grandma really belief that the man wetted with turmeric water by a virgin on a special day like today would be destined to marry her? Nathan was absolutely soaked by two girls not by one, so what then? Gowri wondered briefly.

Then the celebration continued. More water was thrown, and more people got soaked as people's minds were completely absorbed in an extraordinary atmosphere of music, food, and laughter. But, after the ceremony, Gowri felt that something had suddenly dropped into the calm water of her mind, causing a new ripple to be born.

Chapter 8

It was the first week of February. Most children were at school. Shiva had returned to the town, but Ragu remained in the village because of his father. He said he would go back to college in a few days' time.

The fourth of February was Ceylon's Independence Day. The headmaster raised the flag and sang the national anthem. After that, Ramanathan told the villagers to go and see their MP to speed up the building of the school. But the prospect of meeting him posed a problem.

During the 1956 general election, he had won the seat for the constituency on the ticket of the Federal Party, which was Tamil-led. Now he joined the predominantly Sinhalese party, which held power nationally.

The villagers, who were Tamil, had voted for him, although he was a Muslim, because they trusted him as a member of a community that had lived on friendly terms with the Tamils in the region for centuries. There had been very little conflict between the communities during British rule because all the people had been treated oppressively by their rulers unless they were rich or powerful. The Akkaraippattu area was neither powerful nor rich, but its inhabitants were content with tending the paddy fields and reaping the harvests. Batticaloa province in the eastern part of Ceylon was fertile, and rice, maze and sugar cane flourished there.

Most Muslims and Tamils worked in the fields. Some were fishermen or had shops in the market. During the election, many local Muslims had supported an independent candidate. Practically all the Tamils, however, had voted for the Federal Party, which had campaigned for equality for all Ceylonese and worked for a solution to the Tamil national question.

Tamils in Ceylon had been protesting vocally at their unjust treatment by successive Sinhalese majority governments after independence. The Sinhalese had reneged on the understanding that English would be replaced by both the Sinhala and Tamil languages, which had been spoken on the island for thousands of years. Instead, in 1956, Sinhala had become the sole official language. The many who were fluent only in Tamil – including many Muslims as well as Hindus – had been placed at an enormous disadvantage in their dealing with officialdom. That year, a peaceful protest began. Demonstrators had marched on parliament, determined to get a fair deal for Tamil-speaking people.

When the local MP had changed his political position in order to get a ministerial post in the government, those who had voted for him were furious. There were clashes between supporters and detractors.

Grandma had never been keen on strangers and had even more disliked the MP when he visited as a Tamil Federal Party candidate. 'All these politicians with their parties and slogans should do something useful for ordinary people,' she had said. 'If they can't keep promises they shouldn't become MPs.'

Over the past few years, the villagers had attended many rallies and welcome parties for leaders from Jaffna who came to talk about the future of the Tamils in Ceylon. Most leaders could not speak Tamil properly; they had been educated in English. Sinhalese nationalists had been blaming Tamils for the island's many problems, such as the lack of economic development. Leaders had been whipping up this chauvinism in order to win votes and get into parliament.

Grandma had not expected independence to bring so much chaos. As far back as she could remember, she had not faced any problems being a Tamil woman. She had been brought up to believe that she would be in no danger living in Ceylon. When she heard the news that Tamil leaders had been beaten up in Colombo during a peaceful protest, her opinion of VIPs had plummeted. She said, 'Those in high places should have the moral courage to protect their people, regardless of race, religion or political differences.'

She was illiterate, so Gowri had to read the national newspapers to her. Now and then, Grandma would stop her granddaughter and give her own views, which were often inconsistent with her attitude toward Gowri. For instance, when Grandma had said that people in high places should treat everyone equally, Gowri had demanded, 'Why don't you treat us equally? You don't take our opinions seriously.'

Grandma had shouted, 'Women shouldn't want to be equal; they should serve men and keep them happy.'

Gowri had said she wanted to go to school; that had nothing to do with men. Grandma had said that women had the great responsibility of safeguarding traditional values.

Uncle Kasi and Gowri's father Nadesan were worried about increasing Sinhalese domination and the worsening position of Tamils in society. 'How can we live in peace if the state is so cruel to us?' Kasi asked Dad as they mended a fence.

They had both been involved in welcoming Tamil leaders, mainly from Jaffna, who would come to the village during the election times and talk about the great past history of Tamils in Ceylon. In mediaeval times, Tamil-speaking kings had been among those who had ruled, formed alliances and sometimes fought over that part of Asia; and Tamil had been one of the languages in which literary works were composed. The unsophisticated villagers would become deeply emotional about the glorious history of the Tamil people and their gloomy future under the Sinhalese national bourgeoisie. The leaders would speak of monarchs who led subjects under the tiger flags and great poets who created priceless epics about the Tamil nation.

The politicians would talk for hours on end, and some could not speak Tamil at all. Grandma, who did not know any other language, would get cross and shout, 'Hey, sir, first you should learn to speak in Tamil, then you can tell us about Tamil greatness.'

Aunt Indira had said, 'They were educated in English. We should respect English-speakers.' Grandma had become even more cross. 'Why should I respect those who speak a language which I can't understand?'

Gowri and Saratha had been asked to sing songs to welcome the leaders. They had got up on the stage, wearing newly-made silk skirts and blouses, and sang of the glory of being Tamil. The song called on Tamils to rise up and fight for their rights. But what was happening now? Local people could not even save their school through the MP whom they had sent to parliament with such high hopes. He should not have run off to another party because of the lure of a ministerial post and the chance of more money in bribes, the villagers mumbled.

The Tamil villagers expressed their anger against the MP who had changed sides, but the Muslims in town got angry with the Tamils who had voted for him instead of choosing a Muslim from of their own village. Angry verbal exchanges got out of hand and ended in blood and tears. A few Tamils were beaten up by some Muslims youths in the market. Trouble had spread throughout the Akkaraippattu area, and a bloody communal riot had broken out at the end of February 1958.

The weather was hot. The harvest had been poor that year because of the floods a few months before. People were trying to earn much as they could by going to the paddy fields in search of work. Most of the men from the village of Kolavil had already left for the fields when the violence began. Rajah was one of those attacked by Muslim hooligans in the market. When he came back in a gory state, the youngsters in Kolavil were infuriated, since he was the Federal Party youth leader in the village.

In retaliation they beat up helpless Muslim peasants on their way to the fields. Gowri's father begged the young men to stop harassing innocent Muslims, but they were angry at what had happened and took no heed.

Around four o'clock that afternoon, hundreds of Muslims thugs charged the village. They had come all the way from Akkaraippattu town with guns and other weapons to wage 'war on the Tamils of Kolavil'.

Grandma was distraught. She had heard many stories about communal riots in other parts of the country. 'The Muslims will kill all the men and rape the women,' she lamented. Gowri had never been so frightened in all her life. She, Buvana and Saratha were forced to hide behind the rice sacks in the attic for hours as the battle continued on the outskirts of the village.

Old Palipody joined the young men who went to fight the Muslim 'invaders'. There was a shop which sold 'everything' including – according to Grandma – 'illicit *arrack*'. They had plenty of soda bottles in stock. There were few men in the village. Boys who had just returned from school seized bottles and used these as their weapons to chase their adversaries away and protect their village.

That day, Gowri's mother not only felt sick because she was pregnant, but she also had diarrhoea because she was so scared. The village was in chaos for hours. Then a police jeep arrived on the scene. Grandma was loudly critical. 'Is this justice? Didn't the police notice when the Muslim hooligans passed the police station on the way here?' It had been whispered that the organisers of the 'invasion' had slipped backhanders to corrupt policemen so that they would look other way as the march on Kolavil went past.

Palipody stepped forward, demanding justice. Immediately his old teeth were broken by one of the policemen, and the old man was bundled like a cabbage into their jeep. As the police began to drag other villagers in, most ran away to avoid being beaten up. Rajah was badly injured and was sent by ambulance to Kalmunai town hospital. 'Nobody ever returns home if they're taken away by ambulance,' Grandma wept loudly.

The atmosphere was very tense that night. Dad begged the youths not to harm poor Muslims who were passing by on their way to the fields. Usually, the village was filled with bullock carts, bicycles and tractors in the evening; after work, people would go home in these. But today was different. No carts or bikes moved. Often, men and women would sing folk songs to forget their exhausting journey, but now, nobody sang. It was a ghost village. Few households dared to light fires, cook or talk.

'If we hadn't got mixed up in all this stupid politics, we wouldn't have to suffer this way,' Grandma mumbled in the dark. Dad, Mailar and Ragu had all disappeared just in case the police came to arrest them, as they had already arrested almost a hundred schoolboys and Palipody.

'What madness!' Ramanathan came through the dark and sat on the verandah.

'What is?' Gowri whispered the question.

'Politics and politicians are mad.'

Gowri was confused. Was it wrong to ask for the right to speak your own language? Was it wrong to demand equal treatment in your own country? But she knew he would not talk nonsense; he was better educated than anyone else in the village.

'What will happen if the Muslims come tonight?' Grandma sobbed.

'What will happen?' The teacher repeated the question.

'Well... well, they'll kill the men and rape the women. We've got to do something.' Grandma was especially worried about the girls.

'We don't have guns,' Gowri murmured. She had heard that the Muslim thugs had come armed with guns.

'We'll go and ask the *pariahs*,' Grandma said. (Pariahs,

people born into the lowest caste, were excluded by orthodox Hindu society.)

Ramanathan laughed grimly and said, 'You lot never treated them as Tamils until now. You only go to them when you need help.' His voice was full of anger.

'What should we do? We have to follow tradition. We can't throw away beliefs which are thousands of years old.'

'Grandma, nobody has to obey unjust laws which go against humanity,' the teacher protested.

No-one contradicted him. They knew of many occasions in the past when the untouchables had been unjustly oppressed.

'Sir, we never created the caste system or our culture. They're there. What can we do? We're simple women, we have no power to change things,' Aunt Indira said practically.

'When traditional beliefs aren't helpful, when old values go against one set of people, isn't it time to think about change, progressive change?' the teacher stated clearly.

Gowri began to understand him, but her worries about the situation they were in were what most occupied her thoughts. Her great-uncle Palipody had not yet been released from the police station. His wife Theivi, already very ill, was now moaning continually. With no men in the house except for Ramanathan, Gowri was petrified by Grandma's tales of other Tamil villages which had been attacked by Muslims in the past.

It was pitch black; no moon could be seen. Late in the night, the teacher offered to go into town in the morning to find out if it was possible for Palipody to be released as his wife was very ill.

'Please see Rajah, too,' Grandma pleaded.

'Grandma, Rajah is in hospital, not in custody with old Palipody.'

When dawn broke, there was more trouble in the fields and the market. A police jeep moved through every lane in the village, seeking out 'troublemakers'. Boys as young as ten were picked up and dumped in the jeep.

There was no sign of Ragu. Mailar's wife Sathya was close to fainting; she had been weeping since yesterday. Mailar came out from his hiding place and yelled at her to be quieter. He was terrified of police brutality.

The police raided the school and picked up some of the boys, although the headmaster and Ramanathan objected politely. 'Hey, teacher, if you don't shut your mouth you'll teach in the police cell, too,' they warned him.

'Their uniform gives them the authority to talk like that,' he grumbled after they left. Classes could not continue. 'Huh, look at the guardians of the law, what do they do? Nothing but behave like paid thugs. Having their party in power gives them the nerve to think they can get away with this.'

No human voices could be heard in the village. No noise could be heard but the bark of wandering dogs and the tinkle of a cow's bells. Children did not go out to play in the fields or on the bank of the River Thillai; old women did not gather to gossip. There were no temple bells, no songs from passing workers on their way to the fields, no music of flutes played by bullock-cart drivers. Even the dog Amuthavalli stayed under the mango tree and slept all day.

Come the evening, there was an announcement by a man

who drummed the news to the villagers. They would have to observe a curfew – something they had never experienced before. They would have to stay indoors from six in the evening to six in the morning. Most people were used to leaving at four o'clock in the morning for their fields and not returning until seven at night. The state of emergency brought unhappiness and poverty, and anger against the government grew. The villagers did not know what to do except make sure they were indoors well before six in the evening and be miserable.

Chapter 9

One evening one of Gowri's father's friends, Iburahim, a Muslim gentleman, came to visit. 'This injustice is appalling. The police have nothing better to do than make one set of people angry with another set. Here they come to harass the Tamils. In the Muslim areas, they come to harass the Muslims. When you ask for the reasons, they finger their guns. What can we do against guns? Stupid politicians, they're stirring up riots against communities who've lived in this part of Ceylon for many hundreds of years.'

Gowri brought tea to Iburahim. She liked the old Muslim man. She was told, he had been her father's friend since they were ten years of age. She also remembered playing with him when she was little. He would bring lots of fruit from his garden and spicy biriyani rice and meat after the festival of Ramazhlan. He had been to Mecca in Saudi Arabia and become a *haji*, a holy man. He would talk for days on end about Saudi Arabian deserts, camels, and so on.

He had been in Mecca during the dispute over the Suez Canal between the British government and the Egyptian president Nasser. Iburahim practically worshipped Nasser for his courage in fighting British imperialism. When the British prime minister Anthony Eden lost the Suez War, Iburahim came home with Dad to celebrate. 'Western people think they can cut the world into slices so than it can be eaten up by the Americans, the English and others,' he would laugh.

Dad was a deeply religious man. Although he was

politically progressive, he would talk of other things, too. He would remark, 'Power can't last if it's based on violence which destroys humanity. Some people think that they can bomb a place if they don't like it, but in the end, they'll be destroyed, too. There's no justice for the man who doesn't treat humanity justly.'

'Well, I wonder...' Iburahim sipped tea and talked about doing something to bring the community together.

Was it that easy? Gowri wondered.

There were many other things that were easy for Dad and Iburahim to do. She remembered how, when she was small, she would come along when they went to shoot flamingos on the bank of River Thillai. In summer, thousands of storks and flamingos would gather at the riverside to mate. People would trap them or shoot them to roast or fry; their meat was considered to be very tender.

Gowri always disliked the shooting. She could not bear to see the birds dying violently. Her father and Iburahim would bring back as many as ten flamingos on one occasion. The men would clean the birds and give them to Mum to cook. The necks of the storks were as long as snakes. Gowri did not like the business of shooting birds at all. But that shooting had been very different from the shooting which was happening now.

The local candidate at the general election had been Iburahim's nephew. Still, the old man was not annoyed with the villagers for voting the other way. As usual, he had come as their friend.

'Politics has no real value anymore; it's all down to individuals,' Dad said, with hurt in his tone. Gowri could tell that his memory was going back to the days he had been in India with Gandhi and the non-violent resistance movement.

'We'll just have to do what we can,' Iburahim said.

'We'll go and see the government agent and ask him to sort out this mess,' Dad announced in a determined voice. But his determination was shattered within a few hours. More police arrived in jeeps to terrorise the neighbourhood and track down supposed troublemakers.

Gowri was supposed to get up very early in the morning. She was approaching puberty, and it was the prevailing belief in the village that it was bad for a girl to have her first period while she was still in bed. She had been instructed to get up before sunrise and perform the daily rituals such as bathing in cold water and praying.

The crowing of a cock woke her up; other than that, there was little noise. Nobody was going to the fields. What time was it? It was not yet midnight. There were many questions in her mind. What would happen tomorrow? What had happened to her cousin brother Ragu?

Around midnight their dog Amuthavalli barked softly. From the tone of her bark, Gowri could tell that the dog was welcoming someone joyfully. But she was too frightened to come out and see. Could it be the police or army to take her away and...? She did not want to think about it. She listened carefully to what was going on outside.

She could hear Grandma's whisper; it could not be the police. Reassured, she came out. It was pitch dark. There were people near the jasmine bush. Auntie Sathya was crying. Mailar was bossing someone about. Mum was hurrying to prepare something in the kitchen. Ragu was there. He was wearing a black *lungi* and a vest. Gowri wept with happiness to see him.

He had not eaten for a few days, he told them. There were a few other boys beside him hiding in the jungle from police. They had committed no crime except being Tamil boys from Kolavil. If the security forces stopped searching, they would come out soon, he said.

Just as Gowri's mother brought some food, the dog barked vigorously, this time with fear. Immediately, the whole village was awoken by gunfire. Gowri heard the shopkeeper's dog gasping for breath as it died. 'What mad dogs they are, shooting a dog like that,' Grandma mumbled quietly. Ragu vanished instantly. What would happen to him now? How long would Tamils have to run for their lives?

During the general election, Rajah had become a youth leader and a hero in the village by giving emotional talks on Tamil nationalism. He was articulate and forceful. But Ragu had said to her, 'We're not asking for special treatment by the Sinhalese majority government. All we want is to live like other citizens throughout the world. We're one of many minority nations. We all have to struggle for our rights. Today, they're trying to stop us from learning and practising our own language. Tomorrow they may stop us living in this land. We've got to fight. We have no option.'

Gowri thought about the future of the Tamils. She was nearly thirteen years old. There were things she did not understand. Her ambition was to go to school and become a teacher; her horizons were limited. Saratha worried about her 'boyfriend' Shiva and cried silently to Gowri. She could not really comprehend Saratha's feelings about Shiva. Saratha was nearly a year older than Gowri and had in many ways matured more.

For the past few days, the village had been in a zombie-like state. Nobody could talk, walk around or do anything else freely. Gowri could not sleep. Palipody's wife, Theivi, was crying for her husband, who was still in custody. Grandma was comforting her by telling her that Ramanathan would do his best to get the old man released.

When Grandma saw Gowri, she got very cross and frightened. 'What are you doing here?' she whispered angrily.

'I couldn't sleep.'

'So?'

'I'm scared, Grandma.' Gowri could hear what sounded like the howling of a wild fox far away. According to the villagers, the howl of a fox meant that something bad would occur. The old woman closed her eyes and raised her hands over her head to pray. 'Grandma, do you think Ragu might have been captured by the police?'

'Don't talk about it. It's best not to talk or think about bad things.'

Gowri sat in silence. Grandma stroked her granddaughter's hair and said, 'One day they came like this, my great-grandma told me.' Gowri looked at the old woman's face but could not see her expression. The darkness was complete except for a ray of moonlight between the leaves of a banana tree.

'Who came?' Gowri sat and put her arm around Grandma.

'The white men.' Grandma lay on her mat and stared at the millions of stars above her. 'My great-grandma was about your age when they came.'

Gowri knew her grandmother's talent for storytelling. She was a walking library, full of knowledge about the history of the village and many other things. Gowri prepared to listen to her story. If she was going to repeat what her own great-grandmother had told her, the events would have been one and half centuries old.

'My great-grandma lived until she was over hundred years old, did you know that?' Grandma asked Gowri.

Gowri and her grandmother seldom talked alone together, especially recently. She had become very agitated about Gowri's talk of education. Gowri did not like it when Grandma made caustic remarks about going to school with boys, but in other ways she respected her. Gowri admired the old woman's strength and courage in talking about difficult matters openly – although most of her opinions were out of date. Gowri lay next to Grandma on the new mat and curled up against her soft and warm body.

'White men came to take treasure from the village and temples. You know there were priceless statues and jewels in the temples? Foreigners came with guns, riding on mighty horses.' Grandma got up when she heard a police jeep passing by, then continued her story a few minutes later.

'In this village we had a wonderful Hindu temple. It's said it was built by one of the Tamil queens who came to this country when the Tamil king invaded Ceylon from South India. It was one of the most ancient temples at that time. My great-grandma told me about the incident...' She came to a halt and began to cry.

'The young men who fought the white men who were trying to rob the temple were killed, and...and...' She pulled

Gowri close and said, 'Women always have to suffer because of cruel men.'

'What happened?' Gowri squeezed Grandma's hand.

'They... the white men... the brutes raped many young women. Some were killed, some committed suicide, some survived to tell the tale. Later on, some women had fair-skinned babies. Such things repeat themselves over the years, in different ways.'

'Oh Grandma, how terrible!'

Gowri thought about her Grandma, who had lived for others all her life. She had been widowed as soon as Kasi was born. She only had two children, Uncle Kasi and Gowri's mum. Her husband had died when she was only twenty-five years old, leaving her with two small children. She had worked hard to bring them up. Young though she was, she had strongly-held moral values. She had worked hard to bring them up. She wanted her granddaughter to be a good housewife and have lots of children; she expected nothing more.

'I'll pray to the gods for your future. I don't want your life to be messed up by Sinhalese or Muslim thugs or anyone else.' Grandma's voice was cracking with emotion.

'I'll take care of myself, Grandma.'

Grandma chuckled. 'You stupid girl, no woman can look after herself properly without a man.'

'I will.'

'Don't be silly.' The sound of the police jeep was heard again. 'In those days white men came on the horses, now Sinhalese come in jeeps. They commit the same atrocities.'

They could see the River Thillai sparkling in the orange

light of the rising sun. 'I'll go and wash.' Gowri got up and went to the well nearby. Scattered food, prepared for her cousin the previous night, lay on the ground. Her heart ached when she thought about him.

After her wash, she picked white jasmine flowers for the images of many gods in her house and prayed, 'Dear Gods, please keep my cousin safe, and all the Tamil boys who are in danger from the police and army. He's a good man. He treats others with respect; he's never harmed anyone; he's kind. You've got to help him.'

She went to Saratha's house straight away. Auntie was shattered because of her son's disappearance last night. Saratha's younger brother Sangar hurried up and said, 'Go away, girls, the soldiers are coming. They were asking about Ragu at the shop.'

Grandma arrived like thunder, put the girls behind rice sacks and covered them with a big sack which was normally used to cover rice sacks. This was dusty, dirty and made the girls feel like sneezing, but they did not dare. Soldiers were in the house. They heard them calling Ragu's name. The dog was barking fiercely; Grandma shaking with fear.

Gowri held her breath tightly to stop herself from sneezing. The soldiers were asking questions about her cousin, and Auntie Sathya was telling them that he had not been home for the past few days. She started to cry loudly while she answered their questions. They asked Grandma the same questions, and she gave them the same answers.

Saratha whispered she wanted to be sick; Gowri also felt her bowels loosening with fear. Thousands of butterflies suddenly sprang up in her stomach. The waiting seemed to last forever, although in reality the military men were there for only twenty minutes.

'What's happening?' Saratha whispered.

'How should I know?' Gowri sniffed. Both were trying hard not to sneeze.

After the military truck left the lane, the girls came out from hiding. There were broken water pots on the verandah, and Auntie's vegetable patch had been completely destroyed under the feet of the military men.

'I wish I weren't a Tamil girl,' Saratha muttered sulkily.

Gowri glared at her. 'You've always wanted an easy life, haven't you?' she blurted. 'At least he's not been captured by these monsters,' she said, thinking of her cousin. The poor dog Amutha was moaning with pain as she had taken a brutal beating by a police baton. Gowri cursed the army and police: 'They are animals, they don't have any feeling at all!'

Sitting sadly, Saratha mused, 'I hope nothing has happened to Shiva.'

'Aren't you worried about your own brother?'

'I am, I am, but I'm worried about him, too. I hope he doesn't come to the village for a while.'

Gowri kept her amazement to herself. She was beginning to realise the strength of Saratha's love for Shiva. Her own brother was wanted by the army, yet Saratha was perturbed about her boyfriend who was safe at boarding college in Batticaloa.

Throughout that day there were many incidents in and around the houses and fields. Army vehicles from the town terrorised the village the whole day long. Gowri developed a severe headache because of her lack of sleep and her worries about Ragu's safety. Her mother, anxious about the whole business, was nauseous. Grandma had to look after her as well as her sister-in-law Theivi.

Ramanathan came around. He was worried, too. He did not know how to set about getting the schoolboys released from police custody. Until yesterday, he had thought of appealing to the government agent, but today the situation was worse, and he did not think there was any possibility of leaving the village.

The army did not confine itself to terrorising Tamil areas. Now, Muslim areas were being brutalised, too. The whole Akkaraippattu district was seething with anger and frustration. Constantly, news came in about one similar incident or another from various places in the district.

At around four o'clock in the afternoon, Saratha's house was filled with many women whispering gravely to one another. 'What are they whispering? Is old Theivi about to die?' Gowri asked Saratha. Saratha was good at listening in to adults and collecting gossip. If she had the simplest story from an adult, she would dress the story up in a bejewelled saree, even make it come to life and walk.

'They were talking about something awful,' Saratha said with anger in her tone.

'What's the matter?'

Saratha explained to them the news that heard from the grown-ups. The Sinhalese army had raped a Tamil girl in the town of Akkaraippattu!

All three girls looked at one another in tears. 'What will happen to us?'

The girl who was raped by the army was a beautiful and

educated Christian from the town, called Maria. 'Poor Maria!' The girls cried for the victim.

Apparently, Father Thomas and other do-gooders in town had taken the girl to Batticaloa town hospital for treatment, and all the mothers were worried to death about their daughters. Almost all of them wanted their daughters to get away from the troubled area. Saratha's mother Auntie Sathya, Buvana's mother Auntie Indira and Gowri's Mum held an emergency meeting under Grandma's orders and planned to send the girls away to Thirukovil, where Auntie Sathya's family lived. Meanwhile, the girls had to hide in the attic with the rice, maze, *kurakan* grain sacks and mice.

Chapter 10

Gowri thought about fate. The villagers always blamed the stars, the zodiac and supernatural powers for their crises. Should she blame these, too? Was fate really shaped by the stars and gods? No, it could not be!

They were kind, but many men on earth were not kind. It was they who created trouble, bringing calamity to ordinary folks. Poor people suffered more because of these men than rich people. Rich villagers could send their children to school in town. But what would happen to those who were less well off, like Gowri and others in the village?

The god Ganesh had had a hard time, too. He had been damaged by the flood. The poor god had no temple; the girls had no school. Both had to be rebuilt, and soon. But when? And by whom? All the villagers seemed to be at war with the racialist Sinhalese army.

'Do you think all the Tamils will be killed by the Ceylon government?' Gowri asked suddenly. She did not realise that Saratha might not be able to answer the question. Saratha did not read that much news; her reading was mostly about Tamil film stars and the gossip surrounding them.

'I think so.'

'Why do you think so?' Gowri did not like the vagueness of the reply.

'Well, the Sinhalese racialists have already attacked our leaders. It won't be long before they attack the people and kill us all.'

'What a cheerful conversation. Don't be so stupid! The government can't kill all of us,' Gowri protested strongly.

'Well...' Saratha could not say a great deal.

'What's happening? Are they here?' Buvana got up when she heard Gowri's and Saratha's raised voices.

'Go back to sleep, nobody's coming to take you away,' Saratha ordered Buvana firmly.

Buvana did not go back to sleep. She looked at both her cousins and said, 'We'll be in Thirukovil tomorrow.'

'Oh yeah, what an exciting change.' Gowri had no wish to go anywhere; she would have preferred to stay with her parents.

She detested the Sinhalese politicians and army, but she did not know many Sinhalese people. An aunt of her cousin Kamala was one of the few. In Akkaraippattu there were lots of Sinhalese, a Sinhala school and a Buddhist *vihara* (temple). Many Sinhalese and Tamils were married to each other and living in harmony. One of Kamala's aunts was married to one of Saratha's uncles. Her name was Pushpika, and she was very kind and cooked nice Sinhalese meals. She had taken the girls to the Buddhist vihara during the full moon. The visit was enjoyable; the Sinhalese worshippers brought lotus flowers and prayed to the Buddha to grant them prosperity and good health. Gowri also knew a handful of Sinhalese traders in the market. She could not understand why a group of people in uniform should behave so savagely to others just because they were of a different race or spoke a different language.

She could not sleep much that night. She got up early as usual and began to prepare for the journey to Thirukovil, though she hated the idea of fleeing from her own home because of the political situation. If the government could not look after its own people, why bother to talk of democracy?

Because of the curfew and state of emergency, that time of the morning seemed silent and frightening. There were no Muslim peasants or farmers on their way to the paddy fields in bullock carts or on bicycles. The February morning air was nippy, the river misty because of the cold weather. The girls, Dad and Ragu walked at a brisk, steady pace. Two fishermen's boats were waiting for them.

'Please don't come back to the village unless the situation's okay.' Aunt Sathya wiped away her tears as she kissed her son.

Buvana and Dad got into one boat, Gowri, Saratha and her brother Ragu into other. They floated along the River Thillai noiselessly, cutting through the fog. They turned back to look at the village. It seemed hazy and dull with no lights or people moving.

Gowri wept and told Ragu that she loathed the soldiers, who were brutal to Tamil women and chased them from their homes.

'We'll be free one day and enjoy all the rights that other citizens have,' Ragu said.

'Will we?' Gowri asked him in a sad tone.

'Yes. We must have hope that things will improve,' he said, looking through the fog.

'Well...' She hesitated for a moment. She did not know when the Tamils would be all right in Ceylon. She was worried about her pregnant mother and Grandma, who had to work so hard and look after her daughter as well as her sick sister-in-law without Gowri to help her.

The moon had disappeared behind the village to the west.

Aunt Sathya's relatives were warm and friendly. Ragu's uncle was an educated, progressive man with a pleasant manner. His wife was a good cook. Above all, Ragu seemed to enjoy the fact that Kamala was there. She had not gone back to school in Batticaloa because of the trouble in the area. She appeared very relaxed with him. Gowri observed Ragu's behaviour. When she saw his happy smile, she began to understand what was happening, but she had no intention of sharing her understanding with Saratha. Saratha was like a newspaper; she would announce any secret to anyone who was listening.

Buvana could not have cared less what was going on in the world. She seemed to have settled down to helping in the kitchen of the strange household. Neither she nor Gowri had stayed there before, though they visited when they had been to the famous Murukan temple nearby.

The house was situated only a few hundred yards from the sea. Waves continually crashed against the coconut trees on the golden sandy beach, which stretched for miles. Green fields and coconut estates surrounded the house – very different from the homes of the girls, where there were always people around. It was large house with many rooms and with a radio and gramophone so that they could listen to music. Ragu and Kamala spent a lot of time talking and laughing together.

Kamala's mother cooked spicy prawns and creamy crab deliciously. The food, on the whole, was excellent. Saratha marvelled aloud that people should spend so much money on expensive food, but Kamala chuckled and said, 'Life has only a few pleasures, and one of them is good food.' She was very good at experimenting with new dishes. Later, she asked Ragu what his favourite food was.

Gowri could not help noticing their smiles and the meaning behind them, and she was glad for him. She wanted him to be happy; why not? After all, she – Kamala – was his relative and had every right to bring him joy.

Buvana was also his cousin, but Gowri did not think that Buvana understood what was going on around her. Even if she noticed, she was not one to express her feelings. She would never start a conversation or even join in, though she would answer if someone asked her a question. Gowri remembered what Grandma had told her about Buvana. She had been a premature baby, born about eight months into Auntie Indira's pregnancy, and had not grown as quickly as other children. She started to talk late, began school late. Now, she was much brighter academically than Saratha.

Saratha spent most of her time talking or thinking about Shiva. Gowri was preoccupied with various worries. Nevertheless, she was enjoying her stay in Kamala's house.

One evening they all went to the Hindu deity Murukan's temple close by. Murukan was the god of love and strength. He had two wives and symbolised power and romance. The temple was ancient and was well known throughout the region.

While they were there, Tamil youths crowded around to talk to Ragu about the incident in Kolavil. They congratulated him on the courage of the young men. When they went inside to pray, Gowri could not prevent herself from comparing the figure of the god with two wives with

Ragu, who was standing between Kamala and Buvana.

A sudden pain pierced Gowri's heart. She knew all too well how her family were accustomed to arranging marriages for their children. Hints had been made about arranging a wedding between her and Rajah; soon the same would be done for Buvana, Saratha and, of course, Ragu. What would he do?

Gowri thought about a lot during the prayers. It seemed to her that much was being done without proper thought. Uncle Kasi and Auntie Indira were nice people and had great respect for Ragu because of his decency, kindness and integrity. Would they ask Mailar to pledge his son as their daughter Buvana's future husband?

Buvana was the complete opposite of Kamala. Buvana was an introverted and quiet person who expected little from life. Even her birth had been difficult. Her mother had spent more time with her other children than with Buvana, as she was the eldest girl in the family. She had accepted her responsibilities unquestioningly. Although Gowri was also the eldest daughter, she would question things before accepting them, while Saratha was determined and stubborn and would get what she wanted, no matter what stood in her way.

When they returned home, the older women played an old-fashioned game of draughts in the shadow of a coconut tree. Buvana and Saratha chattered in the corner of the portico. Kamala and Ragu read the newspapers. Gowri went for a walk on the beach with some children. The powerful waves echoed what was in her mind.

The days went more quickly than she had expected. The

situation in their village was improving, according to the information they received. Apparently, the soldiers who had been terrorising the area had been sent back to their barracks in Amparai town and replaced by another division. The girls gathered that their fathers, Father Thomas and the Muslim head man Iburahim had been to see the government agent to achieve those changes.

Gowri could hardly wait to get home so she could go to school, and she was deeply concerned about her mother's health. Saratha did not seem to be in any hurry, though. If Shiva had been in the village, she would have been the most eager to return.

Every evening they spent on the beach. They would catch crabs and bring them back to be cooked. They would stroll for miles on the golden sand against the background of crashing waves and fishermen's songs. Often Kamala and Ragu would walk alone without the other children. Gowri, Buvana and Saratha would talk about their childhood when they could play freely in the fields, swim in the River Thillai, climb rocks, trees and dance among the bushes.

One day they walked home from the beach just after sunset. Ragu seemed extraordinarily happy after spending the day with Kamala, and Gowri wanted him to be as happy as that forever. When they reached the house, a couple of people from Kolavil were there. Dad had come and... Who was that with him? Gowri looked at the other person.

It was a dark evening. The new guest was seated in a chair comfortably in a chair, under the margosa tree. Thinking that he must be Uncle Kasi, Gowri ran to him and nearly put her hand on his shoulder. Excitedly she exclaimed, 'Thank you for coming.'

He turned to her. It was not her uncle but Nathan — her teacher Ramanathan's brother.

'Really?' He gave her a lovely smile. Gowri and the other girls never had the chance to talk to strangers except doctors, sanitary inspectors and school inspectors and their teachers. His casual manner made her feel a little embarrassed. She did not know what to do. Her first impulse was to tell him that she had mistaken him for Uncle Kasi, but what was the point of explaining?

He stared at her as she struggled to get words out of her mouth. Her throat was dry, her pulse was fast, her mind went blank.

'What's the matter, Gowri?' His voice was clear as a temple bell, his smile warm and gentle.

'Nothing.' She hurried away.

'Don't bring water to pour on me,' he laughed.

Chapter 11

When she returned to the hall, her father was describing the army's atrocities in the village. Gowri listened, feeling angry. She turned her mind away from the conversation and helped the women who were preparing a big meal for the visitors with a variety of dishes. Nathan joined her uncle and others in discussing politics. The young man spoke of the good things which the prime minister S. W. R. D. Bandaranaike was doing for whole country, such as his policy on education for all and land distribution to landless peasants.

'What difference does it make? He does it mainly for his Sinhalese people. We have to suffer because of the chauvinism of Sinhalese politicians. The Sinhalese nationalists don't think Tamils belong to the country. They're talking about sending us to India,' Kamala's father complained. He worked in one of the Sinhalese colonies – a settlement in the Amparai area traditionally inhabited by the eastern Tamil community. They pondered the recent changes affecting Tamils in Ceylon.

Dad spoke of how Mr. J. R. Jayawardene, at the time a senior figure in the opposition, had mobilised the Sinhalese masses in 1956 against Mr. Bandaranaike when he proposed to grant concessions on the use of the Tamil language in predominantly Tamil areas. Mr. Bandaranaike was from the class of business people and professionals who aspired to take over the economic and political power which Europeans had held – Gowri had heard them referred to as the 'national bourgeoisie'. He had come to power that year with Sinhalese nationalist slogans and promises to treat that ethnic community better than anyone else on the island.

Most Sinhalese were poor and had hoped for a golden future after gaining independence from British rule, and the past eight years of United National Party rule had given nothing to impoverished Sinhalese. When the nationalists saw their frustration, they changed their tactics. To win votes, the Tamils had become the target of their campaign, rather than the upper-class Sinhalese who held power.

Listening to the conversation, Gowri become frightened. She had already witnessed the brutality of the government towards the Tamil people. What would happen in the future? Perhaps it was possible to fight, as Uncle Kasi had put it, 'Instead of living like slaves, let's fight for our dignity.'

But how? She thought about 'fighting back'. She was prepared to fight Grandma over going to school, an issue that mattered deeply to her. Why should the Tamils not fight? They should campaign, too, she thought. She would have loved to discuss the topic with her teacher or with Ragu. He read a lot and was thoughtful; perhaps he could answer her questions.

However, that night the household was too busy. Everyone was glad that the problems in Kolavil were no longer severe, but Kamala said that she was sad to see the guests go. 'No wonder she feels sad if she's going to be parted from Ragu,' Gowri thought.

Kamala was an excellent hostess. She entertained her guests with charm and courtesy. An attractive sixteen-year-old, she had been educated in town and had a self-assured manner. She talked freely with Ragu and Nathan, who also seemed to enjoy her company. Meanwhile, Saratha was livelier than she had been for several days; perhaps she had received reassuring news about Shiva.

Thinking of Kamala and her way of life, Gowri could not help feeling sorry for herself. 'I want to go to school, it doesn't matter where. I want to learn lots of things, lots and lots, and one day I'll be a teacher, or maybe I could go to far-off places, the way Kamala does, and bring back interesting news and everything else I learnt.' She let her imagination wander freely in a world where Grandma could not stop her. Grandma was devout and believed in nearly all Hindu gods, each a manifestation of a single divine presence; there were nearly over three thousand gods according to Hindu mythology. Gowri would worship them, too, if they would help her to carry on with her studies.

After the meal she began to concentrate, 'Dear God, please let me go to school, I'll pray to you for rest of my life. Let me be a teacher, please.'

The next morning, she got up to the sound of temple bells. Saratha ran to Gowri as she was taking a bath. The water was chilly, the air cool, the sea was calm, the temple filled with the sound of praying and singing. Saratha pulled her skirt up to her chest as she washed, a wide grin on her face.

'What's going on? You seem over the moon.' Gowri poured the first bucket of water over her head.

'Yes, yes!' Saratha smiled. In her excitement she seemed lost for words. 'He's home,' she announced happily.

'Oh yeah, who told you that?'

'Nathan told me, he – Nathan gave him a lift from town, and he's home.' No wonder Saratha was happy. 'Nathan told me that he... he's going to Colombo.'

'Why?' Gowri soaped her body while she questioned her.

'He's got a job in Colombo, but I don't want him to go. There could be trouble and…and…' Saratha began to sob.

'What's the matter?' Gowri stopped drawing water from the well and waited for an answer.

'I don't know. People say all sorts of things about young men who go to Colombo. Still, I'm proud of him.' Saratha's mixed feelings about Shiva were understandable, but Gowri was still faced with the problem that Saratha would not talk or think of anything or anyone other than her absent love.

For the moment, Saratha forgot the people around her and her surroundings. She hummed romantic film songs, wiggled her bottom cheerfully, laughed for no reason and walked around without helping the other women to prepare breakfast. Kamala and the women in the house had cooked tasty fish dishes in a creamy coconut sauce and string hoppers (rice vermicelli) and various other snacks for their guests. Saratha did not like the waiting, she wanted to go home. She said, 'Old Theivi may be on her deathbed by now, while you lot are feasting on prawns and crabs.'

What a hypocrite Saratha was! Gowri knew perfectly well that her impatience had nothing to do with the dying old woman at home in Kolavil and everything to do with Shiva. Saratha wanted to go home as quickly as possible to see him.

Ragu was puzzled because his sister was so eager to get ready to leave for home. Normally, she would have spent hours in front of the mirror preparing herself. Kamala bustled about, making sure that everybody had enough food. Her father talked about the famous Murukan temple and its influence and invited Nathan to visit the place whenever he had time.

He smiled and said, 'I don't know much about the Murukan temple and his influence on people's lives, but I've been to your house, enjoyed your hospitality, and tasted one of the most delicious prawn and crab dishes I've ever tasted at your place. I'm certain that I'll visit you when I can.' Kamala blushed with embarrassment when he smiled at her.

'You must come and visit us,' Ragu told Nathan. Gowri wondered who 'us' meant. Nathan noticed the question in Gowri's eyes. She sensed that he was paying more attention to her than any young man had ever paid to her up to now.

'By the way, why did you and your cousins hide behind the rice stores? Couldn't you do something against the army?' Turning to the girls, Nathan changed the subject.

'What could we do?' Gowri did not ask the question aloud, but she realised that he had heard all about their ordeal.

'If you can splash us with cold turmeric water to shock us, why not do the same to the army? Only instead of turmeric water perhaps you could have used boiling water,' he continued, half serious, half joking.

Gowri looked at him. She felt like making a brusque reply. 'The soldiers weren't there to enjoy the puberty festivities, were they?' she wanted to ask him, but she could not. Grandma always said that Gowri had a big mouth because she argued with her a lot. But her big mouth could not open against this stranger. Gowri did not know whether it was because she did not want to get into an argument with him

107

or because she accepted that what he said was correct.

Nathan resembled his brother, the teacher Ramanathan, who was concerned about the progress of the village and women's education. But Nathan had additional qualities: he was more friendly and candid. Above all, he was handsome and elegant. He spoke pleasantly and had a certain grace.

'I am talking to you, Gowri,' he reminded her, as she thought about his personality.

'Are you joking? How can we throw scalding water over the army?'

He looked straight at her. She felt he could go into her heart and mind easily with that look. He replied, 'You wouldn't hesitate to kill a snake if it came to bite you, would you?'

'Well...' She did not answer. Suddenly she remembered the girl who had been raped by soldiers in the town. Did he know how the army treated Tamil girls? He spoke of courage. Talk was easy, but courage was not something to be easily come by. It would have to come with experience and wisdom. She did not know how to counter his argument, but she did not like what he said about fighting back. To the best of her knowledge, men simply did not understand the fear of being raped.

They finished the sumptuous meal which Kamala's family had provided, said goodbye to everyone in her house and got into the car to return to Kolavil. Gowri wanted to go home as soon as possible because she was deeply worried about her mother and others in her household, while Saratha was in a hurry to see Shiva.

In the car, the conversation on the political situation

continued. Gowri was losing her patience. She did not want the political argument to continue. She knew that Nathan would candidly say what he thought was right, but Uncle Kasi would not accept his point of view. He hero-worshipped the Tamil politicians. Like most ordinary Tamils, he had been brought up to respect Tamil leaders who spoke English and had a Western education. They would never accept the fact that the real issue was not the Sinhala language but the struggle over Ceylon's economy.

Kasi was a very sincere man with honest opinions. He could not talk like Nathan, who had an English education and understood ever-changing international politics. His perspective, and Dad's, was that politics was about Tamils having the right to live and practice their religion and culture without being oppressed by the government. As far as Gowri could understand from the conversation, what Nathan was trying to explain was that Tamil politicians were, at the moment, not bothered about ordinary Tamils, like those in the tea plantations or poor people who had no chance of bettering their lives and rising up the social ladder – such as those in her village, who did not have a school.

She knew that the schools inspector who had failed to help them to get the school expanded was an English-educated man from Jaffna region who thought, and said openly, that 'villagers like you should be spending your time in the paddy fields, not wasting on books and learning'. If there were a society in which such leaders were in power, she wondered, would they give village girls the chance to go to school?

As usual, the journey from Thirukovil to Kolavil took about an hour by car because the roads were in such a bad state of repair. For the whole of this time, the men in the car talked of nothing but politics. Nathan did not support the Tamil Federal Party because, according to him, it was set up to represent middle and upper-class Tamils who spoke English, had jobs in Colombo and wanted to send their children to England or America to study. He said, 'I don't like the leaders who manipulate the innocent to vote for them in order to get power for themselves and make profit in the name of politics.'

He did not trust S. W. R. D. Bandaranaike's government. 'So, whom do you support? What are your politics?' Uncle Kasi asked him.

'I respect everyone's views, but I can't condone injustice or oppression. I believe in equality. I hope one day there'll be a society in which nobody is oppressed because of religion, race, caste or sex.'

Gowri wished she could talk with him, while Saratha took no interest in the conversation. She stuck her head out of the window, not afraid of dust getting in her eyes. She was in a hurry to meet Shiva. Buvana slept all the way home.

The car was crowded, and everyone wanted to get out of it as soon as possible. But travelling along this road, between the river and the Bay of Bengal, was a pleasurable experience. The scenery was among the most beautiful to be enjoyed anywhere.

As soon as they reached the house, they could hear a chorus of high pitch wailing and weeping. Old woman Theivi was dead.

Chapter 12

Palipody had only been released by the police a few days before. He sat on the trunk of a fallen coconut tree, crying. He no longer had his front teeth; they had been knocked out by the brutal police and the soldiers. He was making strange noises with his toothless mouth. When he laughed in the future, no one would hear his usual cackle.

Gowri could not help wondering about her great-aunt's death. Theivi had been close to death for weeks, but she had hung on until the old man came home from police custody. Was there any truth in the rural belief that you would meet your loved ones before you die, if you felt really strongly about them? Who knows what could be achieved, if the willpower was there?

As soon as the girls arrived, there was plenty for them to do at the funeral house. The traditional role for young girls was to make tea and look after the needs of the mourners and visitors. Saratha's eyes wandered everywhere, seeking Shiva. He was not there.

Gowri and Poorani served tea; as they had not yet reached puberty and so could move around among men and women. When Gowri saw Shiva, he grinned at her and asked, 'Hey, what's all this? It's like the *Mahabharatha*, with you all running off into the jungle away from the problems.'

She did not answer. Only the girls understood their fear of the army. She spotted Rajah with his head heavily bandaged. He was surrounded by young men from the village. 'Well,'

Gowri mused silently, 'he's a hero to them, now.'

She moved about, many questions on her mind. The dead woman's daughter lived in the 'colonised' area near Amparai, and the funeral would have to wait until she arrived. Someone had gone to collect her.

Grandma's face showed her sorrow at losing her sister-in-law. When she came to the area where the women were embracing each other and sobbing and wailing in rhythm with the funeral rituals, someone asked her, 'What's the matter?'

'Well...' She hesitated for a moment, then continued, 'Well, there's going to be big trouble.'

Some of the women stopped wailing and sobbing and inquired, 'Why?'

'Mailar's a trouble-maker. He's so selfish, he doesn't even show respect at a funeral.'

'What's wrong, Grandma?' Saratha asked confusedly.

'For the past few days there has been some argument about Mailar's behaviour during the food distribution programme. Nayagam (Rajah's father) claims that Mailar has fiddled with money which should have gone to the poor people who were the victims of the flood. On Mailar's part, he says that his good name is being unfairly tarnished by Nayagam, who's spreading this gossip. I don't know what's going to happen now.'

According to other rumours, Nayagam was taking bribes from private businessmen in order to arrange for them to get orders for grain. Normally, the government would set a quota for purchasing paddy from every household; what was harvested from three acres could be sold to the state at a reasonable price. Otherwise, entrepreneurs would buy up the harvest for far less. If Nayagam made arrangements for the state to buy large quantities from businessmen rather than from the farmers themselves, they would find it very difficult to get a fair price for their grain.

'What a monstrous thing to do,' Gowri thought. Uneducated villagers did not understand the quota system. If they were unable to sell much of what they had produced, they would have no option but to sell the surplus to middlemen. She remembered that Nathan had warned that politicians used innocent people for their own benefit.

Nayagam was responsible for allocating quotas throughout the village, but he would have been unable to play such a game without the support of the Divisional Revenue Officer (DRO). Apparently, the D.R.O. from Jaffna had made a deal with Nayagam at the expense of badly-off farmers who had already lost much in the flood. The scandal had emerged when some local people had gone to talk to the 'high-ups' in the Batticaloa office.

If Mailar made a fuss, Nayagam would respond vigorously. Their sons and friends would be drawn in, and the two sides would be at loggerheads. Grandma was furious with Mailar for getting embroiled. She did not want physical violence to flare up in which Nayagam's son Rajah would get involved, since Grandma was constantly praying that Rajah would marry Gowri. The last thing she wanted was for her dream to be destroyed by gossip and scandal. Grandma had seen enough of such things in her lifetime. She intended her granddaughter to settle down in a family of some means, such as Rajah's.

The funeral procession started that evening as the sun was setting in the west, when the old woman's daughter finally arrived. Grandma's face was rigid; she did not want to talk to anyone or encourage conversation. She wanted the funeral to finish as quickly as possible. She hated the idea that her dream might be shattered by Mailar's big mouth and arrogant manner.

She could remember the days when Mailar's family was prosperous and employed Nayagam. She could recall how, during the second world war, young Nayagam had gone away and returned with a lot of money, the source of which was unknown. Nobody had dared to question this emerging businessman, up-to-date in his methods, with a tractor to plough his fields. Moreover, he had plenty of money to lend to poorer farmers, who could turn to him when they were in need. Although Mailar's family had remained the largest and best-respected in the village, his old-fashioned values had faded before the newly rich Nayagam.

Mailar's family's fortune had been split. Some had gone to his brother, Gowri's father Nadesan, who had gone to India and returned with barely a rupee to his name but amply supplied with progressive thinking and Gandhian philosophy. Some of his wealth had gone to Mailar's sister's husband Lingam, who had lost his wife and the baby during the delivery. He, too, had gone with Gowri's Dad to India and returned as a swami. Mailar's wealth was vested in his land, which had now been battered by flood and drought.

Grandma wanted to become more closely involved with the family of Nayagam, now rich, who was also a distant relative of hers. She had gone out of her way to help his wife during childbirth and at other times. The old woman had become very fond of Rajah, who had grown up like a prince – dangerously good-looking, powerful and now one of the most eligible bachelors in Kolavil. He was outgoing and eloquent, wore the most fashionable outfits and had become the Tamil Federal Party's youth representative in the village.

Neighbours had begun to ask Grandma, 'What's all this then? Are you planning on Rajah becoming your granddaughter Gowri's groom?' The joke hit her hard. She was fed up with her son-in-law Nadesan's Gandhian philosophy and simple lifestyle. She was determined that his daughter would be brought up properly, fit to become a member of a rich and decent family. The old woman stopped Gowri from doing many things she wanted; was not the girl intended to marry Rajah and become the richest woman in the village? Gowri's ambition to study and go away to become a teacher irritated Grandma. It disrupted her plans.

Later that evening, the men returned from the cemetery. They gathered under a mango tree to change their clothes and have something to eat. The *dhobis* began to spread out the clean garments. Traditionally the *dhobi* would offer clean clothes to the headman of the village first. But the head *dhobi* Nagan was short-sighted and could not see properly in the twilight. He picked up a white *verti* and handed it over to Nayagam first.

Nayagam took this without hesitation, and Mailar was furious. His family had received the first offer from *dhobis* for centuries. Nayagam knew perfectly well that Nagan could not make out who was who in the fading light of the gloomy late evening. Mailar ran to Nagan, tucked his long hair up, and shouted, 'Hey, you stupid low-caste dog, can't you see who is taking the first offer of fresh clothes?' Nagan was shocked and afraid.

Nayagam laughed loudly and remarked, 'Some people have no self-respect. Although they've lost their dignity, unfortunately they don't seem to be aware of this.'

Everyone knew whom he meant. Mailar's moustache twitched with anger and his lips were trembling. He glared at Nayagam as if eager to reduce him to a heap of ash. But Nayagam continued to laugh with majestic disdain, lit his pipe nonchalantly and boomed, 'It's no good snatching at a piece of clothing to hide one's nakedness. It's better to behave like a gentleman.'

Grandma picked up the message clearly. The cobra was rearing its head to strike in public. She hurried to the men – not usually done in public even by an elderly woman – and she said to Nagan sympathetically, 'Wouldn't it be a good idea to get on with giving out clean clothing?'

She was almost shoved aside as Mailar stormed out of the crowd, waved his hands about in a fury, pointed at Nayagam and said, 'You wouldn't talk like that if you were a real gentleman who had earned his money by hard work. You're a cheap trickster!'

His voice was like that of a roaring tiger, and the three girls behind a mango tree were in fear of a physical showdown between two old and powerful men in the community. They looked at the bystanders and one another.

Uncle Kasi arrived on the scene. He grasped the situation at once and suggested calmly, 'Shouldn't we all be showing some respect for the dead person and forgetting our personal vendettas?'

Mailar's wife came over, her baby on her hip. She hated fights. Stepping between her husband and Nayagam, she said tearfully, 'You stupid men, only a few weeks ago we went through hell because of the army. Now, you seem to want another drama. Will you two let us grieve for the dead and get on with our lives? If you foolish old men provoke the youngsters, they may get into trouble. Is that a good thing to do for those you love?' She broke down and sobbed.

From a distance, Rajah watched his father arguing with Mailar. The youth was not alone, but surrounded by other young men. Since he had been attacked by Muslims because of his activism in the Tamil Federal Party, most of the others in the village treated him as a hero and hung around him like disciples. When he had come out of hospital, they had visited his house shouting Tamil Federal Party's slogans, singing Tamil nationalist songs and were sometimes fed by Rajah's family with tasty mutton curry and rice.

Gowri noticed his expression. If he joined in the row with Mailar, there would be no check on his hot-headed followers. She understood the village mentality. Her neighbours relied more on emotion than intellect. They would not easily forgive someone who disrupted a funeral. They did not often listen to the radio or read newspapers; instead, they listened to, and learnt from, one another. They were not polite like townsfolk.

There was a long silence. Nobody dared to speak. Then *dhobi* Nagan continued to hand out clothing. As the last rays of sunlight died away, an unspoken darkness found its way

117

into people's minds. Though Gowri did not guess it at the time, the rift which had opened up that day would make a difference to many lives.

Grandma's face showed her sadness. She was a wise woman. She knew the games that the men in her village were playing and could predict the outcome.

That night, Ragu came to sing mourning prayers in the funeral house. Nathan was with him, and they talked of the incident before they began to sing. Ragu explained the conflict between his father and Nayagam to Nathan. Gowri was sitting some distance away and could see their faces clearly. From the darker side of the verandah, she listened to her cousin speaking. He talked about the general election and how Nayagam and Mailar had divided the village politically.

Ragu did not particularly like Nayagam or his son, he told Nathan, but they were committed and sincere supporters of the Tamil Federal Party. His own father, however, had backed the independent candidate simply to be different from Nayagam. Gowri came to think of politics as a selfish game played by powerful men, which brought nothing but suffering to people without power or money.

The following day she watched sadly as children left for school. Many of those who had been arrested by the police were now setting off cheerfully. The boys who, because of the past few weeks' troubles, had started studying for their O-levels in the nearest town, were back home now.

Though the local MP had joined the ruling United National Party instead of staying with the Tamil Federal Party and working in the interests of Tamils, the villagers felt they had to go and see him. 'I won't go if Nayagam's going, too.'

Mailar refused to join the deputation if his rival was also a member.

Gowri became angry. 'Why should we become pawns in their game?' she stormed silently. She went to Uncle Kasi and asked him to advise Mailar to go see the MP. Kasi was a forthright and honest man, and he cursed both Nayagam and Mailar for their selfishness. Kasi said that Mailar had even managed to make a mess of Palipody's claim for rehabilitation money after the flood. The poor old man no longer seemed to understand what was going on around him, and Mailar had exploited his debilitation.

She could hardly believe that people like Mailar could exist with no feelings of guilt over their treatment of others. She wondered if there were many who resembled him. She had no wish to meet others like Nayagam or Mailar who would do anything for money.

Would Nayagam's son behave in that way? Her body felt cold at the thought that one day she might be married to him.

Chapter 13

The Tamil and Buddhist New Year in April began with the usual goodies, and the smells of sweets and other foods mingled in the air. People relaxed in swings which hung from large trees around the village. Auntie Indira was making dresses for various people on her sewing machine. Gowri was busy looking after her mother.

Gowri's first period had begun a few days before. Although she was the eldest girl in her family, she had reached puberty while her mother was not that well, and the household was in mourning for Theivi. So, the ceremony could not be as elaborate for her as for Saratha.

Anyway, Gowri could not care less who lopped off the branch of an areca nut tree for her ceremony. 'I bet Grandma will look for Rajah to cut the areca branch,' she thought. But Grandma did not do that; she knew that Mailar would go mad if he heard of any closeness between Nayagam's family and that of his brother, Gowri's father.

Grandma was a little disappointed that she could not do what she had in mind. But Gowri heard her whispering about Nayagam's family to Mum. Mum was very tired as she reached the full term of her pregnancy, so other women accompanied Grandma to the astrologer.

From looking at Grandma's face when she returned, Gowri could tell that the astrologer had not come up with good news. The old woman's expression was angry and impatient as she stalked into the hall. According to her, for girls to reach puberty or be born in April boded well, so why was she annoyed?

Aunt Indira laughed and explained that Grandma was cross because the astrologer had told them that Gowri would never marry anyone from the village or live in the village. Grandma, who had relied since she was young on horoscopes and predictions of astrologers, could not believe that her granddaughter was not going to do what she had planned for her. The old woman had spent many hours consulting the temple astrologer and had shaped her life and the lives of her children to fit what he had foretold. Now, her dream was shattered; Gowri's horoscope was predicting something too extraordinary to take in.

Gowri was confined for nearly two weeks with only Poorani for a companion while the family quietly celebrated her womanhood. While she was inside the house, during the 'isolation period', she read voraciously, as usual. Ragu had brought her many Tamil novels by various famous authors and other reading materials. Much of this reading was about people from other countries and their ways of life. She was surprised to find that her cousin was interested in international matters and social change. There were a few books on women and politics in India, particularly during the independence struggle. In fact, those books and magazines belonged to Nathan, but she was not aware of this. She read them all and began to understand the meaning of freedom, yet had no idea who had provided these books for her.

'There is no freedom without struggle,' the books said. She would have to struggle to be free to go to school, but how?

Grandma was openly talking about proposing to Rajah on Gowri's behalf. Saratha came over and inquired, 'Hey, is it true that the astrologer said you wouldn't marry someone from our village?'

Gowri did not answer. Instead, she talked about going to school after the New Year holiday. Her ambition to be a teacher had become very important to her. She said that she had no intention of spending all her life in a village riddled with backbiting and jealousy.

'All right, you can be like Parames; she went to teacher training college and met her husband Ramanathan. Somewhere, you'll find the right man for you.'

'Come off it, Saratha. Did your mother purposely go somewhere to find your father to marry him? Did Uncle Kasi go to Trincomalee town to seek out Aunt Indira? It's all matter of chance. Anyway, I haven't got boys on my mind all the time, as you do. I've got more important and interesting things to do than wasting time on boys.'

Gowri's snub hurt Saratha's feelings. 'What's the matter with you?' she asked, confused. To the best of her knowledge, what the girls themselves felt would make no difference; their parents would not let them go to school. As soon as the puberty ceremony was over, the families would be arranging marriages for their daughters.

When Gowri thought about the future, she felt unhappy and frustrated. Her dreams were of the beauty of freedom, but to make them come true would not be easy. They were no longer children, allowed to play in the fields, swim in the River Thillai, stuff mangoes up in their blouses and giggle at their make-believe breasts. They had to face the same reality as other girls in the village. They could no longer laugh and joke as they had done a few months before. Their behaviour would have to be above reproach, their speech and movements guarded.

Buvana visited her cousin during Gowri's isolation time. Buvana lived next door to Rajah's family. She heard and understood more about them than anyone else in Kolavil, since her family had no well and had to use Rajah's to draw water for drinking and other purposes. 'Hey, they're going to bring a bridal present for you...' Buvana met Gowri's burning look and did not complete the sentence. Gowri had not realised that Buvana could enjoy a smile and gossip once in a while.

'Go on, say it,' Gowri ordered her cousin like a little princess.

'Er...er...they're talking about you and...'

'Don't get carried away by your imagination, Buvana. All they're talking about is bringing some kind of present. Isn't it traditional to bring gifts to girls who've reached womanhood?' Gowri enquired carefully.

Gowri had no intention of putting ideas into her cousin's head; all she was concerned with was her education. Buvana's face saddened at the abrupt retort. After that, Buvana did not elaborate any further about the expected visit from Rajah's house.

'Listen, Buvana,' Gowri added, approaching her cousin and putting an arm around her. 'Do you think we should be frittering away our time talking about such things, the way Grandma and the others do? Don't you feel we should be trying to persuade them to let us carry on with our studies?'

'But will they let us go?' Buvana questioned.

'We'll just have to wait and see,' Gowri replied reassuringly.

'By the way…' Buvana began, then glanced around, came right up to Gowri and whispered furtively in her ear. 'By the way, Vasantha has stopped going to boarding school in town.'

'Why?' Gowri whispered back. Vasantha, one of their rich cousin, had been at a boarding school in Batticaloa.

'She was involved in a scandal.' The words spilled out.

'What!'

'Yes, she wrote a love letter to a boy in the town, and it was discovered by the nuns at the convent. They refused to let her to stay.'

A love letter?

Only the gods knew what the girls had been through about a year or two years ago. They had begun writing perfectly innocent letters to their pen-pal in Colombo named Leslie.

They had bought a stamp and envelope for the first time in their lives. Then, seated under the jak tree, they had written about themselves, their village and, of course, their grandmother, who did not allow girls to sing loudly, dance in imitation of film stars, swim in the River Thillai, climb trees or rocks near the paddy fields.

They had asked their classmate and confidant Sundaram (the one with rotten teeth) to post the letter in town since the village did not have a post-box. Within a week they received a reply from their pen-pal in Colombo.

After that the girls wrote many letters, about the harvest festival (Pongal) and the rituals taking place in the village such as giving offerings to sea goddesses. Seeing off devotees who went to an ancient temple in Katharagama, a long journey of hundreds of miles through jungles, some of those pilgrims never came back, losing their lives through illness during the journey or getting lost.

Leslie's letters described Ceylon's capital city Colombo, which the girls knew was far away. Leslie wrote to them about Fort railway station, which had many trains carrying people from Colombo in various directions across Ceylon, the harbour with hundreds of ships from all over the world and, of course, Colombo Zoo, with exotic animals from around the globe.

The girls wrote about their paddy fields, which they described as being like green velvet decorated with birds, and ponds full of water-lilies and multi-coloured lotus-blossoms. They would describe the temple's festivals, sometimes the River Thillai and the beauty of its banks. Gowri was the writer, while the other two contributed information. Leslie's letters had not yet stirred up any suspicion nor caused problems with their parents or Grandma, since Saratha used to receive letters from her cousin Kamala who was away at the college in town.

One day, an expensive black car rolled into Kolavil. Usually, strangers and cars would be greeted by yapping dogs, children screaming with excitement and the curious looks of the villagers. Few visited Kolavil in cars other than political leaders during election times, for whom there would be expensive preparations and a feast.

When the black car from Colombo arrived, with its own noise accompanied by the background noise of village children yelling and wandering dogs barking, Saratha's father Mailar had come out of the house to find out who had parked nearby. Sometimes a car would come to advertise a film, music blaring from the loudspeaker. Children would follow the cinema vehicle to the next village, dogs would run after it up to the edge of Kolavil. But this particular car stopped in front of Mailar's gate.

It had been a Saturday, Gowri recalled. Someone had been selling venison, and Gowri's household had bought some, as had most of the villagers. She had been on her way to the shops to get spices to make venison curry when the car arrived.

Mailar had been preparing to have a bath. His body had been smeared with herbal oil and his long hair plastered with a thick sticky mixture of fenugreek and other herbs to relieve tension. He had stood there, paste on his head and oil on his body, wearing nothing but a loincloth to cover his private parts. He had looked like a *maharishi* or some other figure from one of the Hindu myths. The strangers from the capital city who stopped the car had taken a few moments to realise that they had not stepped into one of the legends from the past.

Mailar worshipped men in western costumes. According to Gowri's dad Nadesan, Mailar would willingly wipe the arse of anyone who spoke English and wore western clothes. Mailar had given the newcomers one of his wide, completely artificial smiles.

'Can I help you, gentlemen?' He had wiped his oily hand on his loincloth, beaming.

'Yes. Actually, we're looking for Saratha Mailar, Gowri Nadesan and Buvana Kasi,' the young men had told him hesitantly. They would not have believed that the girls who had written to them lived in such a primitive place.

'Who?' Mailar's smile faded as his confusion grew. Gowri had listened from behind the thatched fence as the strangers spoke, suddenly realising who they were. One of the youths explained to Mailar that they been on their way from Colombo to a wedding in Pothuvil town and had thought of stopping off at Kolavil to see his pen-friends Saratha, Gowri and Buvana.

When Gowri, who was behind the fence, heard that, her mind had gone blank and she had almost wet herself with fear. It was they whom the strangers wanted to see. Gowri had not realised that someone named Leslie might be a boy. They thought it was only a girl's name.

Saratha had only been nearly thirteen years old, but her charm had always turned boys' heads. The well-dressed young men from Colombo had smiled at her just as Grandma arrived on the scene.

After this, a world war nearly broke out. Thanks to the gods, Ragu had come to the rescue and saved the girls from complete disaster and beatings from Grandma with her mighty weapons of a long broomstick and wooden spoons. But although they escaped from Grandma's broomstick strokes, they had been forced to endure her sharp tongue, instead. She had called them all the dirty names under the sun. She shouted that she never known girls from Kolavil village to bring boys over from Colombo.

'I've never talked to a stranger in my life!' she stormed.

'Who'd be interested in talking to you, anyway?' Gowri had wanted to ask, but she had not dared to open her mouth. Grandma was looking for the co-conspirator with rotten teeth, Sundaram, clutching her broomstick, but he was not to be seen.

After that, Gowri was wary of getting embroiled again in any of Saratha's adventures. Poor Buvana had no control over Saratha's actions, but now and again she would get entangled in one of her conspiracies against Grandma. Of course, little escaped her. When Gowri learned of Vasantha's love letter scandal, she could feel butterflies in her stomach because of Saratha's involvement with Shiva.

During the next few days, Rajah's relatives visited with various gifts for Gowri; Grandma was overjoyed, although she remembered the astrologer's prediction. The women in Rajah's family staged a mock wedding in which one of them dressed up as a man and came to ask for Gowri as bride for Rajah.

So, Gowri knew that she and Rajah were now being talked about openly. When Rajah's relatives came around, Mailar and his wife did not visit his brother's house to pay their respects, which would normally have been customary, because of his hostility towards to Rajah's family, particularly Nayagam.

'How dare you be so friendly with my enemy?' Mailar bellowed at his brother Nadesan after he had welcomed Nayagam's family with lavish hospitality.

'How can you say that? This is the first ceremony of this kind in our family. If we don't show some courtesy to people who come to pay their respects, it'll be a disgrace. You can't expect us to be nasty to people simply because you don't like them,' Grandma told Mailar in a firm tone.

Gowri could visualise the future if she were to become

Rajah's wife. No matter what Grandma said, she didn't think Mailar would tolerate his brother's daughter getting married to his enemy's son. Uncle Kasi and Auntie Indira, however, took no notice of Mailar's complaints. Whether they wanted their son to marry Gowri may not have been the real issue. It was possible that the main aim of their behaviour was to provoke Mailar. Perhaps they were right. Why did some people have to play with the lives and feelings of others to prove how wealthy and powerful they were?

Gowri's second ceremony was celebrated in a low-key way. Ramanathan's family came to visit her, bringing a lovely Kashmiri silk saree. They had been away for the New Year holiday when Gowri's puberty ceremony started.

Gowri was wearing a blue silk Bangalore saree and jewels as part of the ceremonial outfit when Nathan saw her. He stared at her in amazement. 'How come you look so beautiful?' he whispered to her with a pleasant and charming smile, while others were talking to each other loudly about some aspect of the ceremony. She didn't say anything; she was afraid to speak to a stranger because Grandma would not approve.

Nathan often visited the village to see his brother Ramanathan and his friend (and Gowri's cousin) Ragu. The local youths did not share of his views on equality and liberalism. He brought more books and magazines, and Gowri received them via Ragu. Some of the books were novels or collections of short stories. Some were about world politicians such as Churchill and Lenin. At first Gowri did not know who they were as she was only familiar with Indian and Ceylonese leaders; she had assumed that they all lived in Colombo and were popular there. As she discovered more about them from Ragu, Gowri began to understand Nathan better. He did not argue with her, but he began to raise her awareness of many issues such as socio-political matters in the world, which she considered important.

While the visitors were there, the conversation turned to the topic of education, and Gowri listened attentively.

Nathan was clearly dropping a hint to her when he commented, 'Unless girls show some interest in the matter, old-fashioned villagers aren't going to take any notice.'

Certainly, it was a good idea. But how could she be firm on her own? Would Saratha and Buvana join her?

While the teacher's family were still there, Uncle Kasi arrived and became involved in the discussion.

Nathan joined in the conversation. He stated that, 'Neither Tamil nor Sinhalese leaders really understand the problems of the ordinary people in Ceylon. The rising cost of living has made people angry with the government, but it has diverted this anger to other targets. For the Sinhalese leaders it's easy to put the blame on Tamils, to claim that all the problems are the fault of the Tamil middle class.'

Uncle Kasi did not agree. He argued, 'The Ceylonese government is against the Tamil nation. They want us to be slaves, that's all there to it. What can we do against the government?'

Nathan was not a person to lose his temper easily, but Gowri could see his expression changing as her uncle spoke. She wondered whether Nathan understood Kasi's view or whether he still regarded the Tamil problem as simply an economic issue.

Ramanathan chuckled as if what Kasi had said was

childish. 'Our religion was made up by rich men who wanted to control others by using concepts like caste and *karma*. If we regarded one another as equals, we'd be able to unite, fight and win a better life in no time. But the rich cleverly divided us along lines of caste and class, making it hard for us to get together in struggle. That's the reason why Sinhalese and Tamils are divided, why we fight one another instead of the well-off and powerful men who exploit us.'

Gowri did not want to listen any more. Political arguments made her head ache. She was fourteen years old and had learnt to trust the opinions of her father and her cousin Ragu. If they said that their mistreatment was because they were Tamils, that was easy enough to understand, but if the teacher and his brother claimed that they were exploited on the basis of class, this was harder to comprehend.

He told them numerous historical stories, which Gowri loved. He asserted that the official version of history was false. It was all about kings and queens rather than about the people who worked to build their kingdom. Grandma also told tales about kings and queens, but, in her stories, kings and princes were mighty and would travel across the world to fight for the woman they loved.

Grandma seldom told stories nowadays. If Gowri spent time with her, it would usually end up in an argument about school and the education of women. There was a radio in Mailar's house, and stories came out of that, too. The plays and stories which were broadcast were always on themes such as love and marriage.

According to Grandma, Mailar had bought the radio to listen to the commentary on the coronation of Queen

Elizabeth in London. The villagers had seen gramophones but no radio until 1953. They queued up to see and listen to the radio. Some of them were overwhelmed by hearing voices coming through the air. 'God behaves in mysterious ways,' they would mumble when they heard prayers being chanted. But after a while, they decided that the broadcasts contained too many corrupting elements such as love stories and romantic songs.

Grandma forbade the girls to listen to plays which had romantic aspects, but Saratha would listen to whatever she could get away with and act scenes out with emotion and humour.

Gowri enjoyed reading. Most of the magazines and newspapers her father bought were from India, and some were against progressive ideas such as liberalism. Many of the books praised women who dedicated themselves to the welfare of their husbands and families. Buvana had become one of them. She would do anything to please her parents. Aunt Indira bought a plot of land next to theirs, where they were growing many kinds of vegetables. Nowadays, Buvana spend more time with vegetables than people.

At the end of the New Year holiday, Ragu, Uncle Kasi, Dad and several others, including Nayagam, went to see the MP about rebuilding the school. Mailar was furious that a delegation on the most important matter in the village had not included him. He came over to Gowri's place and shouted at his brother in the usual way, accusing him of being friendly with Mailar's enemies. Old Palipody had to listen to Mailar's shouting for days and nights.

One evening, there was a lot of noise outside the village

shop. There was trouble. That shop, owned by Gowri's Uncle Balan, sold everything – including illicit alcohol. When important issues were debated, it was usually outside this place, while the youngsters would shop. Old and young people used the shop for different purposes. The old folk would get together to read newspapers and consider national and international politics, while the young ones hung around near the shop front to chat and joke over very sugary cups of tea.

How dense the crowd was would depend on the weather. If it was dull or rainy, only a few of the older people would come, and if it was a fine day, the young ones would also be there in large numbers.

The shop was a valuable centre not only for local residents but also for those who had travelled from elsewhere. Cyclists and drivers of tractors and bullock carts would stop there for refreshments of spicy snacks and milky sugary teas. The shop had a handful of long benches; people would sit or stand there according to their age and position in the community. A youngster would be expected to get up if he saw an old person walking in. When Uncle Mailar began to raise his voice against Nayagam, who was supposedly conspiring against him by going to see the MP, the travellers enjoyed the prospect of a good excuse for moment or two of gossip.

Normally, the quarrels between women over the fences at home could start over anything from poultry to children. Older women might get drawn into such disputes, and they would describe one another in colourful language. A small argument about a chicken or a child could escalate as each family's past was dug up. Most of the old women were walking history books, and they would dredge up all their opponents' family scandals over the past century or two.

Men rarely got involved in the women's bickering, as most would be in the paddy fields in daytime. If they did, there was just a chance that there would be bloodshed, if margosa or other tree branches were used instead of words. Quickly, the women would take over and drag their men home.

In front of the shop, Mailar began to disparage someone whom he did not name, but everyone knew to whom he was referring. It was not necessary to be an old woman to scold one's enemy. Mailar could curse in more foul-mouthed language than any old woman. He dragged Nayagam's family through the dirt, finding the most imaginative ways to insult them.

Grandma had suggested that Mailar was going mad with jealousy because Nayagam was getting more respect than him from their neighbours. Now tales about ghosts were ringing through the air. Mailar was talking about Nayagam's father, who, he alleged, had cheated Mailar's father, in whose fields he worked. Mailar said that his adversary's sinful *karma* would not go away and that his family would suffer because of the crime he had committed in Trincomalee, through which he had made his fortune.

Grandma was talking about witchcraft and the evil spells which Mailar and Nayagam would cast on each other. Gowri's mother, who was cleaning a fish, said, 'Please, Mum, don't talk about mumbo-jumbo. I've heard the Americans are soon going to the moon, and you're still talking about something that doesn't exist.'

Gowri rarely heard her mother arguing with Grandma,

and, even when she did, the old woman took no notice. While they were chatting, they heard Aunt Sathya scream from the shop.

Grandma stopped at once and ran in that direction. Gowri was not allowed to go beyond the front gate since she had just reached puberty, but she raced after Grandma and peered through a hole in the fence.

Almost all the men in the village were there. Some were shouting, some stood by looking confused, while others were bustling about. 'What happened?'

Gowri listened carefully to the grown-ups. She saw some people dragging Mailar away from the crowd. Uncle Kasi was yelling at him, 'You shouldn't have done that!'

Done what? Gowri saw Rajah approaching the shop front with his followers. He was shouting, 'Why don't you stay and fight me? You can't run away after assaulting my father.'

Assaulting? Who had hit whom?

Old man Palipody rushed towards the shop, his long hair unkempt. As he neared the gate, Gowri clutched his never-tied *verti* and asked, 'Hey, Grandpa, what's happening?'

'Your Uncle Mailar assaulted Nayagam with his slipper!'

'Uncle Mailar did what?'

'Yes, your uncle is mad, he's going round the bend.'

'Oh no, oh no, something terrible is going to happen,' Grandma was sobbing.

'Please, son, don't go!' Aunt Sathya implored Ragu, pulling him back to stop him going to the shop, where Rajah and his disciples were standing like angry bulls ready for a fight.

'But Mum, we can't just let Rajah abuse us. I'll go and sort the matter out.' Ragu was usually a very calm fellow, but the

135

situation had become untenable. It was up to him to defend his father's honour, even if Mailar was in the wrong. What else could the eldest son do?

Now Saratha was holding her brother and crying, 'Don't go there, please. Rajah has loads of his thugs with him.'

'Please, my child, don't get caught up in this madman's games.' Grandma begged Ragu not to get involved in a punch-up.

Gowri saw Nathan cycling towards the shop front. She ran to the gate, called him by his name for the first time in her life and urged him, 'Please, get my cousin to go home, or he'll be in bad trouble with Rajah's thugs.'

Rajah spotted Gowri talking to Nathan, but she did not notice him. Nathan went to Ragu and persuaded him to return to the house. Almost all his relatives were there, and Mailar was being told off for bringing the family into disgrace. But he was still raving about Nayagam. Grandma criticised Aunt Sathya for not keeping her husband in order.

'It's easy for you all to blame me,' Sathya complained, 'just because I'm not from your village.'

'Let's not be silly. We have to be careful or we'll be in bad trouble. Can you imagine what would have happened if Rajah and his mob had got their hands on Ragu? We would have had to count all the bones in our boy's body.' Aunt Indira was talking sensibly.

'Uncle Mailar's being unreasonable,' Gowri murmured almost inaudibly. Mum heard that and pinched her to be quiet.

Chapter 14

Ramanathan arrived almost immediately; perhaps his brother Nathan had informed him of the flare-up in the shop.

'What's going on?' he demanded crossly. He hated it when people started trouble for no good reason. He was working hard on the new school project and did not like any conflict among the villagers. 'Ragu, it's better not to get involved in this business. There's a lot to be done. If the village is divided, who will suffer?' He looked at Saratha, Gowri and Buvana.

They could still hear Nayagam and others outside the shop shouting at Mailar and his family. The teacher asked Palipody and Ragu to make sure to keep Mailar at home, then went outside and walked up to the road. There were people everywhere. It was not unknown for peasants to get into fights, but there had never before been a brawl between two such important local figures.

Ramanathan came over to Gowri's place a few hours later. He said, 'Don't think the fight's over; it's only just begun.' By now he knew enough about Kolavil to realise how people were manipulating others and trying to prove their superiority. 'Don't let the situation get out of hand,' he urged sadly.

'What can I do?' Dad was the opposite of his arrogant brother, the biggest local landlord, doing whatever he chose.

'When I was a student at college in Batticaloa town,' the teacher reminisced, 'there were some boys who were always on the look-out for action and thrills. Some of them were impressed by the glamour of politics and joined the youth wing of the Tamil Federal Party. One of my fellow students, who was nothing but an opportunist, is now an influential political leader. Don't let a young man like Rajah win the support of the village. He won't do much for local people, just make a name for himself. You see, nowadays, instead of people choosing their leaders, the leaders are able to manipulate the people because they are so ignorant about the real issues.'

'What are you saying, sir?' Gowri brought him a cup of tea and stood by the door.

'There's not a lot more to say. A lot of things are happening here at the moment that are going to affect people's lives. It's a pity your uncle is behaving in a childish, stupid manner.' He knew that the split was inevitably going to bring unhappiness to many people.

That night Saratha and Gowri sat on swings and talked about what had happened that day. 'It looks as if we won't be able go to school.' Gowri sounded thoroughly miserable.

'So?' Saratha tried to be casual.

'Not a lot will happen. We'll grow up to be like our mothers and spend all our lives staying at home and cooking for other people.'

'I'll have a servant.' Saratha speeded up the swing.

'Maybe, maybe not.' Gowri was not sure what she was trying to say, but her words flowed without too much thought.

'What do you mean?' Saratha stopped the swing.

'If you don't marry Shiva, how will you able to afford a

servant? At the rate your father's spending money, sooner or later the paddy fields will have to be sold.'

'Oh, I'll definitely marry Shiva.' Saratha's tone was firm.

'Otherwise?'

'There is no otherwise.' Saratha got out of the swing and ran home.

Gowri could not sleep that night. The day's events were vivid in her mind. She could not stop thinking of the ruthlessness of Mailar and Nayagam. What would have happened if she had not called to Nathan to help?

She could not imagine Rajah beating up Ragu. When she thought of Rajah, she could not prevent herself from noticing the uneasiness in her heart. Would she be able to refuse to marry him?

She thought of Nathan, so different from the local boys. He wanted her to go to school, study and learn about different things. He was kind, good-looking and witty. Above all, she knew that he understood her better than anyone in her family and indeed the whole village.

She could not get to sleep after pondering all these things. 'Oh, well, one day, as Grandma keeps reminding me, I'll have to get married and have lots of children. Will I name one of them Nathan?'

The following month was May 1958.

The villagers were busy preparing for the festival of goddess Kannaki, the goddess of chastity and virtue. There were many stories about her. A few thousand years ago, she had been the daughter of a rich merchant in Madurai in south India and married to another merchant called Kovalan. Her husband left Kannaki to seek pleasure from less virtuous women. After a while, he split with his mistress Maathavi, and he had no money left. Although he had not treated Kannaki well, she had a duty to help him to get his life in order.

Kannaki gave him a pearl-studded anklet so that he could sell it and, with the money, go into business. On his way, he was arrested by the king's men and accused of being a thief for stealing from the palace an anklet of the queen's. He was subsequently hanged for theft.

When Kannaki heard what had happened to her husband, she went to the king and told him that the anklet belonged to her. They asked her to prove it. She threw down the anklet in front of the king, saying, 'If you are right, I will be destroyed when the anklet is unclasped, but if I am right, you will die by the fire of wrath.'

The pearls in it were shown to be different from those in the queen's anklet. Her curse was fulfilled; the king collapsed and died.

She had stepped forward, torn one of her breasts out, flung it down and exclaimed, 'May the fire of my anger destroy the city which belongs to the unjust king!' The city of Madurai went up in flames. Her chastity and virtuous nature led people, mainly women, to worship her and pray to her to give them virtue and strength.

So, Kannaki worship (*Paththni theyo*) was brought to Ceylon by a king called Kajabahu. There were a few temples of Kannaki in the Batticaloa region, as the region had at one time been administered by the Kandyan monarch. He had been related to those in Kerala in South India, where worship of Kannaki was widespread. There had existed such a temple in Kolavil about a century ago. But, according to legend, the goddess had moved out of the village because it had become unsuitable for one so pure.

Once upon a time, the story went, a young couple had met behind the temple to make love. The had been bitten by the seven-headed cobra who guarded the goddess. The following day, the villagers had gone to the temple to worship the goddess, and they had seen at the entrance not her statue but instead the seven-headed cobra, which angrily chased them away.

A few days later, the statue had been found in the midst of the jungle, miles from the village. The priest had told the local people that the goddess had come to him in his dream and told him that she did not want to stay in Kolavil any longer, as the couple had not respected the purity of womanhood. Having a sexual relationship before marriage was seen as an extreme sin in Hindu beliefs. The lovers' families had been expelled from the village.

Since then, the villagers would celebrate the goddess Kannaki, worshipping at the temple in the jungle. The villagers were not orthodox Hindus in that they ate meat and fish and drank alcohol, but they would change their eating and drinking habits for a fortnight before the festival. Houses and huts would be cleaned and whitewashed, overgrown bushes and grass cleared away, lanes and roads swept clean.

The temple was about three miles away from Kolavil. Old people and children would use bullock carts for the journey, while those who were young and able-bodied would carry items for making *pooja* on their heads. The baskets and other objects had to be new, unused for any other function.

Grandma was very religious and held the goddess in

especially high regard. She had great respect for traditional beliefs and ordered the girls to be clean and proper for the *pooja*. The religious ceremony would take all day and night. They would do *pooja* in the daytime and sing prayers at night to calm the goddess' anger against them. The fifth day would the goddess' 'wedding day'. A special *pooja* would be done, and, that evening, selected devotees would guard the temple. At midnight, the villagers would offer her *pooja* including *pongal* (sweet rice with nuts and fruits).

While the people of Kolavil were busy in the jungle doing *Pathiviratha pooja* (worship of the virtuous) for Kannaki, the country was in turmoil because of communal riots against the minority community of Tamils.

Kamala's father arrived and told the villagers that several hundreds of Tamils had been killed, and their properties destroyed, by Sinhalese thugs who came to Tamil areas from different parts of Ceylon. The worst-affected areas were those where there had been new developments – the colonised areas in Amparai district, where the Tamils were a small minority. Grandma become anxious about her niece, Palipody's daughter, who lived in Gal Oya, one of the colonised settlements.

Radio Ceylon announced that a few incidents had occurred and that a curfew was being imposed. The villagers remembered how they had been affected by the previous emergency only a few months ago. Now they were worried in case Sinhalese thugs came to Kolavil to attack them.

The next town, Akkaraippattu, had a handful of Sinhalese families. Kind-hearted Tamils and Muslims from the area took responsibility for protecting them in case there was a backlash.

Ramanathan told them that violence had spread through the capital city of Colombo and other areas where Tamils lived. The older villagers gathered at the shop and discussed the situation unhappily. News came from travelling Muslim traders; there had been much brutality against Tamils, and those in the colonies had run for safety to predominantly Tamil areas. The villagers heard more horrendous stories from various people. Some Tamils had lost their entire families. Women had been raped in front of their fathers, husbands and children. Small children had been hacked to death in front of their parents.

Palipody started to get hysterical about his daughter Thangamma and her family, who were in one of the new colonies near Amparai. He sank into depression and wept constantly. Thangamma had two children aged ten and eight and had spent all her married life in the colony. Now, there was no news of her. Those who lived nearby said that if they had survived, they would have fled by now.

The situation got worse. According to the radio news, Tamil leaders had been placed under house arrest, and many Hindu temples and Tamil schools had been destroyed.

At a place called Panathura, near Colombo, a Hindu priest was burned alive by thugs, his wife and daughters raped in public. In another incident, a racialist Sinhalese mob cut a foetus from a pregnant Tamil woman, then butchered her on the street.

In another incident a woman threw all her children into a well and jumped in to escape from rape by the mob. They all died, watched by the mob, who stood near the well and cheered happily at the dying Tamil family.

Grandma stopped listening to all these horrible stories, shut her eyes and prayed to the gods to stop the barbarity. Gowri could hardly believe that such things could happen in this world. Grandma told her, 'I won't let any Sinhalese thug touch you, your cousins or the women in my household. If they come here, kill yourself – don't ever let a mob destroy you.'

As Gowri took a bath very early in the morning as usual, she thought of what her grandmother had said. She wanted to go far, far away where there was no racial hatred, no discrimination, no language problem, no sexual harassment, no arranged marriage. Did such a world exist?

One of the books which Nathan had given her asserted that the greedy and powerful used people's weakness to gain and sustain their power. This political manipulation led people to think that destroying another community by oppressing them would give their own community more power. If an ordinary man discovered that he could not achieve what he sought, he might go berserk and commit atrocities in the name of religion, race and language. Hitler created conflict and confusion for his own ends. People like him who were in power manipulated and distorted the real needs of the people, and in the end the whole system would be destroyed. Was this true?

Certainly, the Sinhalese leaders were using race and language to stir up conflict between Sinhalese and Tamils. Did the majority of Sinhalese people really think that Tamils were the reason for their misery? Did such people believe that peace-loving innocent villagers like her neighbours and her were doing better than the average Sinhalese?

She found it difficult to think clearly as reports of violence continued. The Tamil population in predominantly Sinhalese areas had dwindled to almost nothing, and it seemed that there was nowhere to hide.

Chapter 15

One day, some of the women from the village who had gone to collect firewood in the nearby forest came back with the news that they had glimpsed other women hiding behind the bushes, naked. When the village women approached, the strangers ran away into the jungle to hide.

'Emergency or not,' said Aunt Indira, 'we have to go and look for them so we can help them.'

Mum objected that it might bring trouble on Kolavil, if they were being pursued by Sinhalese soldiers or thugs. But, others pointed out, sooner or later trouble might reach them, anyway. In the meantime, they might be able to rescue someone in need of help.

Indira went into the forest with several other women, carrying a lot of clothes. They found three girls; all were naked and had been badly beaten and bruised. One was about eighteen years old, and seriously ill with fever and vomiting. Another, who was about thirteen, would talk to nobody. She bore many scars and marks of beating, biting and bruising. The third, who was ten or so, was also severely bruised in many places. They all had the Sinhala letter 'Sri' – which Tamil political leaders refused to use for their car registrations – marked on their breasts with a knife.

The girls had been cruelly raped and beaten by Sinhalese thugs. The village women looked up at the sky and called for divine power to take revenge on the perpetrators of this unspeakable attack. They brought the girls to the village, fed them, gave them first aid, cleaned their wounds and embraced them with love and kindness.

A message was sent to Father Thomas and other old and wise people around their area.

The young men in the village were furious. They wanted to attack the Buddhist temple and Sinhalese people. But Gowri's father said, '*Ahimsa* (avoidance of violence) is the best in this situation. It's immoral to take revenge, to seek an eye for an eye.'

Ramanathan emphasised to Rajah, 'If you start killing innocent Sinhalese people, there'll never be an end to this problem. It's better to think logically and work politically to solve it.'

Ragu was a peace-loving youth, but, after seeing the condition of the girls, he asked, 'What's the point of being Tamil men if we can't keep our women safe?'

Nathan was there, too. He said, 'We can't go around doing to them what Sinhalese thugs have done to us. One reason is that we'll never achieve anything by using physical force with no political strategy. Another is that such action might affect thousands of Tamils living in Sinhalese areas.' The discussion went on for a long time.

Rajah did not come to Gowri's house, but she could hear his voice, which was full of aggression and racialism. He wanted to take revenge on the Sinhalese thugs for brutalising the girls in such an inhuman way.

The girls were the daughters of a Tamil engineer in Amparai district. When the trouble had started, the engineer and his wife had got ready to leave the house. But thugs had found them, raped the mother and daughters and killed the father. His wife had died from the attack but made the girls run away to the jungle.

The American Catholic priest Father Thomas came over and looked at the girls sorrowfully. He knelt, raised his head towards the sky and asked God to bring an end to the barbarity going on throughout the country. Gowri thought about what she read about religion in one of the books which Nathan had brought for her.

'If there is a god who created all living beings, why did he make some people suffer so much? People who are untouchable or belong to an ethnic minority or are women go through such terrible suffering. Why does God arrange things that way, if he exists at all?'

She wanted to ask Father Thomas why people like him remained silent and obedient to this barbaric government. If a man went around talking of saving people, was it not his duty to raise his voice against injustice? If religious leaders stayed quiet, what right had they to be called 'reverend', 'holy man' or 'father'?

The previous year, Gowri and her cousins had visited a Buddhist temple during a Buddhist holiday; there were many devotees praying. Would those Buddhists kill innocent Tamils? Unanswered questions lingered in Gowri's mind, as usual.

Father Thomas took the injured girls to Batticaloa General Hospital in his decrepit old car. He asked the old men in the village to keep a watchful eye on the young men, who had become very emotional. But some could not control their anger. They went on the rampage, attacking a poor Sinhalese family who lived about a mile away. The old mother came to

Gowri's father, crying that 'Tamil boys have killed my chickens and goats'. Gowri was cleaning the portico when the old woman arrived. She was weeping for her chickens and goats, but how many Tamil mothers were weeping for their children now?

The following few days nothing brought but bad news about the riots. 'When are they going to lift the emergency?' asked Ramanathan bitterly; he was unable to open the school.

'The government didn't declare a state of emergency as soon as the riots started. If that had happened, there wouldn't have been so much killing,' said Uncle Kasi furiously, slicing a papaya. 'No matter who is in office, they all want to wipe out the Tamil community from this country,' he continued.

'When the United National Party was in power, Mr. Bandaranaike's party accused the UNP of giving everything away to the Tamils and promised that, when he came to power, he would stop all our 'privileges'. Then when Mr. Bandaranaike came to power, Mr. J. R. Jayawardene went on a holy pilgrimage to protect Buddhism and the Sinhala language. It seems as if the better Sinhalese leaders are at oppressing Tamils, the more support they get.'

Dad's position was clear. He would never again trust a Sinhalese politician who came to power with hollow promises to the masses, for he believed that justice, peace and freedom for all people were genuinely important.

'I can't believe that, in the civilised world, a minority nation can be treated like this by its own government. We are not asking for anything extraordinary, just our basic rights. The Sinhalese have no right to refuse us what's legitimately ours,' Uncle Kasi said angrily.

'Is there any Sinhalese leader who stands for the right for every citizen in this land?' Kasi asked the teacher.

He replied, 'There are a few progressive leaders who, before independence, voted for the right to self-determination of Tamil people in Ceylon, but their place in politics was replaced by Sinhalese chauvinism on the part of the main parties.'

There was a noise; police Jeeps were approaching. Gowri switched the radio off, and they stopped talking. Grandma was restless and kept glancing over the fence.

'So, why don't the progressive politicians say or do something now about the atrocities?' Uncle Kasi demanded of the teacher.

'It's not easy for those who are progressive to fight the racialist system in Ceylon.'

Gowri listened carefully. She remembered something that she had read: governments were supposed to be elected from among the people, by the people and for the people. But were those in power really solving the people's problems?

She saw Saratha approaching in the moonlight. She did not care in the least about politics. She would rather talk about the lovely blue shirt that Shiva wore. But at that moment Shiva was in Colombo, and she was deeply worried about him. Shiva's father had begged some Muslim traders, who were going to Colombo, to look for his son. But no news came of him, despite regular reports to Saratha by Sundaram in return for spicy snacks and bottles of ginger beer.

Palipody openly cried for his daughter and her family, but Saratha could not shed a single tear for her boyfriend Shiva in public. Everyone was afraid of attack by Sinhalese thugs, who might come from the mountains to their west – a mainly Sinhalese area – to kill the men and rape the women. The villagers had no weapons to defend themselves. They had never kept guns; Dad would borrow one from his Muslim friend Iburahim when they went hunting for birds and rabbits.

Saratha sat with Gowri, listening to the discussion. Gowri felt sorry for her. From what they knew, the situation of Tamils in the capital was far from good. According to the newspapers, hundreds had taken refuge in the Hindu temples and colleges around Colombo. Among the injured and dead were not only people originally from Jaffna but also those whose families had lived in the city for many centuries.

'Will India help us?' Saratha asked.

'Why should India help us?'

'Because, er, because there are a lot of Tamils in India.'

'But the Tamils in India don't have any army or navy of their own,' replied Gowri hesitantly. The teenagers knew very little about the politic of India, but a great deal about South Indian Tamil cinemas and its stars, who now and then visited Ceylon. Thousands of admirers would line the streets to welcome them, especially the top actors in Tamil films, such as M. G. Ramachandran (known as MGR), and famous actresses such Savithri. These stars played heroes and heroines, gods and goddesses, and it was popularly believed that they were as virtuous in everyday life as on the screen.

It was Saratha's opinion that MGR would help the Tamils to win their freedom. Gowri said that she doubted it. Saratha seemed irritable because of her worries. 'These cruel people and the government will be destroyed one day,' she sobbed, a choking sadness in her voice. They both sat on their favourite swing. 'Only the gods can help us. What can have happened to Palipody's daughter?' Gowri pushed the swing into the air.

'Hey, girls, come inside. You don't want to be taken away by the army, do you?' Grandma shouted. They went in.

The following day Nathan came to the village. The riots had not stopped, he reported. He seemed to want to talk to the girls and comfort them, but it was out of the question for him to approach them on their own. So, he spoke to everyone present but smiled at Gowri. Saratha was too preoccupied with her own worries to notice.

Palipody asked him and Ragu to go and search for his daughter, since the situation had improved over the past few days. Saratha went to the temple to pray for her boyfriend Shiva's safe return. Grandma repeatedly cursed the government for its callousness. But what can we do, Gowri wondered to herself? Her main worry was whether she would be able to return to school when the violence was over.

A few days later, Saratha came running. She did not need to explain. Gowri could tell from her cousin's expression what she was going to say. Saratha announced, 'He's home!' She was breathless with excitement. Her beautiful eyes sparkled, her lifeless gaze was a thing of the past.

Saratha said that he had arrived with Muslim traders who had not been affected by the trouble. To avoid being killed by thugs, who were stopping vehicles to look for Tamils, he had hidden in a lorry carrying coconuts. 'I prayed for his safe return.' Saratha was weeping with happiness. 'And I told God that if Shiva died, I would never go to the temple again in my life.'

'If gods grant all that we wish,' Gowri thought philosophically, 'why are there so many problems in the world?' Nevertheless, she was very pleased for Saratha, although she was still worried about her mother's cousin – Palipody's daughter Thangamma – and the people who had gone to search for her.

There was much excitement about Shiva's return. Quite a few young men, including Rajah, went to see him. They asked him about the situation in Colombo.

He told them what he knew. He had witnessed attacks on Tamils and the destruction of their property by mobs. 'Unless we think carefully and do something,' he said, 'the Sinhalese regime will kill us all.'

'What can we do?' the boys asked as with one voice.

'I don't know, but there must be some kind of action we can take. No struggle can take place without people taking part, so we've each got to do something.' He sounded determined.

His father said, 'You're not going anywhere or doing anything. You won't have to face any more big problems just to earn a little money. You can find a job in Batticaloa or work in the fields, but whatever happens you're not going to a mainly Sinhalese area.'

This pleased Saratha. She would cry for an hour over something which upset her, but soon she would get fed up with being miserable and bounce back. She hated it when people were miserable. She was open and outspoken. When she was happy, she filled her surroundings with happiness. Gowri would observe people closely before she spoke and only laugh at something which was very funny, but Saratha could find a cause for merriment in almost anything.

Buvana was busy with her vegetable garden. She had known of Saratha's unhappiness but hadn't sought to probe the reason behind it. Buvana shied away from close involvement with people and avoided difficult issues. Gowri was a fighter, Saratha easy going, while Buvana's character was too complex to be easily understood. Gowri wanted to talk to Buvana about Saratha's elation, but Buvana was more interested in the broad beans in her garden than in Saratha's feelings for her boyfriend.

Chapter 16

The village began to breathe more easily. There had been no attack for weeks, and people wanted to get on with their everyday lives.

One evening an unexpected guest arrived. It was Lingam, who – after the death of his wife, Mailar's only sister, during childbirth – had accompanied Dad to India all those years ago, returning as a long-bearded, ganja-smoking, *mantra*-chanting holy man. He had not come back to Kolavil often. The god who dwelt in the Murukan temple at Kathirgamam in the south had called him, he said, and that was where he stayed. Those who went there on pilgrimage would see him; otherwise, he had little connection with the village.

The evening when he arrived was colourful; the golden-red sun was dipping behind the mountains to the west. Then Swami Lingam turned up at the gate of his brother-in-law Nadesan. Within an hour, almost all the villagers had gathered there.

Gowri remembered him slightly. Whenever he came, Dad would go and buy ganja for smoking and make coffee. Ganja coffee was rather like alcohol; some people would grind the herb, mix it with coffee and drink it as they talked of gods and myths.

Grandma would comment that ganja made people forget the real world. 'She should know,' Gowri thought. When she had been a small girl, there had been a discussion under the jak tree on mythology and religion while she was busy

155

playing with friends.

Grandma had been unwell, and was lying on a mat on the cement verandah. 'Gowri!' Grandma had yelled. Gowri had come, and Grandma asked her for a cup of coffee. People seldom drank coffee in the village unless they were not well; usually, they had a cup of tea in the morning and then, if it was a hot day, a sip from a young coconut. Gowri knew that Dad was making coffee for Swami and so she poured a cup. Unknown to the young girl, it contained powdered ganja leaves.

Poor Grandma! Within an hour after drinking the coffee she was acting strangely. She started to giggle and babble nonsense: the trees were walking upside down, the River Thillai had flooded and the dog Amuthavalli was laughing at her. Grandma was in tears and said their cat was trying to steal her money. When Mum realised what had happened, she gave Grandma a bucketful of cold water to sober her up and persuaded her to drink gallons of foul-smelling herbal water.

Now, Swami Lingam had no beard; it seemed to have been cut off in a hurry. His orange-mustard colour robes were tattered and dirty, his appearance pathetic and pitiable. He had been beaten by Sinhalese thugs in Katharagama, the holy place of the god Murukan, and his belongings stolen. As a Hindu swami he had been humiliated by a Buddhist mob. He looked shattered.

Grandma boiled water in a big aluminium pot and Dad bathed Lingam tenderly; they had respect and affection for him.

He had never harmed anyone. He was free from greed and

jealousy; he was a kind and loving man. Gowri cried for him. Grandma bought out more clay pots to cook a meal of vegetables for the swami, while Mum arranged a new mat, pillow and sheet for him in the portico so he could sleep.

Gowri thought to herself that the house contained not only her immediate family of many kids and parents but also old Palipody, never sober nor fully clothed, Grandma, a strong-minded witch who lives in her own world, and the gentle, wise and ganja coffee-drinking Swami Lingam. What an atmosphere of contrast in which to grow up!

Uncle Kasipathy came to visit the swami. It was rumoured that Mailar's sister had once been love with Kasi, but that her big-headed brother Mailar would not allow her to marry someone poor, forcing her to become Lingam's wife. When she died, her husband had gone to India to become a *sadhu* (holy man), while Kasi had gone to Trincomalee and married Auntie Indira. When he saw the swami's condition, Kasi became furious with the government.

'There's no need to get so angry. If a big fish eats a little fish, one day it will be eaten by a bigger one. We are a small nation; it's our fate to suffer. We have to wait and think what we ought to do. Picking up a knife never solves a problem,' Lingam said calmly.

'Wait, wait, wait! How long will we have to wait? By the time we get on with doing something, part of our nation will have been wiped out.'

The swami smiled and said, 'Nobody wins anything by violence, my son.'

Kasi disagreed. He went away mumbling something about taking revenge on the Sinhalese thugs.

'Swami, won't you be going back to the temple?' Gowri brought him a cooked vegetable meal and sat down near to him. She could hear someone playing the flute far away. Night had just fallen. The breeze was cool and soft, sounds of jollity could be heard in the background, but tomorrow was another day, and unexpected things might happen.

The Swami ate a small meal, then picked up some betel leaves and areca nuts to chew. He signalled for her to come closer, looked at her as he chewed and smiled. 'Did you ask me if I'd be going back to the temple?'

She nodded her head in assent.

He stroked her hair tenderly and replied, 'Temples and gods are everywhere. Why must I remain in the temple to pray? I should stay with my people and do something good for them.'

'But...but we have no temple or...or no proper school either since the flood.'

'Really?'

'They were damaged by the flood.' She could no longer hold back her tears.

'Don't cry, child, every destruction brings a new construction,' he told her comfortingly.

'We had to put Ganesh under the banyan tree to stop him from getting wet.' She continued to cry for herself and her god Ganesh.

'No village should be without a temple,' he said firmly.

'I don't go to school, either.' She was choking with sorrow.

'You will, my child. All we have to do is to build a new school and a new temple. We can do that.'

'Can we?' At that moment, she could believe it.

'Of course, my child. If we work hard in unity, we can get it done.'

'Well...' She hesitated.

'My dear, we've just got to make our minds up. Mind over matter; wait and see. Humankind can achieve a great deal; it's a pity we waste our time destroying one another. You see, my child, love for one and others will bring good things in life.'

She knew it well, but for almost a year there had been nothing but one disaster after another.

'My child, as I told you, sometimes destruction brings creation. There is no birth without pain, no temple without the people's strength, no future without hope. We'll do it. Don't cry for yesterday, smile for tomorrow.'

It was all very well for a *sadhu* to speak like that. What reason did she have to smile? She could not go to school. Could she tell him, she wondered, about Mailar and Nayagam? How could a holy man change the behaviour of powerful men like them? Each showed off the size of his ego by making others unhappy. Their conflict could reduce the chance of the village having a school.

Why should relationships be based simply on self-gratification? Mailar knew the importance of the school; Nayagam, too, was aware of that. With them pulling in different directions, getting support for any project that would benefit the neighbourhood would not be easy. Might Rajah try to persuade his father to act in harmony with Mailar in order to get a school built? That night, she slept with much on her mind.

She could hear the swami and her father talking about the village and its people. Dad spoke of the help given by the

159

teacher Ramanathan and his brother Nathan, and the swami seemed interested in meeting them.

The following morning Nathan and Ragu returned from the colony, where they had been searching for Palipody's daughter and her family. Even before they began to tell what had happened, the others could read the story from their faces. Thangamma and her family had been killed, as had hundreds of her Tamil neighbours who had been unable to escape the mob.

Poor Palipody! He had been having a bad time since the flood. From her early childhood Gowri could remember him as an old man who drank, sang and laughed a lot and who was jolly, despite having squandered most of his wealth. He had been arrested and beaten up, losing most of his teeth at the hands of police during the Muslim-Tamil riots in Akkaraippattu. He had lost his house, livestock and his bullock cart in the flood, and his wife had died. All he had left were his daughter and her family, who had lived miles away. Now he had lost her, too.

He cried like a child. Grandma cried, too. Her brother had nobody but her now. They both seemed worn out, helpless and despondent. Gowri felt sorry for her great-uncle. What a life! He was harmless, laughing at nothing, singing about everything, filling the air with a noise like that of rattling tins; often drunk, seldom entirely sober. What had he gained in life? There was nobody at the end of his life to comfort him, though Gowri's family, including Lingam, and Nathan tried to console him.

Nathan recounted what the survivors from the colony at Gal Oya area had told them. One night during the riots, a mob of hundreds of Sinhalese thugs had arrived, singling out the homes of Tamils. Women were raped, and most of the Tamils who were rounded up by the mob had been slaughtered, burned alive, regardless of whether they were old or young. Property was looted.

Gowri felt that she was going to faint. She did not want to hear any more. She went into a corner and began to cry. She looked at her small brothers and began to feed one of the youngest. How could anyone kill a child like him?

She heard footsteps and turned. Nathan was there. He saw her tears. He stood there for a while. He wanted to hug her and say how sorry he was for their loss, but he would not risk doing this, as such behaviour would be taken very seriously in the village and might even cost both of them their lives.

'We lost not only Palipody's daughter and her family, also hundreds of innocent people just because they were Tamils.' He drew some water from the water pot.

'I can't believe that humans can do such cruel things to other humans,' she wept. It was too much for someone barely fourteen years old to grasp.

He looked at her sadly. 'History repeats itself; the strongest wins every battle, whether justified or not. Here, it is the Tamils who are victims, elsewhere, it is others. Thousands of innocent people are killed just because they belong to a different race, nation, religion, sometime a different class. This happens because of lack of organisation, tolerance, understanding and unity among people in various sectors of society.'

To Gowri, Nathan was not like anyone else whom she had met; he talked in a different way. It was too much for someone barely fourteen years old to grasp. 'I hate growing up in this world,' she said woefully.

'You have no choice; all you can do is walk carefully and try to find a path. It will not be easy, but I believe you can do it,' he said comfortingly.

'I'm scared of the world around me and the future ahead of me,' she wanted to tell him. Though she could be strong when was confronted with Grandma's old-fashioned talk of customs and values, she felt naïve and vulnerable in front of this intelligent young man, the only one who understood her pain.

'What will happen to the Tamils in Ceylon?' she asked him.

'I don't know. All I can say for certain is that we're not prepared, and we've not been serious enough about tackling the problem because of the divisions among us. Do the Tamil leaders who talk about language rights care about the estate Tamils who produce most of the wealth for this country but have no fundamental rights in Ceylon? The Tamil leaders joined the Sinhalese leaders to make the estate Tamils stateless, then, don't they think the estate workers are Tamils, too?'

Mailar arrived with anger on his face and said, 'We have to cut down all the Bo (Bodhi fig) trees, otherwise the Sinhalese thugs will come and place a Buddha statue underneath one and claim the village for themselves.' Uncle Kasi disagreed, but his neighbours had overruled him. They were frightened of Sinhalese encroachment because so many houses had been taken over in the Amparai area.

According to Nathan, Buddhist monks were bringing

Sinhalese people from the south of Ceylon to colonise localities after chasing away Tamil residents. For centuries, places like Amparai had been inhabited mainly by Tamils. In just a few years, it had been practically taken over by Sinhalese settlers.

'Where can we go?' Gowri mumbled.

'Nowhere. We have to fight back against the system,' Nathan said in a firm tone.

She was confused. She had thought that Nathan was against fighting; he was always arguing with Uncle Kasi, who would insist on the need to fight for freedom and justice.

He knew what she was thinking. He explained, 'I never opposed the Tamil struggle, but I am against the way the leaders manipulate people. The politicians are relying on the middle class to resist the system instead of including estate Tamil workers and the untouchables in Jaffna. Of course, not much attention is given to a lot of other Tamils, either.'

Gowri got the impression that he was not particularly keen on rich and influential Tamil leaders in Jaffna. Perhaps, she thought, it was because he had spent a lot of time on the estates while his brother was teaching there. People who worked hard usually wanted to be rewarded, she wanted to tell him, but she was reluctant to speak. One reason was that her Grandma might tell her off for talking too freely to the young man. Another was that he was more perceptive than other people whom she knew; she liked him secretly, but she did not want to admit this in case it led to trouble.

Chapter 17

After the flood, many children had come to school to receive free bread and milk. Now, in the aftermath of the worst riots against Tamils that there had ever been, again, attendance was high. People who had lived in the fields near Sinhalese areas hurried back to the centre of Kolavil for safety. Some of those who had been receiving secondary and further education in town stopped going there because of the army attacks on Tamil boys. The village school could not cope with the additional pupils; it was overflowing.

Temporary huts were put up to keep classes going. The holy Bo tree at the school had been saved, thanks to Ramanathan's determination. Now there was an urgent need for work to be done on the new school.

The racial riots had brought greater unity to the village in the campaign for a school. Town-educated Ragu, Rajah and Shiva had all stayed in the village. None had resumed their old way of life in the towns and cities far away from the village. Nathan applied to a teacher training college, but at present he was working in the town of Kalmunai and spent every evening visiting his brother Ramanathan and his friends in Kolavil.

A delegation of VIPs from Kolavil went again to Colombo to talk to the MP about the school, who promised to look into the matter. The youths in the village said that it was important to lobby him as often as possible or the building would never happen.

Saratha was ecstatic that Shiva was back in the village. 'I'm so glad he's home!' She was practically jumping with joy.

'Well, I'm not,' Gowri remarked stiffly.

'Why on earth not?' Saratha did not like it when Gowri snubbed her. Until the previous year Gowri had listened to, and gone along with, Saratha's wishes. Now that Saratha's relationship with Shiva made her vulnerable, she needed Gowri's advice and help. Gowri knew how to use this to make Saratha join her in going to school.

Gowri looked at Saratha and said, 'Because I do not think that Shiva's family will allow their son to get involved with a girl of our kind.'

Saratha was cross. 'What is our kind?'

'Well, girls who have very little education.'

Saratha knew what Gowri was talking about. 'Will our family let us go back to school?' Saratha's voice was trembling; she wanted to be loved by Shiva at any cost.

Nathan and Ragu were involved in lobbying the MP to get the new school built. The schools inspector, who was not helping the villagers to get the school developed, met with harsh criticism from students such as Gowri when he expressed the view, 'Why do girls like you want to waste your time and energy going to school and studying when, sooner or later, your family will make you get married, and that'll be the end of it?'

Not only Gowri but also Dad was unhappy with the inspector's remarks regarding women's education. Dad always wanted to give the girls a chance to study.

When Nathan came, Ragu was talking to him about the girls and their wish to keep studying. Many young girls at boarding schools in town had stopped going there for fear of further communal riots. Nathan said, 'This time Grandma and others should see how many girls need help. A new school and permission to have classes up to GCE would do wonders for them.' Gowri listened and looked at him appreciatively.

'What can we do if permission isn't given to have GCE and O-level education there?' she asked them.

'Stay put in the school together, and make it clear that you want to study there,' Nathan said firmly, looking straight at her as if he wanted to implant his words in her heart. At the time, it did not even cross her mind that his encouragement would stay with her and that the conversation they were holding that evening would completely change her life.

She liked him very much. 'It'll be no good if I'm the only one who wants to stay at school,' she murmured hesitantly.

'Well then, ask your cousins to stay at school, too; otherwise, they'll have to get married at the next harvest.' He laughed loudly and she joined in.

'Hey. Gowri, what are you doing?' Grandma shouted from the house.

Gowri hurried away from him. When she turned back to see whether he had gone, she could see that he was still there, watching her, smiling.

For the first time in her life, Gowri thought about Nathan a lot that night. He seemed to be there even when she closed her eyes. She liked him for encouraging her to do what she really wanted to do with her life.

She carefully considered how she could persuade Saratha and Buvana to come, as well. Already, two girls who could no longer go to school in town were there.

'Do you reckon our mothers will let us go to school if there are no O-level classes?' Saratha expressed her doubt.

'Well, there's no harm in trying. After all, Shiva and the others are involved in getting permission for the change. If we're at the school, it'll be a strong point in favour of the argument they are making; it'll help Shiva a lot.'

Saratha did not refuse to go school after that. She said that she would make sure that Shiva came, too.

There were many changes in the village. When Gowri, Buvana and Saratha resumed their education, even Grandma did not make too much of a racket. She mumbled something about finding husbands for them. Beyond that, she did not bother, because she had seen other girls going to school, and she knew that she would not get support from any others in the family.

'What am I going to do about the vegetables?' Buvana whispered desperately when Gowri forced her to come with them.

'Bring them with you to school, idiot!' Saratha snapped at her.

Chapter 18

Kolavil, like other villages in the eastern province, had a clan (or caste) system quite unlike the rigidly patriarchal Jaffna society in the north. Most easterners were descendants of the subjects of north and south Indian princesses and others who had married Kandyan kings. According to local tradition, the people of Kolavil, particularly on Grandma's side, largely originated from the Kalinga kingdom in northeast India during the third century BC, before Buddhism came to Ceylon. Also, some in the east originated from Kerala in south India and still had many similar social, food and marital customs, along with clan patterns.

Of the four clans in the village, the *Panikkanar* (priestly or teachers clan), from which Shiva's family came, was first. Grandma's clan *Kalinga rajan kudy* came in second place. The third in importance was the *Padaiyanda kudi* (military clan), to which Mailar belonged. And Nayagam's clan belonged to the fourth, the *Vellala* (farmer) caste, who in Jaffna held the most prominent position.

Nayagam and some of the traders from Jaffna were campaigning to gain prominence in Kolavil. But Mailar and others would not let the village hierarchy be altered. Numerous meetings were held in the village temple's grounds. Both Mailar and Nayagam raised their voices over which of them would lead the opening ceremony, known as *Kumbabishegam* – a very special event. This normally went on for fourteen days, with a multitude of *poojas* and other ceremonies.

Because of the matriarchal system, Gowri's home – like most of households in the village – faced domestic chaos. Gowri had to put up with Grandma's continual criticism of Mailar's family, including her father, who were part of an opposing clan. Grandma would disparage their ancestry and whatever they had done or not done in the past.

Grandma reputedly came from king Kalinga's lineage, whereas Mailar was supposedly descended from soldiers. Shiva's family belonged to the first and most prestigious (priestly or educated) clan, but he and his family took very little interest in these old values and practices.

Gowri took refuge in Nathan's books, rather than listening to this nonsense being discussed in her house. When she mentioned to him that she was fed up with hearing stupid arguments about heritage, lineage and historical bigwigs, he said to her, 'Tamils and Sinhalese have nothing but the past to boast about. Who came to Ceylon first, when and from where, should not be diverting attention from the real issues of unity and developing our country. Why shouldn't we create new theories, new works of art, music, theatre, and an equal society?'

She would rather not get involved in Nathan's ideology of changing society, either, because she didn't think she had any power, she told him. He gave her one of his charming smiles, nodded his head and said, 'Oh, poor Gowri, one day you will understand what I am saying.'

'Why do people have to fight over religion and God?' she asked Swami Lingam naïvely. 'If they're that concerned about God, why can't they come together and get on with the rituals? Why do they have to be so nasty to one another?'

Lingam finished his ganja coffee slowly, closed his eyes as he meditated for a minute or two and opened them again; they were red, due to the drug. 'Dear daughter,' he replied, 'religion is the opium of the people, someone said. Isn't it true? If they did not have something to believe in or cling to, what would happen? I think that the mighty Lord lets people behave in this way to show how much he is above such pettiness. If these people didn't squabble over religion, they think, what is the point of having one? Look at the past, and how many people have died in the name of religion. You don't even have to look back; just think of our country and all the religious fanaticism. If Buddhist monks really believed in *ahimsa* (avoidance of violence) as the Buddha preached, there would be no conflict between Sinhalese and Tamils in Ceylon.'

'He might be right,' she thought; after all he was a swami and knew more about world affairs than she could ever imagine.

The new school was completed just before December 1958. The villagers wanted it to be opened in style, so Mailar organised a large welcome committee to greet the VIPs who were going to arrive from Colombo.

He had contributed a substantial sum for the ceremony and loudly bragged of how much he had spent on the project. 'Why do you have to race with Nayagam? Can we afford it? Saratha's wedding will come soon; we'll need jewels, new clothes and decorations for the house. Please think of your family instead of your personal vendetta against him.' Auntie Sathya's cries, weeps and shouts were ignored by Mailar, as usual.

When Sathya went to her brother-in-law Nadesan and asked him to advise his brother to be more sensible, Gowri burst into laughter. 'What are you talking about, Auntie? Who would tie a bell on a cat? Do you really think your husband will listen to anyone?'

Gowri was right; he would take heed of nobody. Even Swami Lingam was reluctant to clash with his brother-in-law Mailar. Quite apart from the ganja, which Mailar supplied, his contributions were needed for the temple.

Because of the previous year's flood, Mailar did not have enough crops to sell to raise money for his extravagant spending. When Sathya realised that he had sold a few of her pairs of gold bangles without even telling her, she went on hunger strike for a day or two. Mailar did not even notice; he was too busy organising a feast for the VIPs from the capital.

The opening ceremony for the school was splendid. The whole village seemed to be in a jolly mood. Shiva, who worked in Batticaloa, had arrived for the occasion, so Saratha was ecstatic. As soon as she had heard that he was coming, she had asked Auntie Indira to stitch a new silk skirt for her. She had put it on and wiggled her bottom sexily up and down in the lane between Gowri's house and hers, though Grandma was extremely displeased by such behaviour.

Buvana, Poorani and two other girls sang a welcoming song. Lingam gave a speech to greet the visitors, in which he mentioned that because the divine Ganesh had been pleased with the progress in building the temple the village would be able to open the school. He added that the god would grant a bright future to the village, which would be known for its wealth and wisdom.

Gowri believed his words. 'Dear Lord Ganesh,' she prayed fervently as the swami spoke, 'Please stop the fighting between Uncle Mailar and Nayagam.'

'What are you praying about?' someone whispered behind her. She knew it was Nathan. She did not look at him or answer him. They were surrounded by other people; nearly the whole village was there. She was afraid to speak to him in such a public place.

When she was on her way home, he said, 'Well, now you have the new school. You won't have to worry about going outside the village to complete your studies.'

'Beginning to study is one thing; finishing is another,' she responded, thinking of Grandma and her plans.

'Gowri, you're too young to worry about life and your future so much. Why do you have to be anxious all the time?'

'Since when have I told you about my worries?' she snapped at him.

'I have not come to argue with you, madam; it was my observation and bit of a joke,' he said in a sarcastic tone.

She liked him, but she would not dare to show it, except for the occasional quick chat or smile. He was from a different world, where he had learnt about much which the villagers did not understand.

The moon was full, the night was beautiful. It was like a dream or a scene from a film. The breeze was soft. The stars in the crystal-clear sky gleamed like pearls on a soft silk saree. The slowly-moving moon radiated lovely golden magical light and shadows on all created things on earth.

Saratha was still at the school, since Shiva was there. Gowri wanted to get home early as her mother was unwell and walked fast to catch up with Buvana and Poorani, who were a few hundred yards in front of her.

She did not notice that Nathan was following her. When she had turned from the road into the lane, she looked behind her and spotted him. She panicked. She did not want people gossiping about her. She had too much on her mind for additional worries.

'What's the matter, Gowri? Why are you running away? Are you scared of me?' Nathan asked her in his usual casual manner.

When would he understand the village? Gowri walked faster to avoid further conversation with him.

This night was going to be one of the most important in her life, and not just because of the opening of the school. It was also the first time that Nathan had talked to her alone, followed her with the intention of talking to her.

She could see someone ahead. It was Rajah, standing like a mythical monster in the middle of the junction. Her heart began to beat so loudly she was afraid both young men would hear it.

'Hello, hello; I never reckoned our women had to have outsiders brought in to be their bodyguards.' Rajah's tone was ominous and insulting. He spat on the ground and laughed crazily.

Gowri did not need to work hard to fathom the meaning of his comment. He was making it absolutely plain that he did not like to see Gowri with another man.

She became angry. Firstly, her anger was directed against Rajah, who was standing in her way to obstruct her and making remarks as if he owned her. Secondly, she was cross with Nathan, who was following her and playing silly games without really understanding local people and the sharpness of their tongues.

She glared at Rajah as if she wanted to scorch him with her look and told him; 'We don't need guards, sir. This lane belongs to everyone; there is no need to rely on someone else. I think we should learn to respect other people.' She did not wait to hear his reply. She could not stand assumptions being made about her without foundation.

She already knew that next day there would be gossip in the village. And so, what? Even if she were concerned, there was nothing she could do about it. Her anger turned to distress. She walked fast, opened the gate and turned to see if anyone was coming. Nathan was still behind her, walking in her direction. She could tell that he, too, had been hurt by Rajah's remarks.

'What are you doing here?' She wept, the moonlight reflected in her tears. Though she did not know it, he took a step forward to wipe them away but stopped himself.

'Am I just a passer-by on the lane?' he asked softly, his voice silky, tender, loving and stimulating.

Suddenly Gowri realised that she was in a situation over which she had no control. She could not afford this. In no way could she feel relaxed or happy about the whole business of standing there with a handsome man who was whispering tenderly in the moonlight.

'Please go away,' she whispered, begged him.

'Is that what you really want?' He seemed sad, disappointed. She wouldn't look at his face.

'If you want to be my cousin's friend, that's fine, but don't give me a hard time.' She was weeping uncontrollably.

'Gowri, I would never do that.'

'You don't understand this village.'

'Help me to understand.'

'Not on my account,' she wanted to say, but she found it hard to bring the words out of her mouth.

Amuthavalli came, barking in a friendly manner as she recognised Nathan. Gowri knew her mother or Grandma would be out in a minute to see at whom the dog was barking.

'Please go.' The words were accompanied by tears. She watched him leave and cried for herself and for him.

Chapter 19

The next afternoon, Gowri received a letter from Kamala. She described Jaffna town and the nursing school. She seemed to be enjoying herself. She asked Gowri to give her love to many people in Kolavil, including Nathan.

Why had some people begun to ask Gowri about Nathan? Why could Kamala not write to him herself? While Gowri was thinking about Kamala, Ragu, Nathan and also Rajah, Saratha came in gasping. She looked happy though breathless. No wonder; she had the chance to talk to Shiva last night. She had been determined to catch him; otherwise, surrounded by so many people, she would not have hung around him last night.

'Hey, do you know something?' Saratha asked Gowri. Saratha's eyes were darting about all over the place, her glance was shifty, as if she had something to hide. Grandma was on the verandah, taking the seeds out of dried beans. Mum was asleep with her new-born baby boy, and Gowri's younger sister and brothers were playing a silly game under the jak tree. They had painted the chicks with their watercolour brushes in various hues, and the poor mother hen did not recognise her chicks, which ran after their mother with their multi-coloured feathers. The mother hen was making loud noises and scurrying round a jasmine tree. Grandma was chasing the chicks with a stick and flinging pebbles to drive them away.

Gowri was watching the drama and said to Saratha, 'We

used to do that, too, remember?'

Saratha wouldn't answer for a minute or so. Then she said, 'He's gone.' Saratha nearly bit Gowri's ears in her eagerness to reveal the secret.

'What are you going to do now? Chant a *mantra* or say prayers for him?'

'Get lost!' Saratha seemed reluctant to joke.

'What's the matter?'

'Well...' Saratha was biting her nail nervously.

'Well...what?' Gowri sounded irritable.

'Will you do me a favour – a big favour?' Saratha begged Gowri.

'It depends.'

'Oh, come on, don't be so big-headed.'

'I didn't know I had a big head,' Gowri jested.

'You write better school essays than me,' Saratha giggled, still nervous.

'Thank you for the observation.'

'You seem unfriendly today,' Saratha mumbled.

Gowri felt sorry for Saratha, who she knew wanted talk to her about Shiva. 'Well, tell me, what can I do for you? Go and talk to him for you?' Gowri joked.

'Don't see him, write to him,' Saratha replied quickly.

'What are you talking about?'

Saratha looked around again. One of her brothers, Sangar, was giving tobacco to a lizard. It looked forlorn and helpless. There were many small onlookers. Sangar was trying to make the lizard intoxicated, so that he could have fun seeing its unsteady movements – like a drunken dancer.

'Look. Read this.' Saratha suddenly produced a letter from

her blouse.

Gowri's heart stopped for a second or two with shock.

A letter? A love letter?

She remembered the letter which the three of them had written to their pen-pal Leslie in Colombo and the scenario which followed. Another letter? God help her. Gowri was certainly in need of help from beyond this world if she was to get involved with Saratha's adventure.

'What is this letter?' Gowri tried hard to keep her voice at its usual level. She didn't want Grandma to hear the word 'letter'. But Grandma seemed to be occupied with chickens, dogs and the noise made by the children. Sangar was laughing loudly at the lizard's dance.

'He sent me a letter,' Saratha announced proudly.

'For you or me?' Gowri tried to make a joke of it.

'For me, you fool.' Saratha's voice was sweeter than honey from the frost.

'Why do you want me to see it?'

'Well...'

Gowri waited.

'You can help me to write a reply.'

'What?'

A charming smile came from Saratha's face instead of a reply.

'You're grinning, Saratha.' Gowri was confused.

'You write nice articles with beautiful words.' Saratha kept her gaze on Gowri's face.

'Don't be silly, Saratha, love letters are between two people, not three.'

'Of course, I wouldn't tell anyone.' Saratha's voice was soft and plaintive.

Gowri did not know what to do. 'Saratha, this is dangerous. If Grandma finds out, I'll be in trouble.'

'She won't.'

'How do you know?'

'We'll be very careful.'

'Will we?' Gowri was undecided.

'Yes, you silly. Read this letter and think of a reply, then I'll join you in putting it down on paper.'

Saratha had no second thoughts; she had decided that Gowri should help her.

Saratha held out the letter. As Gowri put out her hand, she noticed that it was trembling with fear. To what was she stretching out her hand?

'Be careful,' Saratha whispered.

Be careful? What was she talking about? Did she think Gowri was about to put it on display with the newspapers at the village shop?

'Oh, so it's a love letter, not a paper for national distribution?' Gowri nearly shouted at Saratha, who was sitting elegantly on the swing and singing a romantic film song.

'Anyway, please read it.' Saratha left the letter with Gowri, who sat clutching the letter for a while.

'Saratha is so stupid, she can't even write a reply to a love letter. How on earth is she going to cope with a love affair?' Gowri cursed her cousin for leaving her in this dilemma. She did not even know when she would manage to read this letter.

Grandma was preparing food for Mum and Swami

Lingam. She had to cook separately for him, as he was a vegetarian. Nowadays, she had fewer arguments with her granddaughter. This was partly because Gowri was happy that her studies were continuing.

She had less free time these days. She spent much of her time doing school work, some time with Dad and some time with the swami, both of whom were deeply involved in work around the temple. They had been discussing with others the possibility of bringing craftsmen from Jaffna to build a special section of the temple. The swami would explain to her the significance of different gods and goddesses when she asked questions. Some days she would have time to read novels and other books given to her by Nathan.

She helped Grandma to finish the cooking. Gowri's young brothers and sisters were too absorbed with playing to bother about giving trouble to Grandma. While they were eating, the drama of the hen and chicks was a topic of conversation. Grandma had not been that all pleased.

She said, 'Don't harm living creatures who have no way of defending themselves. God will hurt you in the way you hurt others.'

'They're only chickens,' one of the young one protested.

'Chickens have feelings, too,' she retorted stiffly.

Gowri felt guilty about Saratha's letter. She thought that it was not right to be carrying someone else's love letter around. After the meal, she settled down to her homework. It was hot for December.

That evening, without warning, rain started pelting down. Thunder rolled and lighting flashed. She put the pots and baskets in the portico to keep them dry. She prepared tea for her father and Swami. They were busy discussing matters related to the temple and its committee. Grandma was there, too, making remarks about unity in the village. Mum was feeding the baby and getting the other children ready for bed. The boys slept next to Dad in the portico; the girls slept in the room.

Gowri began to read the letter by the dim light of the kerosene lamp. The letter seemed to have been folded many times and – as it had been hidden in Saratha's blouse – smelt strongly of sweat.

'My dearest loving Saratha,' the letter started, 'I saw you last night. The more I see you, the more I want to be with you. Unfortunately, because of situation in the village, the subject is not suitable to be brought up in my family. The temple issue is very important to everyone at the moment. I think your parents will have to raise the subject with my parents, as is traditional in our village...' The letter contained little of importance except that he wanted Saratha's parents to go and see his about a marriage proposal.

Gowri considered how to reply to this letter. If Saratha told her parents about Shiva, they might prevent her from going to school. If Saratha stopped going to school, then Buvana and Gowri herself...

She did not like the thought of Saratha's love affair getting in the way of her own studies. After all, she had masterminded Saratha's decision to stay at school in order to win Shiva's heart. Now, Gowri had no wish to help Saratha to drop out.

'I suppose, even if I don't help her, she'll be able to find some words from a book and put a slushy letter together,'

Gowri thought. She had no alternative but to keep Saratha's love simmering for at least another year.

The next day, Saratha arrived with a radiant smile, 'What do you think? Did you write a reply?' she asked Gowri.

'Who? I? Did I write a reply? Oh no. But I'll help you to write one,' she replied forcefully.

But how could they cooperate on a letter? They did not usually do their homework together. 'We'll have to persuade the others that we're studying together,' Saratha suggested reluctantly.

'You should have thought more carefully before falling in love.'

'Love doesn't come to fit anyone's plan,' Saratha said, with the assurance of a woman experienced in such matters.

'Oh, yes? We'll just have to find a way to make sure that it continues.' They settled down with their schoolbooks and notes. 'We're writing an essay, Grandma,' Gowri convinced her with a pleasant smile.

Chapter 20

In March 1959, as soon as the harvest was finished, the villagers began to work hard to complete the building of the temple. It was heartening to see them banding together thanks to the god Ganesh. Nevertheless, all four village clans tried to outdo each other in collecting money for temple.

Was it natural for humans to emphasise their differences and strive to prove themselves better than one another? Was it fear of other social groups which caused people to think in a cowardly way? Gowri never ran out of questions in her mind. 'Why do I have to keep thinking about other people? Am I different from other girls in the village?'

On her way to school, she admired the temple. The village seemed to have gained a new dimension since the construction began. It was like a jewel in a crown. Nearby villagers came to visit the temple.

Swami Lingam cried with joy to see the building going up. 'Once upon a time, white men destroyed our ancient temple. Now we've rebuilt it after a hundred and fifty years,' he remarked happily.

The harvest was excellent. 'Local people suffered greatly last year, but God has compensated us very generously this year,' people said.

Villagers were expected to set aside a certain quota of their crops for sale to the government. The quota, which depended on how much land each household owned, tended to be the same, since most only had a small state-allocated plot.

Sometimes poor farmers would borrow money from rich neighbours like Mailar and repay the loan with surplus grain. In effect, their quotas would be bought in advance, an illegal practice.

The government co-operative was in the town next to theirs, where communal violence had erupted the previous year. Now the villagers had gained permission to set up a co-op in Kolavil. They had to elect officials from among themselves. Gowri knew that there would be another drama in which prominent personalities jostled one another to play the central role.

As she expected, Uncle Mailar put himself forward for president. But the villagers voted for Uncle Kasi, since they did not want any more conflict between Mailar and Nayagam. Mailar and Rajah were elected as joint secretaries, Ragu as manager.

For a while everyone was happy about the co-op and its officials. Then, when it was time for the surplus rice to be sold, it was Nayagam's duty to ensure that the correct quotas were allocated to farmers. Until now, they had dealt with the co-op in the next town and had been completely reliant on its revenue officer. Though they were currently able to sell their grain to their own co-op, they still needed his permission.

It was only then that some farmers realised that they could not sell the usual quantity of the rice. The reason was that Nayagam and the district revenue officer had denied them their proper quotas. Dad was one of those affected, and he was very angry.

'No government will get people's support unless it has

honest officials,' he grumbled.

Gowri could have laughed aloud, but she did not. She asked him, 'If you notice corruption only in the co-op, what do you think is happening in the hospitals? Every time we go there, we have to pay five rupees for a penicillin injection.'

He replied, 'That's because the doctors are from outside. They only care about money, not our health.'

As far as she was aware, no government department functioned without corruption. People with money bought the best healthcare and managed grain quotas.

When stories of Nayagam's corrupt deal with a district revenue officer began to circulate in public, people suggested that his son Rajah also might be involved. Gowri asked her cousin Ragu, who was the manager of the co-op, how he could work with people like Rajah, who were directly or indirectly tainted by corruption.

He replied that he trusted Uncle Kasi and that, to date, he had come across no financial maladministration, but he did not want to carry on working there for long because he was afraid his father was using him to spy on others.

Gowri was cross with Uncle Mailar. Perhaps he had planned something like this all along. He had not allowed his son to go to college after the flood last year. Ragu had applied to enrol at the agricultural college, but that had come nothing because of Mailar, who had pressurised the young man into becoming the co-op manager.

'Nathan has got into teacher training college recently; Ragu could have gone, too,' Gowri told Saratha, but said little about the problems in the co-op.

Within a few weeks, Ragu had resigned as manager, as the

trouble worsened and the gossip got spicier. 'You've got to find a job and get away from all this,' Gowri urged him.

He said, 'My father is not happy that I left the post. Let him cool down a bit. He is shouting that I don't listen to him anymore.'

Mailar lamented to the *dhobi* Nagan, 'I never thought my son was a coward who would run away from people like Nayagam.' Mailar was conscious of class distinctions and would trample on people such as washermen as if they were fertile soil on the banks of the River Thillai. He hated people arguing with him; he enjoyed having Nagan as his listener, since he would not dare to answer back.

Ragu said very little that was critical of Mailar, retaining his respect for his father, although he did not see eye to eye with him on a number of issues.

Almost everyone in the village was aware that Mailar wanted his son to follow his example, but Ragu did not seem to be interested in that lifestyle. His personality and aspirations were the opposite of his father's. The young man was scrupulously honest, kind and hard-working. He wanted to be free and control his own life, but he was still reliant on his father for many things and would not argue with him openly.

Grandma was reluctant for him to leave the co-op. She had secretly hoped that the family would become closer to Rajah as they worked together, but this had not happened. He was still active in Tamil politics. He appeared on stage with Tamil political leaders from Jaffna, while Ragu spent his time with Swami Lingam doing temple work. A few years before, Ragu had been a youth leader for the Federal Party, but now he enjoyed being away from politics because of the conflict between Mailar and Nayagam.

The conflict in the co-op also found its way into the classroom. 'It's a pity that politics has been taken over by hypocrites and humbugs who aren't really concerned with the people,' the teacher told the children one day when they heard singing at one of the meetings organised by Rajah.

'People like Nayagam will sooner or later take over from Mailar's type; there's no alternative. Mailar is an old-fashioned control freak, who wants to control the people with his land and power, while Nayagam is a new type who uses new-found money and manipulative methods to have control over them, although he has no glorious past linked with tradition and old customs,' he explained. Gowri did not fully grasp all aspects of the conflict, but she disliked both men. Mailar had been exploiting poor people for a long time, and Nayagam was now exploiting them by giving them loans at high rates of interest.

'Instead of the people creating the leaders, the economic structure gives leaders control of the people,' was another remark from the teacher which Gowri did not completely understand.

As the dispute continued, the villagers prepared to celebrate the Sinhala-Tamil New Year. People boiled herbal water to purify themselves, as was the local custom. Usually, they had plenty of money with which to buy two or more sets of clothing and presents for their friends and relatives. To celebrate the New Year, sometimes the villages would stage a play, usually based on one of the Hindu myths.

Everyone would visit loved ones and have fun. Old

Palipody was drunk long before the festivities started. He sang or recited a poem to everyone who came near him. There were many large swings on the big trees in the village, and people, young and old, would relax on them. They would sing as they swung, making fun of one another with satirical songs.

One afternoon, Gowri and Saratha stood as Grandma sat on a swing, pushing it high in the air and enjoying themselves. Grandma was happy and was singing a romantic song. It was about a girl whose lover had left her and the loneliness she felt. Grandma was in a world of her own when she was singing.

Though Gowri had not talked to or asked anyone about Grandma's past, the girl sometimes thought about the old woman and her hard life after she was left widowed with two young children. No wonder she was a strong woman! Perhaps it was her experience in life which had made her like steel.

She could be good fun. Sometimes she got on well with her granddaughters. She would tell them about the village history and the men who helped to create it. She was an old woman with old-fashioned ideas. She did not intend to be nasty to the young ladies; she simply tried to impose on them her view of the way life should be. She was singing about love when Palipody approached, cackling as usual.

'No wonder you're happy. It's not every day someone comes to ask for your granddaughter's hand in marriage.' The old man leaned against a crooked coconut tree and made himself comfortable.

What was he talking about? Gowri let the swing slow down and began to listen to him. The day she started to help

Saratha with her love letters, she had known that – sooner or later – the romance would be discovered. Then Uncle Mailar would do something drastic, maybe arrange a marriage for Saratha or practically murder her.

Grandma stopped singing and looked at her drunken brother gravely. Because he was always drunk, nobody took any notice of what he said. But when he started speaking of marriage, Grandma naturally became alert and serious. 'What are you talking about?' she demanded.

'You ought to be a happy woman today,' he grinned.

'Oh yes, what for?'

'Your granddaughter Buvana is going to be a bride soon.'

Gowri nearly screamed with surprise but contained her anxiety.

'Are you serious?' Grandma jumped out of the swing and approached the old man.

'Of course, I am. I'm not going to joke about the girl's marriage.' He lit another cigar merrily.

'In that case, we'll have to wait for the New Year festivities.' Grandma smiled brightly.

Would they do that? Buvana was only fifteen years old, but it was not at all unusual for a girl of fifteen to get married in the village. Gowri's mother was only fourteen when she got married. What a pity! Gowri felt sorry for Buvana, soon to be tied up in marriage. At the same time Gowri was worried that, if the news of this engagement were true, her own wedding might come next in Grandma's plan.

Who could the bridegroom be? Would Auntie Indira allow her daughter to marry so young? If Buvana got married, what would happen to Saratha, the eldest of the girls?

Saratha did not seem surprised by the news. 'Did you hear that?' Gowri asked her.

'Yes.'

'Did you know the news already?'

'Not the details.' Saratha's voice was no different than usual. How could Saratha not have informed her?

'Why didn't you tell me?' Gowri concealed her anger.

'I didn't think the talk was serious. I thought Dad was just rabbiting on, the way he does about other things. Most of the time, you know, I don't take too much notice of him.' Saratha was honest, and she might have been right. The proposal was still no more than talk. Nonetheless, it was remarkable that, though Buvana was as closely related to Saratha as Gowri was, Saratha had not thought the subject important enough to discuss.

'Who is to be the bridegroom?'

Saratha looked at Gowri in surprise. 'Don't you understand anything?'

'Such as what?'

'Well, they're talking about my big brother Ragu for Buvana, who else?' Saratha seemed to be enjoying herself on the swing.

'What?'

Gowri suddenly remembered watching Ragu with Kamala. There was no doubt that he loved her. In Gowri's mind she pictured Ragu, Kamala and Buvana together when they had been in Thirukovil temple. Gowri knew with certainty that Kamala, on her part, was in love with him. What would he do now?

'Does Ragu know the latest development?' Gowri asked.

'I don't know.' Saratha's dislike of the subject was evident.

'Oh yeah, you're only interested in talking about your own business and your darling Shiva, aren't you?'

Saratha did not answer her.

'Tell me, would you marry someone just because your father told you to?'

'Certainly not!' Saratha raised her voice.

'What would you do? Surely we don't have much choice about getting married.'

'I have.' Saratha was furious about Gowri's question.

'Have you? How?'

'Well, I'd tell them I won't marry anyone but Shiva, and if they try to force me to marry someone else, then I'll commit suicide.'

'You'll do what?' Gowri became cross with Saratha, who was creating more of a headache for her. 'Why can't she think of something pleasant and positive, not negative and nasty?' Gowri thought.

'What will the grown-ups do if your brother refuses to get married?' Gowri asked Saratha.

Saratha shrugged her shoulders in reply. She did not know, she said. She had little understanding of other people unless she had something to gain from them. Gowri thought that Saratha's behaviour was similar to that of her father Mailar. He would do anything to satisfy his own needs. In the same way, Saratha would do anything to fulfil her ambition to marry Shiva.

Chapter 21

Gowri could not help noticing the rapid changes in the village. The River Thillai had brought floods; it seemed as if the river had washed away most of the old way of life, old customs and the old network of relationships.

After the flood, Kolavil had changed a great deal. Tremendous damage had been done. Many homes had been destroyed; in place of huts, houses had been erected. The old thatched school had been replaced by a new building located next to it. Instead of the thatched temple, there was one of the largest and finest temples in the area.

The people, as well as the village, had changed. Nayagam bought a tractor. Mailar was losing his land because of his extravagant attempts to keep up his lavish lifestyle. Shiva's family had never been deeply involved in village matters, as his father worked as a storekeeper in town; they were basically urban people. Uncle Kasi was busy with the swami.

Auntie Indira had a new sewing machine as people were bringing more cloth from which to make dresses; as the financial situation got better, there were many religious and cultural events for which to dress up. The family also bought another plot of land, as they had four daughters and wanted to build four houses for them. Auntie Indira had always been a good organiser; the land they had bought was near the river and had soil suitable for growing many kinds of crops. As everyone expected, Buvana spend more time there.

The flood had created a new society in Kolavil,

transformed the way that people lived. Gowri could list and discuss, one by one, the changes which had occurred. She relished them.

She gazed with pride at the river, which was completely covered with flamingos and storks, wild bulls, silently floating small boats to catch the fish. The sun was rising beyond, its rays created an illusion of millions of diamonds scattered in the river bed, the scenery was the most beautiful that anyone could imagine.

She walked to Buvana's house one morning, as Poorani had said that Auntie Indira was not well. Gowri was reluctant to go there because it was next to Rajah's house.

The young man was becoming more popular in the village. He could not have cared less whether Ragu left the co-op. Rajah resembled his father; money was very important to both of them. Would Grandma persuade Gowri's parents to go to ask for Rajah's hand in marriage for their daughter?

Change in the village was inevitable, but what lay ahead for Gowri? The suggestion that Buvana's wedding was impending had given Gowri a shock. If her cousin got married, sooner or later Saratha and Gowri would have to follow her example. There would be no more argument about continuing to study.

Gowri asked her mother what Palipody had said about the proposal. Mum was playing a game, rather like draughts, with sea-shells on the sand, where other people's business was often a topic of conversation. When the recent conflicts in the co-op were mentioned, Gowri asked if it were true that Mailar was talking about a proposal for Ragu to marry Buvana.

Grandma and Mum looked at Gowri and replied, 'Why shouldn't it be true? Ragu is Buvana's relation. Mailar has every right to put forward such a proposal. Buvana is a lucky girl.'

Did Buvana know? Gowri went to her house, where she was watering her vegetables. Did Buvana love Ragu? Did she know that he was in love with Kamala? Gowri had many questions on her mind. She prayed that God would make Ragu happy. He was one of the nicest and most important people in her life. Through him she had met Nathan, who had given her strength and courage to continue studying. Through Ragu she had become involved with the swami and his work in the temple. Ragu meant a great deal to her. No brother could have been dearer. Bring him joy, she would pray every day.

Poorani was there with her sister Buvana, watering the plants together. Their characters were completely different; Poorani was an open book, easy to read, whereas Buvana was a closed box, its contents unknown. Would she and Ragu understand each other?

'Hey, young lady, why haven't you told me the good news?' Gowri teased Buvana.

Buvana carried on watering the vegetables and would not look at her cousin. Her beautiful long hair shone in the morning sunlight. 'I have managed,' Buvana began, eager to change the subject, 'to grow a...'

'I know what you've managed to grow.' Gowri watched Poorani fetching water from Rajah's house well. Gowri did not want to see Rajah; just in case he came out, she turned to face Buvana, who seemed overcome with shyness. 'Buvana, the whole village is talking about you.' There was a pause. 'You're lucky.' Gowri looked at her cousin, but she was not looking at Gowri.

'Mum says I have green fingers.' Buvana fingered the young spinach leaves. Gowri made no effort to hide her impatience with her cousin, who was trying hard to avoid the subject.

'Can I ask openly whether she in love with Ragu?' Gowri pondered silently. 'Since she's gone all quiet and keeps changing the subject, I reckon she is happy with the proposal. What else is there to find out?'

Auntie Indira was ill with flu; her joints ached. She was making coriander water for her cold and cough. She was a very busy woman. She had worked hard to improve her life and was concerned about her four daughters. Unlike the other women in the village, who were under the control of their men in their families, she was educated. She was from Trincomalee and earned a lot with her sewing machine. She and Uncle Kasi shared everything; she had a different way of life to others in the village. She was efficient and resourceful and was willing to help any of her neighbours. When she saw Gowri she seemed surprised; young women were discouraged from wandering alone along lanes and roads.

'How are you, Auntie?' Gowri sat on the verandah, which was cool and clean.

'Not too bad, dear. I was going to ask you whether you wanted to learn dressmaking because I'm going to teach Buvana. It's something she'll need to know.' Her cheerful smile confirmed what Gowri had thought.

Oh well, who would not be happy to have Ragu as a son-in-law? Perhaps there were several other mothers in the village who would envy Auntie Indira. He was an ideal young man to marry one's daughter. He was kind, intelligent and handsome, and had all the qualities to make a good husband – except for one.

That was that he loved someone else. Would he tell his parents about Kamala? Or would he let his dominant father rule his life? The two men had little in common. Mailar was like an old king with his heavy moustache, long hair, large earrings and a heavy golden chain with a medallion. His son Ragu was not at all pretentious; he had an easy-going manner. When he began to grow a moustache, Gowri and Saratha had persuaded him to remove it because they hated Mailar's. Grandma had been proud of the moustache and had yelled at the girls when he shaved it off at their insistence.

His neighbours regarded him as a decent, likeable lad. When he resigned from the co-op, they had blamed Mailar. They were pleased that he was taking an interest in the temple. 'Nowadays, how many boys do you see who are so religious and dedicated?' people would remark.

All these things had made him one of the most eligible young bachelors in the village.

One day he came to Gowri's house in a furious mood.

'What's the matter?' Grandma asked, sweeping the verandah.

'What's the matter? You all know what the matter is.' Gowri had never known Ragu to shout. 'Isn't it unfair to arrange a marriage without consulting the people involved?' he demanded.

What was this? Gowri had a period that day and was lying

196

down in severe abdominal pain. Was the proposal a surprise to him? The talk about the marriage had started weeks before. Nearly everyone knew – except, apparently, Ragu himself. Discussion about the wedding had begun in April during the New Year celebrations. Most weddings took place in May or June. She had assumed all along that he knew about it.

What was he going to do? He was shouting that he did not like the idea of getting married at all, no wonder he was furious! Gowri knew that he was in love with Kamala, and she understood his anger.

'What are you talking about? Didn't you know about the proposal?' Mum asked, a little anxiously, although she did not sound too worried.

'Tell me, Auntie, isn't it unfair to…' He was too angry to finish the sentence. Grandma wanted to change the subject. She brought some *thosai* (rice pancakes) with spicy coconut chutney. He would not touch it.

Mum sat down next to him. 'Come on, my dear, surely they don't have to get your permission to go ahead with the proposal to Buvana? From the day she was born, we knew you'd be her husband. After all, she's your close relative; it's your duty to marry her.'

Duty? Gowri was still indoors, lying on her mattress and listening to the conversation. Worse than her period pain was the realisation that Ragu did not seem to have a choice. Everything had been planned, proposed and decided without his consent.

Did adults have the right to do that to their children? Because they were one's parents, did one have to obey their wishes? What would happen if Gowri refused to marry

Rajah? She closed her eyes. She could not visualise any escape. She let her mind wander for a few moments, picturing herself and Rajah together. 'Oh no, I won't,' she promised herself determinedly.

'Buvana's a very nice girl,' Grandma argued.

'I never said anything about Buvana,' Ragu protested.

'She's a decent, well-brought up girl. She'll make you a good wife.' Mum backed up her mother.

'I don't want to talk about her. I'm trying to make it clear that I don't want to get married – not yet.' His voice was strong, but was his willpower?

'Why don't you tell them that you love Kamala?' Gowri wanted to ask him. Why could he not openly say what he felt about the whole issue?

'I don't want to get married now,' he was saying.

'Please,' Gowri urged silently, 'tell them you're waiting until Kamala finishes her nursing training.' Gowri wished Ragu were bolder. Why was he being such a coward? He had already messed up his education for his father's sake and got into trouble with the co-op on account of him. Now Ragu was going to get married because of the man. 'What's wrong with you, cousin?' she wanted to yell at him.

He went home. With support from Gowri's family, the swami went around to Mailar's house and told him of his son's objection to the marriage.

Gowri could hear Mailar's angry voice. 'What wrong with marrying the girl I choose? He is not going to be like his uncle in Thirukovil who married a Sinhalese girl. My family has respect, and my children must listen to me.'

Why was he talking about the uncle in Thirukovil? What

198

did his uncle marrying a Sinhalese have to do with Mailar? Why was he so determined to make Ragu marry Buvana? Gowri had plenty of questions and no answers.

Chapter 22

Gowri set off for Saratha's. She was busy preparing a letter to Shiva.

'Why is your brother refusing to marry?' Gowri put the question in the hope of getting more details.

'I don't know.'

'Do you think he's in love with Kamala?' Gowri had not wished to put the notion into Saratha's head, but now she felt she had no choice.

'You must be out of your mind to think that,' Saratha replied sharply.

'Why?'

'Why? Because...because...well, Dad wouldn't let my brother do anything of the kind.'

'What's wrong with Kamala? She's beautiful, educated, friendly. Above all, I think your brother's in love with her.'

'Maybe, but...' Saratha was reluctant to speak.

'Go on, tell me, why doesn't your father like Kamala?'

Saratha gazed at Gowri for a while, turned her face aside and told her cousin, 'Gowri, I've told you what I know. That's all I can tell you. To the best of my knowledge, Dad won't let my brother marry Kamala.'

Gowri knew Saratha was hiding something. What could it be?

Gowri begged Saratha to divulge the secret, but she only said, 'Gowri, you know perfectly well, Dad doesn't like Mum's family. He won't even talk to them politely. Having

Kamala as his daughter-in-law would be the last thing he would do.' She would not say any more on the matter.

Gowri knew that Mailar did not like many people in the world. He was determined to run his son's life. If Ragu refused to marry Buvana, he would get nothing from Mailar, he told everyone. What a selfish man! Because of him, Ragu no longer had a government job. He had no choice but to rely on the land, and since he had no land of his own, he depended on Mailar's goodwill.

Auntie Sathya wept for her son. She, too, wanted him to marry Buvana, partly to keep her husband happy and partly because she knew that Ragu, if he refused to go along with Mailar's plans, would get nothing from his father. Why did some parents have to use their children to fulfil their own egos?

The teacher felt sorry for Ragu; nevertheless, he could not stop the marriage. 'Why can't they wait for the GCE exam?' the teacher inquired, as he did not want the girls to miss it, but the families did not care whether they took the examination or not. 'I have heard that marriages are fixed in heaven,' he joked.

'In this village everything's fixed by Mailar,' Gowri wanted to tell him. She explained that Ragu was not happy with the arrangement; however, Mailar would not listen to anyone.

'You know, sometimes it seems as if women and people with no money have no rights or power in the world. Ragu has no choice if he relies on his father's money to survive, but he'll be free and strong if he chooses to be independent. People who exploit others always have a way of manipulating them; that's what Mailar does.'

201

According to him, people were exploited by those with the means, who made a profit, since human labour was more valuable than the price paid for it; if oppressed people united, they could fight against such injustice. The schoolmaster might make statements like that, but she could not imagine anyone in the village living in the way that he advocated.

That term was a busy one. Preparations were made for an essay competition in the district. Gowri and Vasantha were taking part. They set off to discuss the matter with their teacher.

There were four subjects from which to choose. Gowri selected 'The modern woman and education'. She was good at writing essays, particularly when the topic affected her deeply.

'Why did you choose this subject?' the teacher asked her. She was nearly in tears. He understood her pain. 'Be strong, be honest, be dedicated in anything you choose to follow in life.' He encouraged her. 'Our society makes use of girls to clean pots and pans and produce babies. Will you do something different?' he asked in a joking tone. She knew that he really wanted her to be different.

'I'll try.'

'Will you? Or are you going to become like Buvana?'

'No, I won't,' she promised him but, in her heart, she was terrified of the future.

Sooner or later, Saratha's love affair was going to be discovered by her parents. Then she would be stopped from going to school. After that, Grandma would definitely not let Gowri continue her studies.

'Dear Lord Ganesh, keep Saratha's secret for another year,'

Gowri prayed to her favourite god. But she wondered if he would. She would have to wait and see.

There was a whirl of activity as preparations were made for the wedding. Although everybody in the family knew that Ragu was opposed to the wedding, nobody took any notice. Gowri wanted to see Buvana and find out what she was feeling. Surely, she had heard about her fiancé's reluctance?

Gowri hated to pass Rajah's house in case she encountered him, but she had no choice if wished to visit Buvana. Gowri made her way through the sandy, narrow lane which led to Buvana's home. If anyone came past, there would be scarcely room to pass. She hoped that he was not around.

She could not forget the night when he had made caustic remarks after seeing her in front of Nathan in the lane. She had not met Nathan for a long time; he had entered teacher training college. Perhaps he would come to Ragu's wedding and might meet Rajah again. It was up to her to try to avoid another awkward situation.

She spotted Poorani in the lane on her way home and felt much happier. Gowri could walk along with her cousin, just in case Rajah emerged.

'Hello, Poorani, hang on. I'm on my way to your place, too,' Gowri called. Her fear had been well-founded. She saw Rajah coming out of his house. She turned her face away as if she had not noticed him, but she could not keep up the pretence for more than a few moments. He wheeled his bicycle just in front of her.

'Hello, Gowri, what a pleasant surprise!' His tone was jolly. She did not say anything.

'To catch sight of you, Gowri, is like seeing a fourth-night moon – a very rare event.'

'Oh yeah? In case you didn't know, seeing a fourth night-moon brings bad luck,' she retorted sharply.

'I wouldn't really mind if you were around so we could share the bad luck together.' He was sharp as her.

Gowri could tell he was serious. Poorani started laughing at their conversation.

He asked, 'Why do you always go around with a bodyguard?'

She became very angry. 'Because there are animals roaming about to harass me.' She really wanted him to understand that she disliked him.

'Then you need a good partner for your protection, don't you?' He continued to be quick-witted, too.

'I know.' She snubbed him.

'Do you?' He had an odd look in his eyes.

'But nobody like you.' She did not want to hear his remarks on the subject.

She thought, 'If he has any decency, he won't give me any more hassle.' She had not realised that he was so keen on making her his wife.

When she arrived, Buvana was in the garden as usual. 'In the very last moment of her life,' Gowri said to herself, 'Buvana'll tend her stupid plants.' The fresh air played with the leaves in the vegetable garden. Buvana was carrying a huge pot of water.

'Hey, don't break your back carrying so much water. What's Ragu going to put his arm around if your shapely hip's not there?' Gowri joked. Buvana seemed shy but unconcerned by the mention of her fiancé's name. If she knew of his feelings, she could have told him to leave her alone and find someone else, but she was obviously enjoying the conversation about her marriage.

What could she do? Gowri tried to put herself in Buvana's position. Did she have any way of saying 'No' to getting married? Though Ragu had objected, all the adults assumed that he was making a bit of a fuss but would be all right as soon as the ceremony was over.

Buvana pointed out that the 'ladies' finger' plants were flowering. Gowri could tell that her cousin was dodging the subject again.

'When is the big day going to be?' Gowri asked, flicking a drop of water at Buvana playfully.

Buvana averted her face and said, 'How should I know? The grown-ups will decide. Do we have a say?'

So, Buvana was not as naïve as Gowri had feared. The bride-to-be knew that if the grown-ups put their minds to something, there was little that the girls could do to prevent it. However, Gowri did not fail to notice the softness in Buvana's tone when she talked about marriage. Who could object to marrying Ragu?

They talked about other topics, such as school; Buvana did not seem to be missing it. She enquired about Nathan, who was not visiting the village as often as he had previously done. Gowri said that she knew nothing about him, her heart aching with pain as she lied. He was at the teacher training college in town, but if he wanted to come, he would find the time.

That night when he had spoken with Gowri had been important to him as well as to her. He had realised that she had major choices ahead of her. She was terrified of many of the people and beliefs surrounding her. She respected him but could not be friendly with him as he had hoped. Gowri could not tell such things to Buvana or anyone else. Sooner or later, he might stop coming to the village, but, if Gowri became the target of gossip it would never go away, and the good name of the family would be damaged. She did not want to take the risk.

'Ragu is very close to Nathan,' Buvana remarked, her eyes on Gowri's face.

'What does she expect me to say?' Gowri wondered. 'That he was also trying to get close to me?'

'Yes, but that's all in the past. Now Ragu's going to get as close to you as possible. Don't keep him indoors all the time; let him come out and talk to us, too, won't you?' Overcome with embarrassment, Buvana covered her face with her hands.

'Whether you care for her not, my dear cousin Ragu, Buvana seems over the moon about marrying you. Please keep her happy,' Gowri pleaded with Ragu in her mind.

Chapter 23

A priest from the temple of God Shiva in the nearby town came to organise the wedding.

Ragu looked extremely handsome in his traditional, silk wedding costume. He didn't look at anyone; instead, he kept his eyes fixed on the ritual fire which burned in front of him. Gowri wondered what he was thinking. Buvana looked like a statue from the Hindu temple in a golden saree and jewels. She was only fifteen years of age, yet appeared grown-up in her bridal costume.

Saratha was the most excited person during the ceremony. Gowri could read her thoughts from her smile and her expression. She was looking forward to the day when she herself would be married.

Ragu tied the holy chain – *thali* – around Buvana's neck while the priest chanted *mantras*. Women made celebratory *kuravai* noises. Mailar looked proud. Auntie Sathya was in tears.

The couple placed their feet on a stone *ammi* to pledge their love and dedication to each other, as solid as rock. The priest asked them to look at the star in the sky known as the *arunthathi* star, which symbolised chastity and purity in women. A silver plate was set before them. Their first meal together was made with seven vegetables, with seven fruits to follow.

The village enjoyed a three-day feast provided by Mailar. Palipody's condition came as no surprise. Drunk and partially naked, he lay under the mango tree singing; no-one understood the lyrics. Sometimes he would dance unsteadily in celebration of the marriage. Auntie Sathya's relatives came from Thirukovil, bringing gifts. Shiva was at the wedding, as was almost everyone in the village. Saratha was flying high with her feelings of love.

Gowri had already sent a letter to Kamala about Ragu's marriage. Perhaps she had received it that day. Would she cry? Gowri did not wish to dwell on the subject or the meaning of her great-uncle's songs. He was unsteady and tripped over Dog Amuthavalli and the lazy cat a lot.

Gowri liked both Kamala and Buvana. Now Ragu was with Buvana. Gowri decided that she would talk to nobody about Kamala; the past was best forgotten.

Nayagam did not come to the wedding. But Rajah and his mother came and shared a meal with the others. Nathan arrived; Gowri removed herself to the kitchen, where she helped Grandma, in order to avoid him. She could see both him and Rajah through the keyhole. She watched them for a while.

Rajah looked and acted as if he were a prince of the village, while Nathan laughed and joked with his brother and sister-in-law as usual. Gowri could see that Nathan's eyes were wandering. Was he looking for her? If he was...

Gowri wiped away her tears with her skirt. Grandma asked if she was crying. She replied that the onions were making her eyes water.

'What a beautiful sight,' people said of Buvana and Ragu. Indeed, they made a beautiful couple. Both had gentle manners and were well-respected in the village. Ragu did not show any emotion; he seemed to be fitted into the new role.

Now the time had come for them to visit relatives, as was the local custom, but Mailar forbade them to visit Nayagam's family. Uncle Kasi did not take well to this. Villagers regarded weddings and funerals as times when people would set aside their differences and grudges against one another.

Uncle Kasi's family had grown very close to Nayagam's. They were distantly related via Grandma's family tree. Buvana was like a daughter to Rajah's mother as she had no daughter of her own. Kasi's household had used Nayagam's well for water as if it were their own, and, over the years, the next-door neighbours had become like one big family. Now Mailar was trying to put restrictions on their way of life because, as the father of the bridegroom, he thought he had power over Kasi's family.

'I gave my son to you, so I thought you'd respect me and keep away from my enemies.' Mailar jumped up and down in rage when Kasi told him he should not interfere with Kasi's daughter's life. 'Your daughter is no longer your daughter; she's my son's wife. She will obey my son.'

Mailar ordered his son not to go and visit Nayagam or draw water from his well. This led to a heated argument between Kasi and Mailar. 'If you arranged this marriage with the idea of manipulating me, I'm going to stay away from you completely,' Uncle Kasi warned that night, raising the possibility that he might resign from the co-op in which everyone had such an interest.

Mailar nearly had a fit when he heard that, and shouted hysterically. The swami had to go over and soothe him by giving him a long talk on philosophy and some ganja cigarettes to smoke – in the company, not surprisingly, of old Palipody and others. Over a ganja cigarette, Mailar came up with another idea for causing a split between Nayagam and Kasipathy.

'My son's not going to bathe in my enemy's well. You must provide water for him,' Mailar demanded.

'What? How am I going to get the water? Connect the pipe to the River Thillai? I can't dig a well; my house is on rocky ground. That's why, all these years, I've had to go to a neighbour's house to get water.' Uncle Kasi was nearly in tears.

'I didn't ask you for any dowry for my son. Surely, it's not too much to expect you to provide him with water. Just use dynamite to break the rock and build a well, as many people in the village have done.' Mailar continued to be nasty.

Gowri thought her uncle Mailar a horrible man for behaving like this. Auntie Indira felt deeply uneasy. Their savings had been used up on Buvana's wedding. Whatever money was left should be spent on seeds for the paddy fields, soon to be planted. Also, it would not be easy to dig a well now, as the rainy season was about to start.

From then on, Mailar's nagging continued almost every day. Gowri's father and the swami were working on the temple and did not want to get involved in 'this business about water'. The whole village knew Mailar's motives; he wanted to break up the friendship between Kasi and Nayagam. One of the underlying issues was control of the co-operative; another was control over Kasi's political activities. A staunch supporter of the Federal Party, he was extremely friendly with Rajah, the party organiser in the village.

Nayagam was a cunning person, too. He gave plenty of contributions to Swami Lingam for the temple, so that he was not in a position to support Mailar in trying to cut Nayagam off from village activities. The swami preferred anyway to join his brother-in-law Mailar over a ganja cigarette to keep him calm.

According to local tradition, a bridegroom had to join his wife's household. Also, he was not supposed to work for at least three months after the marriage. In other words, a girl's family had to provide everything for the groom during the first few months, while the couple were enjoying their honeymoon period.

Ragu would take his bath at Gowri's house every morning and go to his father's fields or hang around with the swami doing temple work. Mailar gushed with sorrow at the suffering his son was enduring because there was no water supply in his wife's house.

One day the water issue went much further than anyone in the village had anticipated. Nathan came to the village and went to see his friend Ragu. As he walked along the lane to the house that evening, cows in their hundreds were on their way home.

It was very hot, and the passing cattle were stirring up dust. When Nathan arrived, he was dusty, and his feet were covered with cow dung. Poorani took him to the well at Rajah's house to wash off the dust and dung.

Rajah was there and came out of his house to see who was with Poorani. Nathan could vaguely recall the remarks Rajah had made that night when Nathan spoke to Gowri. He had been resentful of Nathan for some time. Rajah's anger had been inflamed by Nathan's remarks about the Federal Party; some of the village boys had reported that Nathan had mocked this party and its middle-class leaders from Jaffna for exploiting innocent Tamils by stirring up communal sentiment.

Rajah watched as Nathan approached with Poorani. 'Hey, Poorani,' Rajah called as she drew water from the well for Nathan, 'We let your family use our well because you don't have one, but we never said you could bring in people off the street to use our water.' His tone was sarcastic.

Poorani did not know what to say. She stood there for a while, looking at neither man. She had never been addressed by Rajah in that tone before.

'It's okay, Poorani, I'll wash at Gowri's house.' Nathan spoke loudly and clearly to make sure that Rajah heard.

Ragu spotted his friend walking away from Rajah's well with dirty feet, and Poorani told him what had happened. He did not shout or even raise his voice, as his father would have done, but instead went to the fence and called to Rajah.

'What do you want?' Rajah snapped at Ragu.

Ragu answered, 'I don't want anything from you. I'd just like to know why you insulted my friend? He has done nothing to annoy you.' He was polite, as usual.

'Oh yeah, is that so? Well, I'm not running a charity here for anyone to walk into my house.'

'It's only a little water.' Ragu's anger rose at the sound of Rajah's arrogance.

'What's the matter with you? Why are you getting so worked up about this stranger? Are you about to invite him to marry your sister-in-law or your cousin Gowri?'

Ragu knew Rajah dislike Nathan for some reason, but did not want to find out the details, preoccupied as he was with the battles around his marriage. He was furious about the whole business.

He went into the house, angry, and asked his father-in-law to dig the well as soon as possible. 'What's the hurry?' Kasi thought that Mailar had persuaded Ragu to make the demand.

'Because I'm not going to let my wife bathe next door any longer, as those people have no manners or respect for others,' Ragu said firmly.

'That's nonsense. Buvana's been having baths there since she was a few months old.'

'But not anymore.'

'Why not?' asked Kasi.

'If my friend isn't good enough to wash his feet in their well, my wife isn't good enough to bathe there, either.'

'Well...' Uncle Kasi had not been aware that Nathan had been insulted by Rajah. 'He's...'

'He's what?'

'He's an outsider,' Uncle Kasi replied.

'What? He's my friend.' Ragu stopped eating and glared at his father-in-law. Ragu had never before argued with Kasi, whom he liked very much.

'There's no need to get upset about things like your father. That's what you always advise, isn't it?'

Kasi should not have said that. Ragu was livid. 'It has nothing to do with my father. I'm talking about my wife, not him.'

Uncle Kasi was a good and honest man, but he had his

faults; he was emotional and quick-tempered at times. He became cross with his son-in-law, who had become so insistent about the well. He said, 'Well, you'll have to put up with not having a well until I'm able to dig one.'

'Until then, my wife's not going to stay here.'

'What?' Kasi was practically screaming.

'I'm taking my wife home with me.'

Auntie Indira hurried in. 'This is her home.'

'Yes, hers, but not mine. She should live with me, wherever I am.'

'Don't be silly,' Kasi protested. 'In our village, no woman goes to her husband's home.' Kasi was angry.

Ragu looked at him and said sharply, 'My mother and your wife came from outside to this village.'

'So, you're trying to bully my daughter into coming with you, the way your father bullied your mother into coming with him? I didn't bully my wife to come with me from outside, she lost her both parents before our marriage, and she had no choice.'

Ragu did not want to continue the argument. He went inside and looked at Buvana. In barely two months of marriage, she had not overcome her shyness about talking to him. She got up to show her respect for her husband, as it was village tradition that no wife would sit while her husband was standing.

'Will you come with me?' he asked sharply. She had never seen him that angry before.

'No, she is not going with you,' Uncle Kasi shouted, frenzied as a mad dog.

Auntie Indira began to cry quietly. She knew what the

outcome of the quarrel between the two men would be.

'My home is my wife's home. Will you please come with me?' Ragu begged his fifteen-year-old wife. She did not know what to do. Tears fell on her cheek as she turned her face away from him.

'Oh, no, she won't. You can't drag my girl from her own house. If you're a decent man you should respect village tradition.'

'Stuff tradition! I can't respect a tradition which makes me your slave, having to put up with insults from your friend next door.' Ragu stepped out of the house.

The River Thillai was still. Millions of golden spots shimmered on its surface in the light of the moon. It was not yet completely dark. The lowing of cattle and bleating of goats could be heard in the lane. The road was bustling with bullock carts, bicycles and people.

Ragu waited for few minutes; he had expected his wife to come with him. He had refused, at first, to marry this girl but had done so because of his family. Today, she was refusing to join him.

'I'm asking you for the final time. If you don't come now, I'll never have anything to do with you until I die.' His tone made it clear that he was in earnest.

She came to the verandah and stood there watching her father. For fifteen years she had been surrounded by her parents' love, living in their house. In the past two months she had come to know this man and the pleasure of being a newly-married woman. She gazed at both the men in her life.

'Please come,' Ragu whispered to his wife.

'Don't go!' Kasi yelled at his daughter.

She screamed with frustration and ran indoors.

Ragu waited for a while; then he left. Before he shut the gate, he looked back at the family with whom he had lived for two months.

He walked with his head lowered. The lane was scattered with cow dung. 'Shit, shit, my life is shit,' he mumbled.

Nathan had been dirtied by cow dung, Ragu by Rajah's dirty mouth. Why was Rajah so angry with Nathan? Ragu asked himself that question. Suddenly he remembered Rajah asking, 'Are you about to invite him to marry your sister-in-law or your cousin Gowri?'

'Oh, is it all to do with Gowri?'

Chapter 24

Gowri had nearly finished evening prayers and was humming a hymn tune as she went onto the verandah. There, she came face to face with her cousin Ragu, with a sad expression on his face. She could tell that something in his life had gone seriously wrong.

What was the matter? Was it to do with Mailar and Kasi? He sat down on the stump of what had once been a towering coconut tree. His eyes were fixed on the sky. Was he consulting the stars?

'What's up?' She went to him. He looked at her. 'Has there been an argument?' she asked.

'Yes,' he replied.

'With whom?'

'With my fate. I'm in dispute with my life.' He smiled sadly.

'Tell me what's happened.' She did not have time to question him; Grandma was approaching. Gowri fell silent.

'What's the matter? You seem to have lost a ship.' Grandma put her arm around him to cheer him up.

'Yeah, I lost my ship on a stormy sea,' he erupted. He was close to tears.

'What's the matter, my darling?'

'Go and ask your son. Ask your daughter-in-law. Better still, ask Rajah, your favourite relative-to-be.' Anger reverberated in his tone.

She did not wait a minute longer but dashed to the gate to

go to her son's house. Her eyesight was not particularly good. If she had to go anywhere at night, she would usually ask the small children to help her to find her way. Now she ran with nobody to guide her; perhaps she was relying on the brilliant moonlight.

Mum had been at Auntie Sathya's place, gossiping about something interesting. She arrived with a happy face. Gowri took her mother aside and explained what she thought had happened.

Mum did not get angry as Grandma had done. She smiled at him and asked, 'Are you sure you want to be without your wife?'

He did not answer.

'Imagine that. Look at the full moon, smell the fresh air blended with jasmine fragrance. Who would want to spend such a lovely night without one's beloved?' she joked.

He did not want to hear.

Mum lit the charcoal cooker to prepare the evening meal. 'Hey, son, can I cook something special for you? Go and bring Buvana over for a nice meal.'

Grandma returned, walking briskly. Usually, she would take Rajah's side in any disagreement, but, after hearing from Poorani what had happened, the old woman was little annoyed with him.

'You can refuse to give anything in the world but water. A man who refuses to give water to someone in need is definitely not a good man.' Whom was Grandma talking about, Gowri wondered. Could it really be Rajah? Could it be that Grandma could tell the difference between right and wrong?

Gowri helped her mother to prepare the meal, while Ragu was still seated on the tree trunk.

Mailar came running to see his son who had left his wife but did not want to return home. Mailar was looking for an excuse to abuse anyone who got in his way. Now he smelled a dead fish. He began to talk about get-rich-quick types in the village who had no respect. About whom was he shouting? Did his words apply to Mailar himself or Nayagam or indeed both?

What kind of man would do something like this to a young couple? Who was talking about fair play and justice now? Gowri was disgusted at her uncle's hypocrisy. He had nagged Ragu day and night to marry Buvana.

'If she loves you enough, she will come after you just as your mother followed me.' Now, Mailar was speaking about love. Gowri had not known that Auntie Sathya had followed her husband from Thirukovil; she'd assumed that he had brought her. Gowri's curiosity was aroused.

Mailar left after a long talk with his son, threatening to take revenge on the people who were behind this plot to humiliate him. What was he talking about? Who was humiliating whom? Nathan had been humiliated by Rajah, and Ragu seemed to have been upset by his wife, but who was humiliating Mailar?

Gowri decided that she would never fully understand adults. She asked Grandma about Mailar and Auntie Sathya. Grandma was angry with everyone that evening. She needed someone to talk to and was only too happy to tell her granddaughter what had happened all those years ago.

The old woman said that 'Mailar did not like anyone'. This

was a well-known fact. When he had married Sathya, Grandma continued, he had been very happy and had stayed in Thirukovil with his wife's family, until one of her brothers had moved to a mainly Sinhalese area and married a Sinhalese girl. Mailar was highly conscious of race and class and jumped up and down with fury about the wedding. He had no objection to his in-laws getting married as such – but Sathya's brother's fiancé was already pregnant.

Mailar had found himself isolated. Sathya's brother was in love; that the young woman was carrying another man's child did not matter to him. Mailar could not tolerate his brother-in-law marrying someone 'immoral' and would not talk to Sathya's family for a long time. Grandma told Gowri, 'Mailar is a stubborn man.'

'By the way, Grandma, what happen to the child the young girl was carrying?'

'Oh, that baby was Kamala – a bastard child, who was brought up by Mailar's brother-in-law as his own child.'

Kamala! Gowri began to understand why Mailar would not allow Ragu to marry her. 'God, help me to get over this shock,' she prayed.

Gowri could not sleep. Buvana had been married for only two months. And poor Ragu. What would happen now? She got up and sat for a long time, thinking about the situation. She felt sorry for both of them and annoyed with parents who played silly games with their children's lives. What a world! What was the point of growing up?

She came out from the room. The full moon was brilliant. Between trees and houses, she could see the River Thillai bathing itself in the moonlight. The river seemed unreal and extraordinarily beautiful. Life was beautiful unless others interfered and made a mess of it.

She sat on the tree trunk on which Ragu had been sitting the previous evening. 'Will they force me to get involved in something like this?' A chill went through her heart. 'God, give me strength to resist unjust demands,' she prayed fervently. The future seemed bleak and fearful to her that morning.

After hearing what had happened to Ragu, the schoolmaster felt guilty and saddened, especially when he learnt that the problem started because of his brother. He went to Uncle Kasi to apologise.

Kasi did not blame either Nathan or Rajah but carried on complaining that Ragu was under the influence of Mailar. The teacher pointed out that Ragu was not acting under Mailar's influence; the decision he had made that Buvana should come with him had been his own, not his father's. But Kasi would not accept that. He said that he had known Mailar long enough to recognise his ruthless game of hurting people.

The schoolmaster went to Ragu and told him, 'You'd better go to your wife. Whatever has been said and done, it's all over. It's better to forget the past and get on with life.'

Ragu replied, 'I'm not going back there. She doesn't have to come to my house. Tell Uncle Kasi that I'll find a place of my own for Buvana and me.'

Ramanathan went back to Kasi and told him what Ragu had said. It made not the slightest difference to Kasi; he said that he would never let Buvana move anywhere until he died.

A few other prominent people in the village tried to help

bring about a reconciliation, too. The swami approached both sides, but he did not have any luck. He did not want to upset anyone; to finish work on the temple he needed everyone's support. In the end he said, 'Whatever happens is because of fate. If the young people are suffering, it's destined to be.'

A few weeks passed in this way. Auntie Sathya talked to some of the people seeking reconciliation between both parties, but she failed miserably. After some weeks, Auntie Indira – Buvana's mother – came to talk to Grandma, looking pale with worry. Nobody in the village had ever left his wife after just two months of marriage.

Auntie Indira lamented Mailar's unkindness in keeping Ragu at home. 'How can a fifteen-year-old girl go through pregnancy without her husband's love?' Auntie Indira cried. Gowri's heart nearly stopped when she heard that Buvana was pregnant. She was a child herself. Poor Buvana!

Auntie Sathya learned of Buvana's condition and begged her husband to go and talk to Uncle Kasi.

'Go and talk to him? Over my dead body!' Mailar stormed.

In tears, Sathya pleaded with her son Ragu. 'I'm not angry with Buvana – she can come to me any time she wants to,' he snapped at his mother.

Sathya became deeply depressed over the whole matter. She cried for her son's fate and Buvana's future.

Saratha was very annoyed with everyone in the family, including Buvana. According to her, Buvana should go to her husband if she really loves him.

'Would you run away with your boyfriend if your family opposed your love?' Gowri asked Saratha.

'Of course. I'd go anywhere in the world for Shiva. If you can't do that what's the point in being involved with someone?' Sarātha asked Gowri with her seductive smile.

Gowri realised that, until then, people had worried about Mailar and Nayagam. Now she had to worry about Rajah and Ragu. 'Am I one of the reasons for Buvana's unhappiness?' she wondered. She knew she had no control over matters around her and the behaviour of Rajah or Nathan, but yet she felt responsible for the break-up of Ragu and Buvana's marriage.

Had Nathan come to village just to see his brother's family and his friend Ragu? She knew the answer well, but accepting it was painful. Nathan could not understand the village way of life. She would never be free to put her feelings into practice. So why would she hurt herself and him by keeping up the relationship?

What relationship? She could hardly speak to Nathan. She could not talk to anyone about her agony. There was no point in confiding in Saratha. She would never keep a secret. Gowri might just as well put up an announcement on the village noticeboard at the shop. Did Ragu know why Rajah was jealous of Nathan? Did he blame Gowri for his break-up with his wife? What could she do if this were the case?

Gowri went to school as usual, though her mind was in turmoil. At school, there was much talk about Buvana, Ragu and their marriage. Mailar was criticised. So was Rajah, but he was also given credit for his political activism in the village.

The Ceylon general election would possibly take place at the end of the next year. The Federal Party was trying to get its candidate elected in the constituency; Rajah was busy campaigning to achieve this. The 1958 anti-Tamil riots had left the Tamil population more determined than ever to fight for their right to self-determination.

People like Rajah had seized the opportunity to promote themselves. They led double lives; personally, they were dubious characters, but politically, they created an image of heroism. This appealed to emotional Tamil people who needed someone to lead their struggle. Rajah was a very important person now. He inspired the village boys; they would go to any lengths for the Tamil Federal Party.

'By singing songs and chanting slogans, will we get equal rights?' Gowri asked her teacher. She strongly supported the struggle for equality, but the way the movement was being run and the choice of leaders made her think carefully.

There was a large meeting one day. Through loudspeakers, the speakers declared, 'We have pledged we will die for the Tamil cause if we have to.'

Gowri remembered that, with Uncle Kasi, Ragu had been the first in the village to join the Federal Party. Now Ragu was not active in any political work. He did not talk to many people, either. He spent most of his time with the swami, joining in temple work. Most of the local young men hung around with Rajah.

Nathan came to Kolavil more often. He helped Ragu get over his agony. Every time she saw Nathan, Gowri prayed that God would help her to keep away from trouble and gossip.

Nathan was neither stupid nor selfish. He understood that what had happened to Ragu had something to do with him and Rajah and also had to do with his own feelings toward Gowri. Nathan felt very sorry, but Ragu said, 'Even if you hadn't been there, something else would have sparked off a blow-up between my uncle and my father, and I would have been in the middle, anyway.'

He was right. Mailar would not leave Kasi in peace until he dug the well.

Chapter 25

Uncle Kasi appeared on a platform with Rajah, who gave a speech about Tamil language rights. The schoolteacher was reading the daily paper; Gowri and Saratha were at his house, being taught how to knit by his wife. Now and then, Nathan would make a remark about the speeches booming out from the meeting via the loudspeaker.

'How much longer is Uncle Kasi going to go on about language rights?'

'Well, what Uncle Kasi doesn't realise is that Tamil leaders don't reckon the language is that important,' the teacher responded bitterly.

'Why do you say that?' Gowri inquired.

'Because Tamil leaders speak English; that is their language. Even their dogs would rather bark in English than Tamil.'

'You mean to say that all the Tamil leaders are liars and cheats?' Gowri asked the teacher.

'Oh, no, I wouldn't say anything like that. I have nothing against them. But politically, they're muddled, and the Tamil and the Sinhala politicians are playing dirty games by manipulating ordinary poor people to achieve their political goals.'

'So, who gets the best out of the political system?' Gowri stopped knitting a scarf.

'Who gets the benefit?' Saratha joined the question panel.

'People like Rajah.' Nathan looked directly at Gowri, but

she felt too uneasy to return his gaze.

'Why – why should only some people benefit?' she asked him naïvely.

'Because, when the rich fight for control, for power, who gets jealous? It's like this. Because the rich Sinhalese want more power, they are using poor Sinhalese against Tamils. Because the Tamil leaders want to hang onto their power, they're using the poor Tamils as sacrificial goats,' Nathan explained to her.

'That's a lie,' Gowri protested.

'Why is it a lie?' He was not smiling now.

'Because whether we fight or not, the Sinhalese in power will treat us badly. Why shouldn't we stick up for our rights instead of keeping quiet like cowards?' She was furious with Nathan now.

'Your cousin Rajah must have told you those things,' he teased her.

Gowri nearly exploded with anger. She had never discussed politics with Rajah. Since they had been little children, they had exchanged a few words, had the occasional quarrel. Apart from this, she had never had a proper conversation with Rajah.

'Nobody has had to teach me these things. I don't think there's anything wrong in asking for the right to live, the right to speak my mother tongue, the right to exist as a citizen of Ceylon.'

Nathan had never known her to get that angry. He decided to moderate the way he was putting across his political viewpoint.

Ragu came in. Ramanathan told him, 'You've just missed a

major political discussion between my brother and your sister and cousin.'

Ragu looked at Nathan, Saratha and Gowri. He had never known Saratha to talk about politics.

He turned to Gowri, who wasn't saying much. She knew that Nathan was trying to provoke her by talking about Rajah, but she wanted to avoid his name in front of Ragu. She changed the subject to knitting. Gowri had very carefully diverted the conversation, the teacher thought.

Work on the temple was almost complete. The villagers were jolly, full of joy to see their temple coming on nicely. For the past two years, they had faced one disaster after another. Part of the reason, according to village beliefs, was that they had no temple in which to perform rituals for their god Ganesh. They wanted to please him as much as possible. They had suffered enough; they did not want to suffer any more. They made him all kinds of promises to demonstrate their feelings for, and belief in, him.

Gowri's father decided to stage a play – a traditional activity – prior to the religious ceremony which was to be held soon. The swami was very happy about the idea. Kolavil village was famous for its street theatre (*Naatu koothu* folk drama), too.

The villagers used to write all their old documents, including stories, using the ancient method of writing on specially treated palmyra leaves. Dad spent years transcribing these valuable songs and poems, with Gowri as his secretary, copying old writings onto sheets of paper. Grandma was happy about Gowri's work copying the old myths and folklore. Gowri joked, 'Grandma, you didn't want me to go to school to study. Now, can you see what I can do with my education?'

Grandma was still none too pleased that the girls were going to school. However, the O-level examinations were not that far away, so she did not really mind her granddaughters continuing their studies for the moment.

While Gowri worked on a play adapted from the *Mahabharata*, with its war scene, she thought about the village. The epic was based on two families and their greed to defeat each other. When the baddies gained the upper hand, Lord Krishna came to the rescue of the goodies. Well, there were problems in the village, and two families were in trouble. Who was going to help them? In the *Mahabharata* the heroine Draupadi's honour had been saved by Krishna. Who was going to rescue Buvana and bring her Ragu to make her happy?

Gowri's father Nadesan was the opposite of his brother Mailar. Instead of making others miserable he got involved in being constructive – helping people, developing the arts, helping to build the temple and so on. Once his idea of a play had been fully accepted, he set about choosing the cast. Ragu also helped Gowri with the transcription. He was keenly interested in literature and Tamil culture and spent much time working on the play.

Meanwhile Saratha was enjoying Shiva's love letters. When the girls were together, Grandma thought the girls were studying hard and determined to do well in their forthcoming exam. Of course, Gowri was studying, but Saratha kept her boyfriend's letters in her school textbooks on subjects such as the Hindu religion and Tamil literature and read them many times a day.

Auntie Sathya was waiting for the school exam to finish to organise a wedding for her daughter Saratha. She said that she would prove to the village that they were still capable of proposing a marriage for their children with good families. Gowri's mother heard that Mailar was talking about finding a good match for their daughter and told Grandma, 'It's time for us to talk about Saratha's future.'

Perhaps Mailar had not noticed her affection for Shiva, but the villagers were not all fools. Many had noted Saratha's new clothes and hairstyle every Friday evening, when Shiva returned from his work in town to spend the weekend with his family in the village. He would travel along her lane many times during the weekend for no particular reason.

Her great-uncle Palipody even sang songs about their romance in public. But Sathya and Mailar took little heed; the old man often sang when he was drunk.

Ragu's separation from Buvana had caused Auntie Sathya much pain and anxiety. He was her elder son, and she had high hopes for his happiness. He had been unable to continue his education because of Mailar and forced to get married because of him. Her right to argue for her children's welfare was disregarded.

Sathya was none too pleased with her children at the moment. Her second son, Sangar, was the complete opposite of Ragu. Sangar was more like his father Mailar, arrogant and violent. He beat up other pupils at school. Auntie Sathya had to face a number of parents whose children had been assaulted by Sangar. Every day, she would have to deal with the problem of Sangar. He was only fourteen but was already notorious for his outrageous behaviour towards other youngsters. Sometimes she wept over her disappointment.

Chapter 26

One day, after seeing Shiva's bicycle in Saratha's lane, old Palipody began to croon romantically. Sathya remarked to her husband that the old man was singing about Saratha and Shiva, and that it would be worthwhile having a word with him to find out why he was cycling along the lane with no obvious purpose.

Mailar said, 'Who cares about no-good types? Do you think I'll give my daughter to someone from this village? No chance! One marriage like Ragu's – that's more than enough. I've no intention of pleasing anyone in this village any longer.'

The *dhobi* Nagan and Palipody were, in effect, the mass media for the village. They were enthusiastic spreaders of news; they loved chatting with people. Nagan would carry not only dirty and clean clothes but also unsought snippets of information, while Palipody was garrulously drunk. Nagan had carried more gossip from Mailar to his enemy Nayagam than clean garments to their neighbours. When Mailar stated that he did want any of his other children to marry someone local, Nagan conveyed this to Shiva's family, since he had heard the rumours.

Shiva wrote a long letter to Saratha. He did not try to hide his displeasure at Mailar's remark. 'If your father can boast about his integrity (if he has any), my family can also say a lot, too.'

What could Saratha do to stop her family's verbal

diarrhoea? She was in tears for days. 'If he stops loving me, there's no point in living,' Saratha cried for her love.

Whatever she was involved in now, Gowri had been there from the start. Furthermore, if Saratha made any drastic decision, it might affect Gowri, too. Why couldn't Ragu go back to Buvana? If he did, the villagers would be happy and would forgive Mailar for his big-headed remarks. But Ragu did not give any sign of returning to his wife.

When a girl got pregnant, her relatives and friends would prepare whatever foods she fancied. Auntie Sathya was locally renowned for her cookery. If she cooked king prawns in a creamy coconut sauce, the whole village would sniff hungrily at the aroma she created. She was also known for her delicious savoury and sweet snacks.

One day, she prepared some food for her beloved daughter-in-law. Mailar began to object, but stopped when she spilled some tears and sneezed loudly. Ragu did not say anything regarding the sweet, savoury and tearful drama in his house.

Gowri asked Mum's permission to visit Buvana with Auntie Sathya and Teacher Parames. Gowri had not been allowed to go for a while because of the conflict between her uncles.

Auntie Indira had not expected her visitors. At first, she seemed confused, uncertain whether to welcome them, then she invited them to enter.

'Are you angry with me too?' Gowri asked.

Her aunt forced a smile on to her face and replied, 'Not really.'

Nobody knew what to do. There was silence. Gowri and Saratha went in to look for Buvana. They found her in the garden; she was getting big and breathless. She had a puffy face and big breasts and was wearing an open-neck cotton maternity dress. Prominent blue veins in her neck and hands were visible.

'The doctors say she has high blood pressure,' Auntie Indira said in a worried tone. Gowri did not know what this meant until she asked her teacher's wife, who explained that this was one of the symptoms of stress and pain.

Indira looked at the food which Sathya had brought and said, 'The doctor asked us to give her a salt-free diet.'

Auntie Sathya cried for her daughter-in-law's fate, touching Buvana's belly and lamenting, 'This baby has brought bad luck to both of you. We must offer gifts to God and ask him to remove the bad luck.'

'Wouldn't life be easy if God could be bribed with presents,' Gowri mumbled to herself.

They talked about many things connected to the pregnancy. When Indira asked Aunt Sathaya, 'Won't my son-in-law come?' Gowri looked at Buvana; she was crying. Gowri could not bear to watch her distress. What a world, to play such games with these young people lives! She wanted to run to Ragu and bring him there to show him Buvana's condition.

'You must dig the well. Until then, he won't come,' Auntie Sathya whispered to Auntie Indira.

'How can we do that? The rainy season is about to start, and skilled people are difficult to find in ploughing time.'

Gowri realised that Uncle Kasi was becoming less stubborn and might well concede what Mailar wanted. But would Buvana and Ragu have to live apart until the well had been dug?

There could be nothing worse than carrying a baby without its father's love. Gowri remembered when her father had put his ear against her mother's pregnant stomach to listen to the baby inside. Gowri also recalled the time when her mother had been sick during the night and her father held her, stroked her hair and boiled herbal water over a charcoal fire. Buvana had not had the chance to enjoy such a loving caring friendship with her husband.

Near the temple, there was an open-air theatre stage on which the play based on the *Mahabharata* was to be performed. Over the years, Kolavil had attracted many thousands of drama-lovers from all over the Batticaloa region. The people would come in their hundreds, from all walks of life. They would arrive in bullock carts, on bicycles and by foot. From the school, Gowri watched the villagers decorating the stage. This had been the scene of more meetings about local matters and Tamil politics than of traditional drama based on mythology.

The ways in which the outdoor stage was decorated varied, depending on the activity. Now that a mythological play was to be staged, the adornment was colourful and meaningful. It was always the responsibility of men to do the decoration; women were never allowed to be involved.

Dad chose good-looking, musically capable and skilled actors. The swami helped to select them. Rajah was one of the leading characters in the play. That meant Rajah would be visiting Gowri's house frequently in order to discuss the play with her father. There might be gossip if he visited often. 'How am I going to avoid it?' Gowri wondered.

Rajah would play Krishna and would rescue the heroine

Draupadi. 'Oh, Rajah is so handsome, like a real cinema actor,' Grandma praised him.

'Grandma, you don't like cinema,' Gowri argued.

'Of course, I don't like third-rate films, but I like religious ones,' Grandma said. The schoolmaster was there, smiling at the conversation between the old and young women.

Swami Lingam also had a low opinion of Tamil cinema. He claimed that Indian films were spoiling young minds with emotional story lines and escapism. But the teacher told him that Hindu myths themselves were escapist. He said, 'I don't like Indian cinema, but there's nothing else which poor people can go and enjoy.'

The subject was one which was discussed often, whenever Grandma spotted a movie advertisement. She was longing to see a good old open-air play based on Hindu mythology and performed by her kith and kin.

The swami usually came near the charcoal cooker in the morning to warm himself. He would talk about justice and injustice, good and evil. The preparations for the play reminded him of the controversy.

'Why do most of the films about religion or morality continually portray women suffering for men as virtuous?' Gowri asked him, as she reckoned he would give a well-thought-out answer.

He looked at her sharply, covered himself with a shawl against the cool breeze of the early morning and replied, 'My dear girl, all these films are produced by men. They portray what's in their minds. They like women to be dependent on them. It boosts men's egos to think women can't live without them.'

Could they not? Grandma had lived with no husband since she had become a widow. Buvana had lived with no husband since she was fifteen years old. As far back as Gowri could remember, there had been many women living without men's help in the village. She told him this as she poured him his early morning ganja coffee.

He smiled and explained, 'Yes, my dear, in real life that's the case. But myths, films, novels – most of those are created by men. In these, women have to please men, suffer for men; a good woman has to sacrifice herself, her happiness, freedom and her whole life for a man to show that she loves him.'

Gowri thought of Rajah. 'Will I do that? Will I sacrifice myself to him in order to eat good food, wear a silk saree, have a nice house? Oh no, not I. I want to finish my studies, be a teacher, teach children about good things such as being oneself and not giving in to anyone the way Ragu has done,' she murmured to herself.

'Why can't these men write about real life? Make a film about real issues?' she asked the swami, who was enjoying his morning dose of strong ganja coffee.

'Listen to me, my lass. Art is not only the means of expression of the artist, it's also big business. It can also change the way people think. Nowadays, I don't see many honest works of art. Artists and writers use their talents to make money, promote political propaganda, exploit humanity.'

She understood the point he was making. She wished people would create more works in which women were respected. She considered the cheap Indian magazines with women in provocative poses on the covers and whether there would be any protest by women against these. After all, Tamil culture was reputedly based on respect and decency.

Developing and staging a play gave most of the young people an opportunity to learn about ancient history and street theatre. The episode from the *Mahabharata* which had been chosen was the war with which the epic ended. The villagers identified strongly with the characters in the play. They saw it as a metaphor for their own plight. They themselves were the victims, while the Sinhalese people in power were the forces of evil, from whom they implored Lord Krishna to rescue them. An important person in the Federal Party, Rajah, was playing the role of Krishna, rescuing the victims.

Gowri knew what Rajah had done to destroy Ragu and Buvana's life by provoking them with his third-rate comments. But the villagers did not know that. Gowri wanted to cry when she thought about the hypocrisy of powerful people.

An old man would generally come on first to introduce the play. He would dress like a clown in the circus and would play tricks to bring merriment to the audience. On this occasion, nobody had much difficulty in guessing who would take the part; it was Palipody. He daubed himself with thick make-up to make himself appear younger. Although he had no teeth, he looked splendid in a costume made out of Grandma's silk saree.

Rajah came on, depicting Krishna's rescue of the Pandavas, the five great kings who were the goodies. Young Sangar played the part of the heroine Draupadi, who was married to the five kings Dharma (law), Arjuna (beauty), Bhima (strength), Nagulan (knowledge) and Sahadeva (wisdom), but she and their kingdom were lost in a gambling game by her husbands to the evil king Duryodhana and his hundred brothers. The worst humiliations were forced on her by the evil brothers. Due to these humiliations, she took a vow of revenge that the five brothers should destroy the baddies; until then she would not tie her hair, which had been touched by the evil brothers. The goodies had to go into exile in the jungle for fourteen years before they returned and fought their war of revenge.

When the wicked brothers refused to give the five brothers back their kingdoms, the war began. Krishna took the Pandavas' side and helped them win. Sangar was excellent in his wonderful female costume. In the play Sangar, as the heroine, performed brilliantly, and Grandma burst into tears begging Krishna to help her to maintain her respect and decency in public, when the evil brothers tried to humiliate her in front of the crowd.

Gowri could not prevent herself from noticing Buvana, who was sitting far away from them but looking at her husband and crying. Was there a Lord Krishna who could come to her aid?

The play took five days to complete. As each scene was staged, Grandma would be very happy that Rajah was visiting their house often. He was watching Gowri's behaviour, but she avoided him when he came. When Grandma saw Ragu's sadness, she prayed that God Ganesh would bring him and Buvana back together and that they would be happy. She had no idea of Rajah's role in causing Ragu's sorrow.

Grandma's vision was not very good, but she would still go

every night to enjoy the play. One evening Gowri and Saratha had to go with her. They met Shiva on their way to the temple grounds, where the stage was. Gowri could tell that he wanted to talk to Saratha. 'Oh, God help us,' Gowri thought, 'does he really have the guts to talk to her in front of Grandma?' She glanced at Saratha, who was looking very nervous.

When he reached them, he smiled at Grandma, touched her gently and asked her, 'Grandma, are you enjoying the play?'

'Who's that?' Grandma did not recognise him. It was only then that the girls realised that she did not know whom she was talking to because it was getting so dark and also because she does not see Shiva that often.

'What's the matter with you, Grandma? Because I work in the town, you've forgotten all about me, haven't you?'

'Oh, is it Shiva?' Grandma laughed, put her arm around him and asked merrily, 'Hey, boy, when are you going to get married?'

'I'm ready, but the bride's not lined up yet.' He smiled at Saratha.

'Well, my dear boy, I have a couple of girls to marry off, but I don't understand them. They say they want to study.' There was bitterness in her voice as there usually was then this subject came up.

'Don't rush them, let them take things as their own pace,' he said with a witty smile at the girls.

'You'll have to wait for a while, then we'll see what we can do.'

'We don't mind waiting, Grandma, but your family seems

to be looking for boys from other areas.' He was hinting at Mailar's remarks about not considering any villagers as possible partners for his children. Gowri and Saratha giggled.

'Get away! You're worth more than some outsider from goodness knows where. What's the matter with people, that they say such silly things? Don't worry, when the time comes, it's all going to work out okay.'

'I hope so, Grandma.' He tossed a flower to Saratha when the old woman was not looking.

'Come, Grandma, we're going to be late for the play.' Gowri hurried her away, to avoid any uncomfortable scene.

Chapter 27

When they reached the temple grounds, Gowri could see Ragu and Nathan at the gate. When Nathan saw Gowri, he asked, 'Rajah is playing the part of Lord Krishna, but who is going to be his beloved Ratha?' The goddess was Krishna's consort in Hindu mythology. Gowri did not reply. Ragu smiled understandingly at her.

She kept her words within her, knowing that if Ragu had not been there, the scene would have been different.

Why did men have to keep making remarks about each other? When she saw Rajah, he passed comment on Nathan, then when she saw Nathan, he talked about Rajah. What was wrong with these men? Did they assume that a girl had to be thinking about a man all the time? She wanted to tell them that she had far better things to do than to think about stupid men. Maybe Saratha thought about Shiva a lot. This seemed possible, from the way she carried on about him.

Saratha told Gowri, after whispering with him in the dark on the way to the temple grounds, 'He's asking me to tell my parents about him.'

'What?' Gowri had known it was going to be difficult to be involved with these lovers.

'Well, he says that his family is looking for a bride for him, as he's old enough to get married and has a good job and all that.'

'What are you going to do?' Gowri had no idea how to advise Saratha.

'I don't know. Because of my brother, I can't talk to Mum at the moment, as she's in tears most of the time. It's no good talking to Dad. He's busy causing problems in the village. If I can't get married to Shiva, I'm telling you, I'll kill myself.'

'Oh, no, please don't say stupid things like that.'

'Why not? All those greatest lovers in the world killed themselves when they couldn't live together,' Saratha's tone was firm.

Good heavens! Gowri looked at Saratha carefully. She felt sorry for her cousin, so deeply immersed in her love affair, but hated to think that she might make that sort of decision. Nobody in the village had ever killed themselves for love. Why did Mailar's family have to pioneer so many things? Ragu had left his wife, which no man in the village had ever done. Now Saratha was writing love letters and threatening suicide. What would their naughty brother Sangar do?

'I don't care who does what, because whatever they do is their problem, not mine. But please Saratha, don't kill yourself. That's very bad, a sin against God.'

Gowri prayed, 'Dear Lord Ganesh, please let Saratha learn how to cope with the situation and not think about killing herself.' She thought, 'Many people in Kolavil are poor and have problems in their lives. But they do not go around killing themselves, do they?'

Old Palipody and his wife had been married for fifty or more years. It was a well-known fact that he had given her little other than irritation. In return she had started to nag him. One day, according to villagers, he had run to the River Thillai to kill himself by drowning. But unfortunately (or fortunately) it had been a very hot summer, and, instead of water, the river was full of mud. Poor Palipody had got stuck. His *verti* had come undone (when had he ever been properly dressed?) and he screamed for help when a wild bull chased him through the muddy water. Half of the village had to wade in, chase the bull away and bring him home. He never again attempted suicide.

Apart from this, no-one in Kolavil had ever tried to end their life. Gowri felt sad when she thought that Saratha might die because of her love for Shiva. 'Dear Lord Ganesh, please help Saratha to get married to Shiva – but not before the GCE exam,' she prayed.

In September 1959, the village was to open the temple with a special *pooja*, known as the *Kumbabhishegam* ceremony.

The best Tamil classical band was hired from Thirukovil to play for the occasion. A priest was hired, and what was needed for the ceremony was acquired. The leaders of the community were organising the ceremonies.

The problem of deciding who would lead the rituals led to an argument. Each rival clan was trying to prove how high it was in the local hierarchy by producing obscure 'evidence'. Since there was no written evidence, everything was based on oral history, poems and folklore. Those people with more sense argued that this was all nonsense. But there were some, like Nayagam, who were obsessed with their social position.

The argument was echoed in the school, as usual. 'Why do you all have to fight to show you're superior to one another?' The master was fed up with tussles and squabbles regarding these caste and clan oriented hierarchical arrangements; he hated it when time was wasted on such matters. 'You believe that stuff, do you? Then do you defend what the white colonialists did to the black people whom they conquered? Do you really support Nazism, which was based on the psychology of superiority to others?' he asked angrily.

'Oh no, no, but we have to hang onto our identity by keeping our traditions,' said Suresh, a student who was a keen supporter of the Federal Party and read and enthused about many writings on Tamil kings of the past and their glories.

'If you believe that you're better than someone of your own race and religion, then why are you against those Sinhalese racists who oppress Tamils because they're minorities and less powerful? The racists use the same type of ideology, as if Ceylon belongs to them. Ceylon belongs to everyone who was born here. We are all Ceylonese citizens. All our ancestors came from India at one time or another, and we all have to fight for equality and unity, not difference and destruction.' Suresh could not answer this, but some of the students disregarded the teacher's words as if they were mere socialist hysteria.

'The Sinhalese never show any evidence they want to unite with Tamils,' some argued with him.

'We have to work on that. It's hard, as we're a minority, but people can achieve anything if they honestly want change. Fighting among the groups in the village over who will open the temple is going to create more chaos, but if you young people advise your families to focus on having a good ceremony for the temple, maybe we can avoid further misery,' he said firmly. Gowri thought he was right.

The opening of the temple was a splendid occasion. Thousands of people from all over the Batticaloa region came to enjoy the ceremonies, which involved music, dance, prayers and other events. It was the most exciting day in the lives of many villagers.

There were various offerings to the god – including physical pain. Some practised 'nail *kavady*', when a beautiful decorated object was fixed to the human body with nails and pins. Unbelievably, no blood could be seen on devotees pierced in this way.

Gowri had to carry a fire-pot, as her mother had made her vow to do when she was a little girl seeking to be cured of eye disease. She carried the pot on her head, after having a shower in the temple well, with a wet costume and wet hair.

'What are you asking God for at his new temple?' Saratha whispered softly to Gowri.

What was she praying for? 'Well...' She hesitated for a moment. If Kamala had been there and had asked this question, Gowri would have answered honestly. But revealing her inner feelings to Saratha sometimes led to problems, as she would laugh at Gowri's dreams of the future.

'Go on, tell me,' Saratha nagged like their Grandma.

'I'm...I'm asking the gods that all of us should be happy, especially Buvana and Ragu,' Gowri said – which was partly true.

'What about you? Aren't you praying about...?' Saratha's eyes sparked with naughtiness.

Gowri did not let her finish her question but quickly interrupted, saying, 'Yes, I'm praying that I'll do well in my studies and become a teacher.'

'Like Miss Punitha?'

'Yes.'

'Then be careful.'

'Careful about what?'

'Well, if you leave home there'll be plenty of men like that naughty and dirty inspector to bother you.'

'Don't worry, Saratha, I know how to look after myself,' Gowri replied confidently.

'Lots of girls have love marriages – they meet a wide range of people,' said Saratha, who had more knowledge about the outside world.

'Maybe.' Gowri was trying to ignore Saratha's talk of love and marriage.

'Will you?'

'No. If anyone bothers me, I know how to get rid of them.'

'Oh, yeah? You'd better ask Grandma to give you one of her wooden spoons or her mighty weapon, the broomstick.' Saratha laughed at her own joke. Gowri laughed, too. She detested quarrels and fights. Family quarrels and Buvana's situation flashed into her mind for a second.

'I wish Buvana were with us,' Gowri said sadly.

'So do I.'

'Don't be a parrot, just repeating what I say,' Gowri snapped.

'No, I'm serious,' Saratha protested.

'Are you? Then tell your brother to go back to Buvana.' But Saratha was more worried about her own future than that of her brother. For some time, Gowri had wished that she had a really good friend to whom she could talk. Saratha was only concerned about herself, like her father Mailar, who thought himself the centre of the world.

Chapter 28

Gowri received a letter from Kamala. She described her second-year nursing exam and the exciting life she led in Jaffna. Had Kamala forgotten Ragu?

She mentioned him, too. She wrote, 'People like Ragu, who haven't got the strength to take a stand on anything, will have miserable lives. Why doesn't he make up his own mind when other people are trying to put pressure on him?' Kamala was right to ask this. Why had Ragu never thought of standing on his own feet?

Gowri was anxious to visit Buvana, but she felt uncomfortable about the possibility of facing Rajah on her way to her house. During the temple ceremony she knew that he kept his eyes on her and Nathan. Rajah was rising higher in village circles. He was good-looking, rich, famous, influential – and according to many people, including Grandma, he was the best suitor for any girl from a good family. Would she say no to her parents when the time for a marriage proposal arrived?

She was fifteen years old now. Next year she would be taking her O-level exam. After that, Grandma would get into the full swing with seeking a prospective partner for her. No girl in Kolavil had yet gone to work outside the village. Girls from well-to-do families might go to boarding school, but, when they were over sixteen or seventeen, the family would make sure that they settled down and got married.

Grandma would stand upside down to stop Gowri leaving

home to do teacher training or anything of the kind. 'What is going to happen to me?' This question was a constant irritant in Gowri's mind.

On the last day of the Temple ceremony, the village heads had to discuss next year's festival. The past fourteen days had been a memorable time for all the local people. The different factions in the village had vied with one another to provide the biggest event. Fancy lighting, skilled craftspeople, dancers, and musicians all turned up for the celebrations in Kolavil from various towns.

The first clan, the *Panikkanar* (educated or priestly) caste, to which Shiva's father belonged, were quiet and restrained and held a simple, more or less trouble-free event.

The second, of which Kasi, Gowri's mother, and Grandma were members, the *Kalingarajan kudi* (king's clan), held a pleasant, medium-scale celebration with a special guest from Batticaloa who gave a one-man musical show.

Not to be outdone, the third clan group, Mailar and his lot, the *Padaiyanda kudi* (military clan), brought an elephant from somewhere to carry the god Ganesh's statue for the ceremony. There were puppet shows and dancers and a fancy dress competition; it was an extravagant event.

Many in the fourth clan, the *Vellala* (farmers' caste), to which Nayagam belonged, rich landowners with support from the Jaffna merchants in town, they wanted to prove that they were better than everyone else, so they produced documents to show that they were going to build a leisure hall near the temple. But the other villagers insisted that, if a building was to be put up, everyone should be involved.

Poor Swami! All he had wanted was to hold a religious

ceremony to complete the rituals for opening a new temple. Now, he was fed up with the constant arguments and competition.

'God, whatever you're going to do to this lot, please make sure you do it to all of them equally,' Swami Lingam prayed for all the villagers. He could hardly wait for the final day to finish, so that he would be able to relax. Gowri teased him about having to guard over God Ganesh who was supposed to protect them, while the villagers fought over their superiority to one another.

Grandma did not like Gowri's remarks about abolishing the clan system in the village. 'You ought to be proud of being a *Kalingarajan kudi*. Wherever you go, you must keep your head held high. You come from an exceptional breed.'

Gowri laughed at Grandma and said, 'There's no such thing. The teacher said we all came from apes. It's a pity that you're trying to prove your superiority to one another by using God.'

'God created people in different ways because of their *karma*, and he wants us to go through life differently,' Grandma shouted.

Gowri had no more to say to her on that matter. She could not believe that the whole village had suffered during the flood because their misdeeds in a previous life doomed them to this fate.

The last day arrived, when the temple rituals would be completed. After the night-time *pooja*, the heads of the village got together to discuss how things had gone for the last fourteen days. They were happy and proud to have held the most wonderful celebration in the whole district.

Some of them thanked Swami Lingam for having initiated the whole project. The swami replied, 'It was God's will this should happen.'

After a few formalities, Nayagam began to talk about abolishing old ways of thinking and beliefs. Almost everyone actually agreed with this, but when he spelt out his plan, not many people liked it.

He said, 'We must respect what other people do.' This statement was rather odd and seemed to contradict what had been said earlier. However, everyone continued to listen to him and asked him to clarify what he was saying.

He went on, 'In other Tamil areas, the *Vellala* caste takes first place at social events. The other castes must respect them and recognise their position as the elite in Tamil society.'

Kasi said, 'There should be no such thing as choosing one clan to control the others.'

Mailar could scarcely believe what Nayagam had said. Mailar would not give first place to him until he died, he declared forcefully. That was it!

The meeting could no longer be controlled. Verbal attacks led to physical violence. Grown-up, educated or uneducated and religious men hurled *pooja* objects at one another. Silver trays with offerings to gods, pots of holy water and various other religious objects were used as weapons. Some slipped on banana skins, some were hit by flying trays, some were drenched with holy water. There was large-scale chaos. The swami was trying to calm the men who were shouting and throwing objects. Poor Lingam could not get them to listen to him.

He joined the young men waiting outside. When the

grown-ups had finished their meeting, the plan for tomorrow – when the villagers would take statue of Ganesh for a holy bath to the sea – was to be discussed.

The argument and fighting was still going on when people saw Palipody coming towards the hall. He was drunk as a fish and wanted to get involved in the fight. He stumbled into the hall. As he walked slowly and unsteadily, he lost his *verti* and staggered on, exposed as usual.

'Oh no!' someone screamed, catching sight of the old man standing naked in front of the statue of the god Ganesh. People began to accuse one another of having invited him to the temple to insult the ceremony. Mailar claimed that old Palipody had been sent by Rajah to disrupt the meeting, as the old man had been hanging around with him during the drama. Nayagam accused Mailar of keeping Palipody as a servant in his house and making him do things of this kind.

The fight became fiercer, and the noise woke the wild dogs, which had been sleeping around the temple after feasting on scraps from the *poojas*. They barked like the chorus in an Indian movie.

The fight moved away from the temple and up the street to the village shop, the stage for most brawls. The owner, as usual, shut his shop as soon he heard the uproar.

The ruckus continued until about four o'clock in the morning; the whole village was awake.

Women had already prepared turmeric water in large brass pots for cleansing the path for God Ganesh on his way to the sea. These had been placed in front of their gates, with ceremonial lamps, to welcome the procession from the temple. When they heard the uproar the women came out and took their pots and lamps inside to prevent them from being used as weapons of mass destruction in the ongoing battle.

The musical group from town ran away from the battlefield with their instruments, leaving behind one local player who had played a minor part in the disturbance. Some people had to chase after them to persuade them to remain to play for the final day's ceremony. Abuse – mainly verbal – continued to be bandied about until sunrise. Farmers from the next village who were passing by on their way to the paddy fields stopped to witness the impromptu drama. Women were crying and cursing their menfolk for their behaviour. Half-asleep children, frightened by the noise, were wailing.

The rituals were supposed to be completed before midday. The old women got together and arrived at the village shop to stop the fight, demanding that the men take the god to the sea for the ceremony. The old ladies brought the battle under control. The fighters were still mumbling and swearing but calmed down when they saw the crowd of old ladies around them.

Gowri and Saratha went to the temple early in morning. They knew half the story of the battle at the shop, and cursed Palipody for being naked in front of Ganesh and causing the fight. But he was nowhere to be seen.

'I wonder if God really exists?' Gowri asked Saratha.

'I, too.' Saratha hated conflict. 'I thought that the temple was going to bring unity and harmony, but see what's happened.'

When they reached the snake-god's (Naga) temple to worship the famous seven-headed cobra, what did they see? Palipody was fast asleep under the bush. His breathing or snoring sounded like hiss of a snake, 'Ss-ss-ss'.

'You stupid old fool, do you know what you've done?' Saratha threw a pinch of sand at him, but she must have been crazy to think that a little sand would wake him up.

The procession from the temple started at nearly noon. It contained more women than men, some of whom had been kept at home by their wives and mothers to prevent more fights. The drummers drummed with no rhythm, as they were in a hurry to escape from any further trouble.

Hymns and prayers went on at the seaside. It was late September but still very hot. After the statue of God Ganesh had been immersed in the sea, they had to complete the *pooja*.

As they were finishing the ceremony, Sangar arrived at the seafront, gasping. 'Trouble, trouble, big trouble – hurry up and go home!' he was shouting.

'What kind of trouble?' Within a minute, a large crowd had gathered near him.

'Mr. Bandaranaike, the PM of Ceylon has been killed!' Sangar was gasping for breath as he had been cycling fast to reach them.

'What?' There was a chorus of questions.

'The prime minister – the radio says that he has been shot dead. It was announced just now.'

'Are you sure?'

'Yes, there are lots of police about in the town.'

'Who shot him?'

'A Buddhist monk called Talduwe Somarama Thero.'

'Thank God, he wasn't killed by a Tamil,' the crowd said. They quickly gathered up the statue of Ganesh and hurried home.

Chapter 29

The joy of the temple ceremony was overshadowed by the news of the prime minister's death. That night, people were terrified that a Sinhalese mob would invade the village and create carnage. Two years ago, the villagers had faced a flood. Just after that, there had been riots between Muslims and Tamils. A few months later, the main riots against the Tamils in 1958 had taken place.

'Oh no, I can't face more communal violence,' Saratha sniffed. Shiva was still in the village, so she did not have to worry so much about him, but the whole village was scared that the army would arrive again to terrorise the ordinary people.

'Why did they have to kill the prime minister?' Saratha asked the teacher.

He answered, 'Mr. Bandaranaike was brought to power by Sinhalese chauvinists. Although he called himself a socialist, he let himself be ruled by religious fanatics. They didn't achieve everything they wanted, such as wiping out the socialists and minority Tamils. I think that's why they wanted to get rid of him.'

'Do you think they'll bring in someone like Mr. Bandaranaike again?' Gowri asked him.

'Maybe, or they'll choose someone worse,' the teacher replied. He was a wise man.

Grandma was worried for the safety of the girls, who had to go to school. They had studied hard. However chaotic was the national political situation, they did not want to make fools of themselves by failing. She commented, 'Ah well, it's because of Mr. Bandaranaike that thousands of Tamils died during the riots. God always punishes the wicked. If you kill someone, no matter how long it takes, you'll die yourself because of the way you led your life.'

'What about the people here in your family who make others unhappy?' Gowri wanted to ask her, thinking of Buvana.

Grandma talked to both families, seeking a reconciliation, but both were stubborn. 'No man has a future if he brings grief to a woman,' she angrily warned both families.

Was this true? Ragu had hurt Kamala by not standing up to his father to get him to accept their love. Maybe God was punishing him for that? Gowri suggested this to Saratha, who said, 'Ragu should go back to Buvana, no matter what Dad says.'

'What about the well? Ragu won't go back until they dig the well.'

'That's not the real problem. I think my brother just doesn't want to live near Rajah. I noticed them both during the recent drama. They dislike each other, but not many people know that,' Saratha said.

Perhaps he did not want to live near his enemy, but what would happen if Gowri were married to Rajah? Would her cousin Ragu refuse to see her, too? Gowri thought about this a little, but she could not imagine herself in this situation. She suddenly felt frightened about her future. Destiny was unpredictable. One did not know what was going happen, whom one was going to meet.

'I want to study, go away somewhere, be a teacher and look after my family,' Gowri said to Saratha without looking at her. When she looked, Gowri was in tears.

Grandma was determined, too; she intended to make Ragu go back to Buvana. After going backwards and forwards between their families, she discussed with Auntie Indira the idea of going to a witch-doctor to find out whether Buvana had been cursed by an evil power. Kolavil was well-known for its folklore, drama, music and poetry. Also, the village had a reputation for ghost stories, black magic and casting spells. There were old men who practice black magic and spells.

Since there was no electricity in the village, it was not normal for people to wander around lanes and roads after dark. Old ladies talked about seeing ghosts at night. In particular, some of them believed, ghosts had taken up residence in old trees scattered around the village. People from other villages were often scared about upsetting people from Kolavil, not wishing to encounter sinister forces. Also, the village had an unusual type of raven, bigger than the usual ones seen in other villages. These Kolavil ravens made people even more afraid of magic. According to Grandma, there were constant cries from the ravens at Buvana's house which indicated that they were trying to warn them about something bad happening in the future.

Uncle Kasi had told off his mother – Grandma – many times for her belief in magic, but she somehow persuaded Auntie Indira to agree to a ritual to exorcise Buvana. Generally, this kind of witchcraft took place at the cemetery near the sea. Gifts were given at the *pooja* to angry evil powers to please them and grant a bright future for the supplicant.

Ragu was angry when he heard that Grandma was doing such *pooja* to get him back with Buvana. 'My darling boy, some people have the evil eye. Maybe someone put a spell on you to separate you from your wife.' Grandma was in tears when he threw away her offerings, which she had brought home from the ritual. He walked out without a word, angry and frustrated at all this mumbo-jumbo.

After the temple festival, while the adults were busy planting seeds in the paddy fields and school pupils were busy preparing for their O-level exams, the whole country was in turmoil after the prime minister's assassination.

The newspapers were filled with his murder. The Ceylon government asked Britain's Scotland Yard to carry out an investigation. His family life had been serialised in national newspapers, and there was much gossip about his wife Srimavo and children, too. In March next year, there was to be a general election; the newspapers stated that Mr. Bandaranaike's widow, Srimavo Bandaranaike, was to be a candidate.

'A woman is standing to become prime minister?' Grandma was incredulous. She believed that woman should not be allowed to go out alone and mix with men. Yet, now, not only were Gowri and Saratha about to take their O-level exams, but also the country might be the first in the world to have a woman as prime minister. Grandma could not sleep properly for many nights when thinking and talking about it.

'*Kali yuga* – it's all to do with *Kali yuga*. As the Hindu wise men prophesied, the world is going to end. Ha! How can the world be ruled by women?' Grandma was nervous about all the changes.

'When she comes to power, she must punish men who are cruel to women.' Gowri's expectations were naïve.

'She won't have real power, she'll be manipulated by men behind the scenes,' the schoolmaster told them.

He tried to conceal his pleasure that she was contesting the election; he had always supported equality for women, and, without his support, Gowri and Saratha would not have had the opportunity to study.

Mrs. Bandaranaike began to appear on numerous platforms. She eulogised her latest husband and his inspiration to turn Ceylon into one of the finest countries in South Asia. She poured out promises to the Sinhalese masses. She committed herself to crushing the Tamil struggle for freedom. She claimed that the United National Party (UNP), led by Dudley Senanayake, would hand over the country to the Tamils if it came to power, giving them whatever they wanted. The UNP, in turn, claimed that, if the Sri Lanka Freedom Party won power, it would give the Tamils whatever they wanted. Both increasingly propagated racism.

Due to this, formerly friendly Sinhalese people became suspicious of and bitter towards Tamils. On the opposition side, the Federal Party was pledging that its MPs would work towards a federal system in which mainly Tamil areas would be granted devolution. The socialists were not very strong at that time and had no clear position on minority issues. They said that Tamil nationalist parties were led by middle-class Tamils from Jaffna who sought to satisfy the aspirations of their class, as they did not care about the plight of the estate Tamils or educational needs of the poor Tamils in rural areas. Most socialists failed to recognise the increasing communalism in Ceylon.

Saratha could not have cared less what was happening in the country or even in the village. She was fully occupied with writing and receiving love letters from Shiva and imagining her future with him. She would talk to Gowri about her plans of living in town with Shiva, having seven children, building a house near the seaside and so on.

Buvana went through hell with giving birth. She was not a large woman, and her labour continued for days. Grandma stayed at her house to take care of her.

The girl was gravely ill, her body weakened by depression and high blood pressure. Auntie Indira prayed to all the gods and goddesses she could think of. Uncle Kasi was shattered to see his daughter in that condition. Rajah's family was there most of the time to give support to Buvana's family.

The swami had talked at length to Ragu, trying to persuade him to go back to support Buvana, who needed his love and help during the confinement. He refused. He saw Rajah's family running around in Kasi's house as if it were their own, and he left the village for a few days to escape the pressure from everyone. Grandma blamed him for Buvana's situation. Auntie Sathya cried, as usual, over her son. Palipody spent his time preparing holy water for Buvana. All the family was in a state of anxiety.

Grandma did not believe in Western medicine, as she mistrusted everything modern. She said she had taken care of all her grandchildren when they were born, and none had any problems. 'Having a baby is a natural thing,' she told everyone. She would not let a doctor be summoned until Buvana had started to bleed heavily.

After four days of pain and suffering, Buvana's baby was delivered. It was a baby boy, stillborn. What a punishment! Had she not suffered enough? She was too ill to understand what was going on. She was nearly in a coma when the baby finally emerged.

The doctor blamed the stupidity of the people who had refused to call him earlier. 'What happened is due to fate,' Grandma said to people. Buvana's parents looked grey and pale with the extreme pain of losing their grandchild.

Auntie Indira was the elder daughter in her family, as was Buvana. Similarly, Ragu was Mailar's elder son. This meant that there was a possibility Buvana's son's body might be stolen from the graveyard by witch-doctors to make magical oil which could be used for enchantment to bring sexual desire. Grandma organised a team of young men to guard the graveyard for the first three days. All the arrangements had been made, but the baby's father was not there for the burial.

People went to look for Ragu. Ramanathan and his brother Nathan got hold of him at the house of one of his old friends. After listening to the swami's advice, he came to Buvana's house. He went straight to the dead body of his baby, which was wrapped in white silk cloth, took it and walked silently out while others followed him.

He kissed the dead baby before he placed it in the grave and cried silently. Nathan comforted him. On the way home, it started to rain. The whole village thought that he would go back to his wife, but he returned to his parents' house, instead.

'What kind of man are you?' Palipody yelled at Ragu.

'Why don't you tell your friend to be sensible and go back

to his wife? After all, you're the reason for this break-up,' someone in the crowd shouted at Nathan.

'Don't shout at him. My life is my own business. Whatever connection I had with Buvana is no longer there, that's all,' Ragu said calmly.

After the funeral, the housework was usually done by cousins. Gowri and Saratha spent a lot of time at Buvana's house, cleaning and generally helping. Gowri had no choice but to see Rajah next door, though she kept herself busy. She cursed him for what had happened to Buvana.

Chapter 30

Buvana ate little and did not talk much to anyone. 'These are symptoms which many women experience; this is called post-natal depression,' the teacher's wife Parames explained to Gowri and Saratha when they mentioned Buvana's condition to her. Gowri wanted to give love and support to Buvana, but Saratha thought that Gowri was spending time at the house in order to see Rajah.

Gowri was not in a mood for joking with Saratha regarding Rajah or anyone. She prayed to the gods for Buvana's recovery. Until then, Gowri had secretly believed that Ragu would go back to Buvana during the delivery of their baby. Her dreams had been utterly shattered. She wondered if fate or destiny was really responsible?

Grandma still believed an evil spirit had cast a blight on Buvana. She told the girls a story about a fire ghost which appeared near the River Thillai.

Once upon a time, when Grandma had been a girl and Palipody a boy, they had been walking along the river bank towards their paddy field. It was late evening and getting darker by the minute. Suddenly, young Palipody had spotted a flame chasing him. He started to scream for help. His sister turned and saw what was happening. She said to him, 'My dear brother, it's a *mohini pisasu* (seductive ghost which chases men in the dark). You should embarrass the ghost.'

'How?' he asked.

'Embarrass the women devil which is chasing you by

taking off your sarong (*lungi*) and putting it on your head.'

So, he took his clothing off (he never kept it on, anyway) and kept it on his head until the *mohini* ghost let him go.

When the girls repeated the story and suggested that an evil spirit might have harmed Buvana, the teacher called them idiots for believing such mumbo-jumbo. He told them that they should learn to look at things scientifically. They asked him for an explanation of the *mohini* ghost. He explained that most river banks had rotten sedimentation underneath the earth which produced methane gas. When someone walked through the muddy areas, the holes allowed gas to escape. Sometimes it would come into contact with the atmospheric gases outside and it would ignite. This was the explanation for the fire ghost.

Then why did the gas chase men?

'Because, you fools, most of the time only men go to and fro from the paddy fields near the river banks in the evening.'

'Then why should they put their clothes on their heads?'

'To stop them from catching fire.'

The teacher may have been right, but he could not convince Grandma to stop her preparation for Buvana's exorcism. Grandma laughed at the idea of methane gas and its chemical reactions and went ahead with the rituals to drive evil spirits away from her granddaughter.

Uncle Kasi and Auntie Indira were so upset about losing their grandson and about Buvana's condition that they took very little notice of Grandma and Palipody's preparation for the exorcism. Many varieties of fruits and cooked food were provided to appease the evil spirit. Women who claimed they could talk to mighty unseen powers, a very old *poosari* (witch-doctor) to perform the rituals, drummers and a *mantra*-chanting crowd all went by bullock cart to the shore near the cemetery.

The chanting and drumming created a mystical atmosphere. A medium invoked the spirit-world, saying that Buvana was under the spell of the goddess Mariammal, who was harsh and often brought unhappiness. Grandma ordered the witch-doctor to do a special *pooja* to this goddess.

Buvana still would not raise her head or talk to anyone. The ritual made no difference at all to her life. She sometimes spoke a few words to a member of her family; she seldom went out of her house.

'Buvana is apparently possessed by an evil spirit which won't allow her to talk to us,' the girls informed their teacher.

He got cross with Grandma for making the girls confused and fearful. He said, 'Buvana is not talking to you because she is upset over losing her baby and not having her husband around. She is sad because she has had to deal with all these horrendous issues. How would you feel in her place?'

The girls felt sorry for their cousin, but they did not know what to do. Gowri cursed the grown-ups who made Buvana and Ragu get married for their own reasons.

Ragu had also become something of a recluse. He spent much of his time with Nathan, if he came to visit, or in the paddy fields. He had no friends in the village now to whom to open his heart.

Local people said that Nayagam must have put a spell on Ragu to take revenge on Mailar. After Mailar had beaten his rival with a slipper, they had heard him threaten, 'Just you wait, I'm going to destroy your family!'

Nobody dared to speak to Ragu about this evil spell. They said, 'Unless the person wants to do something about it, there's no point in trying to persuade them.'

General election fever spread through the country. The March 1960 election was crucial in Ceylon's history, and Rajah was busy organising meetings for the Federal Party. But in March, no political party in Ceylon gained an overall majority. This meant that another election had to be called in June.

Gowri was sixteen years of age and waiting to take her O-level exam in December. Saratha was excited about the exam, too. She said that, sooner or later, she was going to tell her parents about her love for Shiva since Auntie Sathya had said that, as soon as her exam was over, they would arrange her marriage.

In June, the election did not produce a local Federal Party MP. Someone on an independent ticket won the seat and immediately went over to the government's side. This made Rajah very angry. He blamed people like Mailar, who had had voted for the independent candidate.

There was a fierce argument at the village shop. One day, Rajah and Mailar quarrelled heatedly and attacked each other verbally. Ragu went to the shop to bring his father home, as his mother had begged him, and Rajah hurled insults at him: 'Hey, look who's coming to rescue his father? A man who couldn't be a husband for more than two months is coming to his father's rescue.'

The two young men went for each other. Ragu was beaten up badly and had to be taken to hospital by car after receiving a head wound.

Auntie Sathya wailed loudly as if someone had died, gathered together as many people as she could and dashed to the hospital. The injury was minor, but Ragu was kept in for observation for a few days, 'I hope the person who beat up my child gets bitten by a cobra,' she cursed Rajah.

'Don't say that, Mum. His hand is going tie a holy *thali* with someone who is special to us and whom we love very much.' Ragu gazed at Gowri, searching for a reaction.

She turned her face away but met Nathan's questioning eyes. His expression asked her, 'Will you marry Rajah?'

She looked at him for a while, very angry, nearly in tears, and wanted to declare in public that she had no intention of marrying a man who was an enemy of her beloved cousin Ragu and who was the reason for destroying Ragu and Buvana's happiness. She answered through her expression to Nathan, 'No, I'll never marry Rajah.'

Nathan understood and smiled at her, pleased. However, she had a message for Nathan, too, which she could not deliver there.

In June, Srimavo Bandaranaike became the first woman prime minister on earth. The island celebrated this with confusion and conflict. She had to form a coalition with leftist political parties. This caused them to splinter into factions with different political perspectives. Some called her a representative of the national bourgeoisie, while others described her as a Sinhalese chauvinist. Whoever came to power, the problems faced by the Tamils were not about to be solved. She was sure to curry support from the Sinhalese masses by curtailing the rights of Tamils.

Grandma still did not believe that a woman could rule a

country. When Mrs. Bandaranaike was elected, the schoolmaster urged Grandma, 'You should be proud that a woman can do whatever a man can.'

'I don't know, the world is changing in amazing ways. I hope it doesn't lead to another disaster for our country.'

December 1960.

At the end of the year, when Gowri had taken the exam in her last subject, she came home very tired. She played with her little brothers and sisters.

'Well, now you've completed what you want to do.' Grandma gave her some sweet rice to eat.

'Yes, Grandma, one chapter is finished; another is about to start,' Gowri said, thinking about being a teacher in the future.

After the Christmas holiday, Gowri and Saratha and their classmates went to school to wait for their O-level exam results. A few boys from their class were looking for a place in the school in town to continue on to A-level studies.

'Why don't you do A-levels and go to university?' Ragu asked Gowri.

'I have many brothers; let them go to university. I'd rather be a teacher.'

Saratha was sending more letters to Shiva, asking him to persuade his parents to approach hers with a marriage proposal. Meanwhile Buvana's parents were building a house for Poorani, their second daughter. Nathan often visited Ragu to comfort him. Grandma did not like Gowri accepting books from Nathan and told her to stop talking to him.

'I don't talk to him, Grandma, except to say thank you when he brings me books.'

'One word or look from you will be enough to start people gossiping in this village.'

'Grandma, I don't do anything to invite gossip.'

'You don't have to, my girl, others will be ready enough. Justice has a different meaning for men and women in the world. Men can go anywhere and do anything, but women have to be careful. What we do can lead to disgrace for future generations.'

'I'll be good, Grandma.'

Gowri told Ragu what their Grandma had told her. 'You can get books from Nathan for me,' she said to her cousin.

At that moment Ragu was writing a poem. He was a talented writer. 'Why? Are you scared of Rajah?' he asked her.

'Why, should I be?' she asked him in return.

'Well...' He hesitated.

'Go on,' she insisted.

'He may marry you sooner or later.' He was looking at her.

She looked at him sharply and said, 'I won't marry him.' Somehow those words slipped out of her mouth, although she had not intended to tell anyone. Now she had said it.

He stared at her. He did not know what to make of his sixteen-year-old cousin. 'Are you in love with Nathan?'

She did not answer this question.

'Rajah has made you two unhappy.' She said, starting to weep.

'That's my fate.'

'We make our own fate,' she said. He looked at her. Suddenly, he realised that she was no longer a little girl but a young lady who knew what exactly what she wanted in life. He smiled at her, admiring her honesty, determination and most of all her self-belief.

'Good luck,' he almost whispered in her ear.

'I need that.' She tried to smile, but her tears continued.

Chapter 31

In early 1961, the Federal Party staged a peaceful protest against government oppression of the Tamil community in Ceylon. They began in front of government offices and town halls. Hundreds of boys set out from the village under the leadership of Rajah.

They had held many meetings to discuss their plans. Rajah had made an emotional speech about the situation of Tamils in Ceylon. 'If we don't do something now, we may be wiped out by the Sinhalese any day.' He was a brilliant speaker with a wonderful ability to gather young men and students behind him. Suresh, Sangar and many teenage school children joined him and worshipped him as their absolute leader.

Ragu was a strong supporter of the Federal Party, but he was not part of the village crowd nor impressed by Rajah's attitudes. Ragu was very worried about the teenagers going to the rally. He feared that the police might arrest them, and the boys might be put in cells, as had happened during the local riots a few years before.

Ragu watched Suresh, his brother Sangar and others writing slogans all over the village. Old trees were daubed with lettering. After the flood in December 1957, the village had lost some big trees but gained a school, temple, library, co-op and other buildings. Now, these bore striking slogans about Tamil glory in the past. Increasingly on the island, people were seeking inspiration from ancient history.

In mediaeval times, that part of Asia had contained a

number of kingdoms such as the Rajah Chola kingdom. Their ruling dynasties, some of them Tamil-speaking, at various times coexisted peacefully, fought one another, formed alliances and intermarried. Meanwhile, scholars, craftspeople and builders created masterpieces, some of which had lasted through the centuries.

Kolavil had long been known for producing folk poets. Now, Suresh was following in the path of his ancestors. He talked a lot, sang a lot and got on people's nerves a lot. He seemed to be Rajah's most devoted follower. He organised the trip to Batticaloa town to join the *Ahimsa* (peaceful) protest and wrote slogans to encourage people to come with them.

'Declare *Ahimsa* struggle now.'

'*Eelam* (a proposed independent Tamil state) belongs to everyone.'

'Non-violence until we die.'

'Live with dignity, or die for the Tamil nation.'

These slogans inspired many, including Grandma, to join the protest. In a meeting held on the stage next to the temple, where Rajah had played the part of Krishna, he explained the importance of everyone's participation. Grandma was very pleased with Rajah's involvement in a Gandhian *Ahimsa* struggle like that which made the mighty British leave India about fourteen years ago. Grandma agreed with Rajah.

He told the crowd, 'Women and children, old and young, we Tamils must show our frustration at the Ceylon government's lack of understanding of our demand for equal rights. Please come in your thousands. Prepare yourselves for a long march. I implore you, don't let yourselves get disheartened in the struggle. Be strong, be steady, we will achieve victory soon.' Grandma was moved to tears.

Only a few people did not go on the *Satyagraha* – the peaceful protest. The schoolmaster and his brother Nathan were especially critical. The teacher said, 'This kind of protest only gives the people an illusion of freedom and equality. Unless they're politically aware of what's happening, it's a waste of time.'

Gowri did not agree with the schoolmaster. She thought that the *Satyagraha* would be the ultimate act to show the government what the Tamil people felt.

'Who are the Tamil people? The Tamils on the estates who work for this country's wealth have very few rights of any kind. The British brought them here and let them live like cattle, making them work for their profit. After Independence, they were made stateless. Why did these Tamil people not make any noise then?' Ramanathan asked her.

'Yes, but the Federal Party split from the former Tamil leaders because of that, didn't they?' she pointed out.

'Oh yeah, then why didn't the party campaign for the estate Tamils? Because they didn't vote for the Jaffna leaders, who get votes from you all to go to Parliament,' he erupted angrily.

She was confused about politics, but she was so scared when Tamil nationalist leaders warned that Tamils were not going to be allowed to speak Tamil, and the Tamil community was going to be wiped out of Ceylon, that she supported her father and Grandma in going on the *Satyagraha*.

Gowri went to the meeting with her former classmate and the constant letter-carrier between Saratha and Shiva, rotten-toothed Sundaram. Saratha was very glad to join the trip to Batticaloa, where Shiva worked. Rajah and his followers welcomed the group with pleasure. They declared their victory over Mailar, as his daughter Saratha had joined them; only Sundaram and girls knew her motive in going to Batticaloa. It had nothing to with freedom for Tamils but was to meet her boyfriend in town.

Like his daughter, Mailar was an opportunist. He claimed that he had never been against the Federal Party. During the election he had only helped the independent Muslim candidate because he believed in encouraging local harmony. However, Rajah referred to him as a traitor and a parasite within the community and asked the villagers to destroy such people like worms infesting their crops.

Gowri was not happy with Rajah's attitude to those who did not support him. Mailar was indeed a selfish man who wanted the old values to be upheld. But Rajah was not free of faults himself; he was ruthlessly determined to be a leader, no matter who got hurt or how dishonest his political stance was. Ragu was not against politics at all, but he could not stand the people who were at the forefront. Grandma urged him to join with the boys who were going to Batticaloa. He would not.

Grandma made tasty snacks to take to the sit-down protest in front of the government building. She bought a new saree to wear for the protest, polished her jewellery and arranged her hair elegantly. 'Grandma, are you really going to fight for the rights of Tamil people or are you going to have a jolly carnival with extravagant clothes and spicy papadoms?' the teacher teased her.

Grandma was reluctant to let the girls come. But hundreds of students from all over the province were going to be there. She wanted them at least to be separated from the boys. However, Rajah said it would be good to give everyone a chance to mix. He got onto a bus in which girls were the majority. Mailar had arranged for a second bus to transport more people. Between them the buses contained over a hundred villagers. Vasantha, Rajah's friend, led the girls. Grandma did not like Vasantha and her political alliance with Rajah. However, she wanted Gowri to draw closer to Rajah.

'Grandma, let's get on with the politics and not get it mixed up with what's personal,' Gowri wanted to tell her, when she noticed her watching Vasantha with envy.

Poor Grandma, she had dreamt of seeing Gowri and Rajah engaged, but Gowri gave no indication that she shared Grandma's dream.

Special food, new clothes, high spirits, folk songs and jollity filled the bus. People shouted slogans and sang about Tamil aspirations. It was very early in the morning when the buses left Kolavil. Most of the villagers had never ventured as far as Kalmunai town, let alone the province's chief town Batticaloa. The villagers were thrilled to see the villages and towns on their way. People knew of Batticaloa's reputation for good food, especially fresh fish, prawns and tasty crabs. On their way they saw the taverns in Kalmunai where liquor was served. Now these places could be experienced at first hand. Palipody was excited to be with so many old women and cracked jokes. Now he had a chance to show off his talent as a performer.

The distance from Kolavil to Batticaloa was about thirty

miles and usually took about three hours as the roads were bumpy and dangerous. The bumps and dips jerked and shook the small children, so that some felt sick. The bus stopped at Kalmunai, a small town which had a variety of shops and places of entertainment, with a mixed population of Muslims, Tamils and Christians. The protesters had a cup of tea and snacks, then continued their *Ahimsa* journey. They were displaying flags and banners celebrating non-violent protest.

Saratha was excited; she put her head out of the window and happily gazed in the direction of the place where her boyfriend worked. She could hardly wait to reach Batticaloa.

Gowri wished Buvana were with them. But she refused to go anywhere now, spending all her time in her vegetable garden or on the sewing machine.

Usually, as soon as the harvest finished, local people would spend their money on the wares of traders who would travel around with clothes, kitchen utensils and jewellery. Since the riots, few had come. Gowri loved seeing their goods, but now people had to travel to town for new clothes and other items. Villagers would buy two or three sets of clothes for their children. Buvana was a skilful machinist and earned enough money to live on. Uncle Kasi had declared that he had waited long enough for Ragu, and that the time had come to consider taking him to court to divide up the marital properties. No one in Kolavil had ever before taken legal action over matrimonial affairs and maintenance. The whole village had been shocked to hear what Kasi intended to do.

Mailar had bellowed with rage. 'How dare you take my son to court?' he had yelled in the street. Some people in the village thought that taking Ragu to court was a conspiracy by Rajah.

'I'll make sure that I get a brilliant lawyer from Jaffna to teach this family a lesson,' he snarled at everyone who had inquired about the case. Gowri did not know why he could not hire a lawyer from Batticaloa town.

At the time of the *Satyagraha*, Kasi and Mailar had drifted further apart because of the court case, and Ragu was keeping out of the arena of village politics. He stood and watched the bus leave. Gowri thought about him. Nowadays, he was more involved with the swami and religious matters and was reading the most important texts in the Hindu religion. Grandma had begun to realise that the marriage of Ragu and Buvana might not survive. All her hard work to bring them together, even using magic, had not worked.

Now she was turning her attention to Rajah and Gowri. She joined them in the bus. Some of the old women noticed Grandma's grand outfit and jewellery and asked her, 'Are you attending any weddings in town or are you really going to sit at the protest?' Everyone in the bus laughed. One or two inquired about Ragu and Buvana and the forthcoming court case. She did not want to talk about the problems of her family in public, but she answered, 'What has happened is God's will.'

The journey was long and tiring. Some of the children kept throwing up, as it was the first long journey on a bumpy road in their life. Gowri and other girls had to clean up; Rajah's comments on equality for all did not show itself in practice when it came to dirty vomit on the *Satyagraha* bus.

Most of the youngsters had stopped singing freedom songs

within an hour of leaving Kolavil as they felt sick. Suresh and his friends carried on with rousing songs about the glory of Tamils and their history. 'How long do we have to sing to get freedom?' one asked naïvely.

Saratha whispered something about Shiva. Her mind was fixed on marriage. She had thought, after the O-level exam, she would tell her mother about Shiva, but Ragu's court case had disturbed everything.

The bus was full of boys and girls. Halfway through the journey, the crowd really got mixed. They seemed to be enjoying one another's company very much. Some may even have been falling in love. The upsurge in Tamil nationalist activity had changed many things in Kolavil. Five years ago, nobody would have dreamed of organising a mixed trip like this. Then, the only people who would have raised their voices on any subject were old people. But now, Rajah was one of the village leaders. He could sway local opinion quicker than a bullock could flick its tail, so strong was his support among the youth.

Ceylon had gained independence thirteen years before. During this period there had been more rioting and killing than in the previous one hundred and fifty years of English rule. The country had been transformed in political, if not economic, terms.

Mr. S. W. R. D. Bandaranaike had expelled the British Navy from Trincomalee during the late fifties. However, he had been unable to take economic control from British companies completely. Most tea and rubber estates still had white owners. Indian Tamil plantation workers still worked in conditions little better than those of slaves, as they done in the eighteenth and nineteenth centuries.

Now Tamils had to sit in the hot sun to demonstrate their anger against a government which was supposed to protect them. What else would Tamil people have to undergo?

The bus stopped at the junction just before Batticaloa Town Hall, and the villagers walked towards to the building. Tamil people had come from all over Batticaloa province to participate in the protest. Students had organised a separate march. The atmosphere was emotional. Chanted slogans reached the sky, songs filled the town. Old and young, men and women marched along the route. Rajah led the students from Kolavil.

While the marchers were passing the police station, the officers outside their barracks stripped off their *lungis* to expose their genitals to Tamil children. Gowri and others had never expected this insult, and felt very angry and sickened; was this a reflection of the attitude to their protest among Sinhalese chauvinists?

'Let's run to the barracks and beat them up,' Sangar raged.

'No, our protest is based on non-violence, don't get provoked by them. Please move on quietly.'

But boys like Sangar insisted, 'We've got to show those mindless officers our anger.'

Rajah got annoyed with him and said, 'Please don't think this is Kolavil village.'

He retorted, 'Yeah, you can carry on talking about non-violence, even if they f... your woman in public.'

Rajah nearly hit Sangar, but people from other villages showed their displeasure at his language.

The marchers reached the front of the building and sat

down on the grass under a makeshift canopy. Volunteers offered the youngsters coconut water. Some leaders arrived to greet the protesters.

Gowri thought about Nathan's remark that 'the Tamil leaders aren't developing the people's political understanding but are simply stirring them up emotionally'. Was it true?

She felt that it was unreasonable to expect the Tamil people to do more than what they already were doing. 'Why does Nathan have to compare the Tamil struggle in Ceylon with struggles in other parts of the world? Does he see our future in a different way from the rest of us? We're only ordinary people, we go along with our leaders.'

The weather was hot that day, and Gowri's mind, too, was overheated. She watched Rajah. In the village she did not often see him. Now he was being ostentatiously friendly with Vasantha. Maybe he was trying to make Gowri jealous, or perhaps he was genuinely fond of her. If he were married to Gowri, would she let him keep up his friendship with Vasantha?

'I'd rather not get involved with him at all,' Gowri thought.

At lunchtime, Nathan and Shiva arrived. Nathan, as usual, came over to say 'Hello' to Gowri and Saratha, and found himself face to face with Rajah, who was boiling with anger.

'Hello, hello, is this a VIP visit?' Rajah spat on the grass as he put the question to Nathan.

'Are you speaking to me?' Nathan smiled at Rajah briskly.

Rajah smiled back at him bitterly. Meanwhile Shiva was engrossed in chatting with Saratha. They were laughing and joking together openly in front of thousands of people.

Sangar came and told Nathan about the incident at the

police station. Sangar shouted. Some of the young women from the town schools clearly disapproved of the way in which he talked.

'How can we expect justice from those people?' he continued furiously.

He was obviously not behaving like an *Ahimsa* follower. Rajah told Sangar to 'Shut up!'

Gowri was tired, and her head ached; she wished she could go home. Nathan was aware that she was uncomfortable. But he wanted Rajah to get the message that he was not scared to talk to anyone, even Gowri, though everyone knew that Rajah had his eye on her. She wished she had never come. She did not want to be the cause of two young men's conflict.

She was concerned about what Rajah might think about her and Nathan; she was already conscious of his suspicions. While she was talking to Nathan, she noted Rajah's behaviour. He looked at her sharply, as if to cut into her heart. She felt angry with him because of the way he was staring at her; on the other hand, she could not help but feel sorry for him, wasting his time on her. She could sense his anger, too. He had been waiting for her for a long time; maybe he had begun to realise that she might not agree to marry him. This would be a major shock to him. Besides his status in the village would be at risk if he were turned down.

Already, people were wondering why Gowri was not married to him. She did not feel responsible for what they thought; as far as she was concerned, she had never given Rajah the impression that she was interested in him.

Sometimes she imagined what might happen if her family tried to force her to marry him. She feared that the whole village might try to make her get married, as they had done to Ragu. 'Well,' she thought, 'I'm not going to marry Rajah. I want to be free from the village's pressure and the family's decisions.' But to her, the word 'freedom' meant upsetting many people, some of whom she loved. What was the alternative?

'What's the matter? Thinking about the future?' Nathan was in front of her, disturbing her deep thoughts as if he were trying to discover what she was thinking at that moment, but she stopped him quickly with a sharp, fixed stare.

'I don't have to tell you what I'm thinking, but, if you know me, then you know perfectly well what it is,' she told him, a smile on her face in case anyone suspected that she was annoyed. She did not want the people next to her to have the pleasure of gossiping about her.

The people from Kolavil had begun to get restless. They wanted to go and look at a train, since many had never seen one in their life.

Chapter 32

That evening they went to Batticaloa railway station. Most could hardly believe that so many wheels could move along the track at the same time. Grandma placed a finger on her nose (she was wearing a beautiful ruby nose-stud) and opened her mouth wide with surprise as a train shunted backwards and forwards. She knew that her son Kasi sometimes went to Trincomalee during the war in one of those monsters; he said it was two days' journey.

Grandma commented, 'The world's changing faster than we realised.'

'The world's changing all the time, Grandma. The only thing is, we don't always recognise the changes,' Gowri said.

It was a lovely evening, just right for a stroll. A cool breeze blew from the Batticaloa lagoon, and music came from a nearby temple. Gowri thought that she might live in a city in the future.

'Are you coming tomorrow?' Nathan asked Gowri, while Rajah was trying to persuade Grandma to step into a railway carriage for fun.

'No, I have a headache.'

'Rajah may miss you.' Nathan's tone was serious.

Gowri turned around and looked at him. She knew the gossip about Rajah and Vasantha was escalating, but Nathan was trying to tell her something else.

'I wish you'd stick to the facts,' Gowri snapped at him. 'Religious personalities have devotees to follow them, Rajah has political devotees such as Vasantha. People like that think that seeing and being with political leaders like Rajah will give them pleasure. I am not here to please or get pleasure from being with Rajah.'

He laughed at her. She did not want to continue her conversation with him while Rajah was only a few yards away.

She was quiet; what was the point of discussing anything? He moved on to talk to Saratha and Shiva.

When the villagers got onto the bus, Shiva and Nathan got in with them. This was the last thing she needed, but many things happened which were outside of her control; what could she do? When Rajah saw them aboard his eyes were like glowing coals. Gowri ignored him and tried to behave as normally as possible.

Nathan came to sit in front of Gowri and started to talk about the protest. She thought for a moment about Rajah's reaction if she continued her conversation with Nathan. But, she thought, after all, this was a common bus for everyone. She asked him what he thought about the *Satyagraha*.

He said, 'It's like a carnival. There's no fighting spirit against the oppressor, it's more like an open-air theatre show directed by the Tamil politicians.'

'Why do you have to oppose the Tamil nationalists?'

'I'm not against the fight for equal rights for Tamils; I'm only trying to express my views on the subject. Such politics is based on emotion not logic. If people can sort out political disputes with songs and slogans, why should we bother with other means? The Tamil leaders don't know the next step forward. They always thought they would hold the balance of power between two major Sinhalese parties, but now they know those parties don't need them anymore.'

'Yes, and the so-called progressive MPs such as N. M. Perera and Pieter Keuneman are going with Mrs. Bandaranaike, who is the greatest Sinhalese chauvinist in Ceylon.' Gowri repeated what she'd heard from her Dad.

'She wants to take back economic control from the former colonialists; that's why they are supporting her.'

She said, 'It's a simple fact that any family, village or country cannot achieve prosperity unless there is unity and harmony among its people. Unless Tamils and Sinhalese are united in Ceylon, how can you expect any improvement in this country?'

Her question made him give her a lovely smile. She felt too shy to meet his gaze and asked him, 'What's the smile for?'

'You're beginning to understand politics.' He sounded happy.

He got off the bus when it reached Kalmunai. By then, most of the children were sleepy. Vasantha and Rajah were drawing attention to themselves with their loud laughter and jokes. Gowri guessed their game and closed her eyes. She could only see Nathan's smiling face.

In the back of the bus, Saratha and Shiva were engaged in a solemn conversation, careless of the crowd. Grandma was fast asleep next to them.

When they arrived in Kolavil, Amuthavalli barked at them happily. Ragu and Swami Lingam came out to welcome them. The swami was not well, but he was smiling as usual under the influence of a strong ganja coffee. 'When you have your Tamil government, will I get a job?' Ragu quipped to Gowri.

'Before we Tamils win our demands, the bloody Sinhalese thugs will rape all our women.' Sangar was still angry about the event at the police station. 'Tomorrow, I'm going to take chilli powder with me to blind the fellows who insult our girls.'

'Hey, you became a militant in one day,' Ragu made fun of his brother.

'I wouldn't mind shooting anyone who insults women.' Sangar's voice was grim.

The following day, everyone was exhausted. Nobody had the energy to go the *Satyagraha* in town. Mailar was furious with Saratha for talking to Shiva in public, having heard the news of them together on the bus. Auntie Sathya wanted 'the truth, the whole truth and nothing but the truth' from her daughter: 'Were these allegations true?'

While this was going on, Sangar came home after a fierce argument with Rajah, who had refused to take Sangar with him, because he was carrying a parcel of chilli powder to attack the police. Rajah had accused him of being a militant thug who was violating the Gandhian principles of *Satyagraha*. Sangar had shouted back at him, 'Gandhi played only a tiny part in bringing freedom to India. It was people like Subhash Chandra Bose, who fought militantly against the British, who made it impossible for them to continue to rule. The Tamil struggle needs people like us to gain freedom.' Sangar had been thrown off the bus by Rajah.

'Shut up about your wretched freedom. Who cares about freedom when the family is being disgraced by this silly girl?' Auntie Sathya was angry with Saratha.

It was only then that Sangar discovered the situation. He

started to laugh at his parents, who were quite unaware of what had been going on for the past few years between Saratha and Shiva. Sangar was one of the best-informed teenagers in the village. He knew a lot of gossip about local girls and boys, especially those who were writing to one another. He told his parents about the relationship in detail, including the exchange of love letters via Sundaram.

Love letters?

Auntie Sathya wailed and screamed and nearly fainted with shock. She ran backwards and forwards, screeching like a mad woman. She hit herself to punish herself, then she pulled Saratha's hair and shrieked at her.

Mailar blamed his wife Sathya for being too stupid to realise what was happening with her own daughter. Sathya blamed her husband for taking the business of the whole village on his head and not being interested in family matters. Sangar sat down and had a good breakfast, while his parents were busy shouting.

The racket from Mailar's house woke Gowri. She had gone to bed last night with a severe headache and stayed there since. When she found out that Mailar's family knew about the love letters, she felt her stomach somersaulting with fear. When all was said and done, she had played an important part in the affair. To persuade Saratha to stay at school, Gowri had persuaded her that Shiva might love her more if she kept studying.

She could hear Auntie Sathya sobbing and Uncle Mailar bellowing. If Gowri's involvement were known, what would happen? Grandma would roast her alive on the charcoal fire.

Gowri was terrified. If Saratha revealed how the whole

business started, and who had helped her, it would mean the end for Gowri, too. She did not dare move.

There was almost a riot going on at Mailar's residence. 'How could she write love letters? I thought Saratha couldn't complete an essay on cats and dogs without your help. She wrote love letters?' Ragu asked Gowri repeatedly. She did not answer but stayed indoors, petrified to come out.

'Did you hear that, did you hear that? I told you all, girls shouldn't go to school at all. Now look what's happened. Did anyone listen to me?' Grandma joined the chorus in Mailar's household. The shouting, blaming, yelling and crying went on all day.

'Oh, come on, did she write a letter to some stranger? After all, the boy is her distant relative. He has every right to marry Saratha,' Gowri's mother pointed out rationally.

'Ah, well, these things are natural. If you can stop the sun from rising or the moon from shining, you can stop young lovers from being secretive.' The swami sipped another ganja coffee.

Early the next day, about six o'clock in the morning, Auntie Sathya arrived at Gowri's home, out of breath. She had run all the way from her house. She woke Ragu, who was sleeping near the swami in the portico. Amuthavalli started to bark nervously when she started to cry loudly.

Mum came out of her room, her baby still feeding at her breast. Dad had already left for the field, so he did not witness the drama. Grandma emerged from the kitchen and said, 'Stop crying and yelling, tell us what has happened.'

'Oh, how can I say it? It's a disgrace! Nobody in the village has ever done such a thing.' Auntie Sathya's opening statement left everyone in suspense.

'What's the matter?' Ragu asked his mother irritatedly.

'Your sister...' Auntie Sathaya was wailing as if someone had died.

'Oh, no,' thought Gowri, 'that blasted Saratha isn't dead, is she?' She felt a lump in her throat.

'She...she's not at home.'

'What?' everyone chorused in unison, as if they had rehearsed it.

'I think she's run away with him,' Auntie Sathya wept, slapping her own face and head as she wanted to do to Saratha. She looked pitifully miserable and helpless.

Within a minute the whole village was woken up and had learned the news. They had never before heard of such a thing. If a boy fell in love with a girl, he would tell her parents through his parents or relatives, both sides would talk things over, and a marriage would be arranged. If there were any problems, an intermediary would try to sort them out. It was unknown in Kolavil for a young couple to elope.

'Maybe they've gone to the protest in town,' was one suggestion.

'They may be at one of Saratha's uncles' places at Amparai or Thirukovil.'

'They may have killed themselves, like many famous lovers.'

All these suggestions made Auntie Sathya cry more. Gowri felt so sorry for her. She had to put up with so much with her husband Mailar, her son and his broken marriage and now her absconded daughter. Mailar was screaming at her and yelling at his family to try to offload all the blame onto someone else.

Gowri was angry with Saratha. That bloody Saratha had always claimed that she would do anything to be with Shiva – and now she had gone and done it.

Gowri did not dare even to poke her head out of the room or get into any conversation, just in case anyone asked her about Saratha's most recent movements. In the midst of the flurry of action was Grandma, promoting her view that girls should not be allowed to go to school.

Chapter 33

Gowri prayed to all the gods and goddesses she could think of to bring Saratha and Shiva back home safely.

She promised, 'I'll never get involved in a love affair again. Please bring them home.' She did not know what to think; she had not seen Saratha since they had returned from Batticaloa. One thing Gowri dreaded was bad news — for instance, a newspaper headline announcing 'The love story of the century from Kolavil: village lovers found dead in the Batticaloa lagoon' or something similar. She looked at the River Thillai. It seemed too shallow to drown in; the muddy water was filled only with wild bulls and flamingos.

Gowri thought about famous lovers; Romeo and Juliet in Italy, Laila and Majnu from Arabian tales, Anarkali and Salim's story during the reign of Emperor Aqbar in India, and all the star-crossed lovers in recent Tamil films who ended up committing suicide.

Whenever she heard Mailar, he was threatening to kill Saratha if he saw her. My God, Gowri thought, he is a rough man at the best of times. Now faced with humiliation, would he do something drastic? She wondered how he might set about killing Saratha. She was too pretty to die at the hands of this stupid man.

Ragu would be upset to witness the murder. How would Auntie Sathya cope? Would Sangar join in or try to prevent it? What would be Grandma's role in the murder plot? After all, she was against every love affair in the world.

'Please, holy Ganesh, help me,' Gowri prayed with such heat that she ran up a fever. She was terrified.

The swami and Dad organised a search-party to look for the lovers. Old Palipody was sent off to Pothuvil, where one of Saratha's uncles who was married to a nurse, lived. Sangar went to Amparai, where Kamala's father worked. Ragu made his way to Batticaloa to find out if Shiva's friends had any news.

That day nobody ate. It was humid. Children carried on playing silly games as usual. Gowri's little brother was busy burying a mouse which he had found dead under a rice sack. It seemed to have been killed by the lazy cat which had never seemed interested in chasing mice.

The villagers appeared to be shocked at discovering that such things could happen in Kolavil. The shop was crowded that day with those who were for and against love marriages and women's education. 'If a woman can rule the country, why shouldn't a girl choose a husband?' The young men who raised the questions were silenced by their elders, who clung to old-fashioned values.

When Poorani went to the shop, some asked her, 'When are you going to run off with your boyfriend?' When she came back, she reported this to Grandma, who stormed off to quarrel with them for talking such nonsense to a young girl.

Mum hinted to Gowri that she would not like it if she were to do something similar to what Saratha had done. Grandma openly urged her, 'Gowri, don't ever do anything like this and bring disgrace to the family. Please tell us if you're in love with someone.'

'Oh yeah?' Gowri thought sceptically. Would Grandma really help if she were in love?

'Don't ever run away,' Grandma pleaded.

'Run away with whom, Grandma?' Gowri did not ask this question aloud, in case her Grandmother came up with any unexpected answers.

The following day Palipody came back. He brought plenty of mangoes, jak and other fruits, but no news of Saratha. Ragu arrived, also with no news of Saratha, but with Nathan, who was happy that Saratha had defied Mailar.

'Please keep your mouth shut, otherwise, Grandma will kill you,' Gowri warned him quickly.

'Don't be daft, Gowri. Why shouldn't a woman choose her partner? Why should women be sold on the marriage market like objects? Getting married to someone is a lifetime's commitment. You wouldn't marry someone unless you'd be happy to spend the rest of your life with him, would you?' The question was put in a casual manner, but she could not answer. 'Gowri, falling in love with a person whom one likes is the most wonderful thing in the world. But it's sad if you can't be with that person. Very sad, indeed.' His voice was clear, his tone brisk. She got the message.

'Gowri,' Grandma called. Gowri went to her grandmother, who was struggling to chop firewood. 'What are you doing, speaking to him? Don't you know that everybody in the village is talking about Saratha. I don't want anyone gossiping about you.'

Three days later, a car drove into the village. People there did not hire cars unless they were really ill and needed to go to hospital. Sometimes a local person would be visited by someone driving in from town. Otherwise, cars just did not appear in Kolavil. The car pulled up at Mailar's gate.

People were expecting Saratha and Shiva to return together. Within a few minutes, half of the village had gathered nearby. Gowri dragged herself to the fence to see what was happening at her uncle's house. Her heart was beating faster than ever before. She wanted to faint, even die, rather than to have to watch Mailar commit murder. The swami, Mum and Dad emerged and stood next to her to witness the scene.

Mailar was sitting in an easy chair, reading the newspaper as he usually did in the morning. Auntie Sathya had been indoors, but she emerged from the kitchen with an oily face and stared, her eyes fixed on the car.

There was a sharp iron stake near the coconut tree on which shells could be scraped; it was a fearful-looking object. Gowri imagined that Mailar had erected it on that spot just to have a murder weapon.

Ragu had been in the hall. Now he came to the verandah with Nathan. Amuthavalli barked in a friendly way as soon as she caught sight of Saratha.

When Auntie Sathya saw her daughter, she screamed as though she had seen a ghost and shouted, 'I never want to see you again, I'd rather kill myself.' She dashed towards to the well to jump in, but Ragu was quick enough to catch her and stop her from doing so.

The swami moved forward towards Mailar. By then, nearly all the villagers had assembled in the lane and were peering through the holes in the fence made of coconut tree leaves. Sathya was still shrieking and gabbling incomprehensibly.

Mailar got up.

Saratha stepped out of the car. She wore a radiant smile. She walked with great elegance, leaving Shiva to follow her. She went straight to her father, knelt in front of him, touched his feet and said, 'Forgive us, Appa, we had no choice.' People could not hear clearly what she was saying.

Shiva looked at the crowd, approached his father-in-law and said, 'We went to the registry office in Amparai and got married. Please bless us.'

Auntie Sathya was still in state of shock. She cried out, 'I'm not going to look at her; she has destroyed our reputation. I'm going to die.' Again, she ran towards the well.

'What are you talking about? Are you mad? It's all finished, Saratha is a married woman now.' Ragu pulled his mother back again.

Gowri did not understand her aunt. What was all this about destroying a reputation? Everyone knew that Saratha had run away with Shiva. The fact that she had obtained a marriage certificate had now been publicly announced. Almost everyone in Kolavil had crowded into the lane; some people had even climbed trees to get a good view of the drama. What was the point of grumbling about respect and dignity?

'Who can alter fate? God made you search for your destiny, and you did.' Now the swami was talking philosophy. But would a philosophical approach to this problem work?

'Why did you have to do something like this? I wanted to arrange the grandest wedding in the district for you. Now, look what you've done!' Uncle Mailar's comments seemed somewhat out of place.

'Well, what has happened has happened. We'll have to think of the next step,' said the swami.

A few village VIPs escorted Shiva to his house. The details of the religious ceremony were talked about for days.

Gowri was confused and amazed at the talk and hypocrisy surrounding the issue. Couples were not supposed to consummate their marriage until the religious ceremony had finished: the legal side was not so important. But Saratha's wedding was exceptional. She was doing things the other way around. As the villagers put it, everything new seemed to start at Mailar's house.

The religious wedding was not bad, considering that there had only been a week's preparation. Saratha sat on a decorated wedding chair like a princess, resplendent in a gold and red silk wedding saree and jewellery. Mailar was in tears as he gave her hand to Shiva.

Gowri remembered Buvana's wedding, just two years before. Buvana's family were not present at Saratha's wedding. Rajah's family did not send a representative to the wedding, either.

During the wedding, Saratha said to Gowri, 'Thanks for your help in writing those letters – he loves them. He says he thinks I ought to be a writer as the letters were lovely.' Gowri did not reply.

Saratha settled into her new life as she has planned. She enjoyed showing off her new clothes and jewellery. The sight of her happy face made Gowri think with sorrow of Buvana.

While Saratha was enjoying married life, the villagers were still engaged in the *Satyagraha* in town. There had been many complaints about the way the protest was organised. The money raised for the rally, it was said, had not all been spent correctly, proper accounts had not been kept. Nevertheless, Rajah continued to recruit young people to take part in the protest.

Tamils were not willing to give in to government intimidation. Politicians were preparing to sell their own postage stamps in predominantly Tamil areas to divert from the real political issues of Tamil people. The young wanted action; they were no longer willing to wait. Ceylon's prime minister was abroad, but she cancelled the visits on her schedule and returned to sort out the crisis.

In the village, people were still deeply emotional about the peaceful protest. The Tamil leaders would come and give powerful speeches to encourage people to get involved. Activists such as young Suresh were creating many songs and poems for the peace rally and went everywhere singing. Vasantha came to try to persuade Gowri to take part in the student march. Grandma was very angry seeing Vasantha, as rumours about her and Rajah were now circulating openly in the village.

'Why do some women go around seducing men?' Grandma asked Mum while she was grinding chillies.

Knowing whom Grandma was attacking, Gowri inquired, 'Why are you being nasty about Vasantha?'

'Women like that ought to be shot.'

'Why?' Gowri brought her ginger to grind with the chilli; they were making lamb curry, so the spices had to be perfectly mixed.

'Why? Why, indeed? Because women who go around seducing men are no good.'

Gowri laughed at her Grandma.

'Why are you giggling?'

'Grandma, are men really so stupid that they need to be seduced?' she asked jokingly.

'Men's minds easily stray to women. It's women's responsibility to stay away from men.'

'Grandma, that girl who was raped by Sinhalese soldiers had kept herself away from them. Women are the victims of men's lust and violence. Please don't say that it's women seducing men that makes them rapists and murderers.'

Grandma retorted that Gowri was going to have a lot of trouble when she got married, if she carried on talking in that way.

'I don't think I'll ever give respect to a man who doesn't respect me,' Gowri wanted to say but did not, as she did not want Grandma to continue talking about women's subordination to men.

Chapter 34

In the evening, Palipody was telling one of the tales from the *Mahabharatha* to the children. He explained how the baddies were defeated by the goodies with the help of Krishna and how they felt sad when, to bring law and order, they had to battle with their relations who were on the baddies' side.

Grandma was mending someone's shirt, although her eyesight was not good. At times, she would ask Gowri to thread the cotton through the needle for her. Mum was bathing the boys when Gowri left for the students' rally. Grandma was close to tears. She knew that Gowri no longer accepted what she told her. Grandma's dream of turning the girl into a good wife and home-maker had been shattered, and she could not prevent herself from crying silently at her defeat.

Gowri, who was nearly seventeen years of age, spent the next few days travelling to and from town to participate in the *Satyagraha*.

Saratha was very happy being married. She was eighteen and had got what she wanted in life.

Buvana, who was nearly eighteen years old, remained at home. Uncle Kasi announced that he was about to take Ragu to court over maintenance. Mailar's household was not happy about this. They had thought Kasi was bluffing about the court case, and they suspected that Rajah was behind the move.

It was nearly two-and-a-half years since Ragu had left his

wife. Nobody now thought it likely that he would go back to her. But the news that the matter was going to court gave the villagers a shock. Some of them began to say that something should be done to bring about a reconciliation. Ragu refused to discuss the topic.

'I feel so sorry for you,' Gowri told him. It was rare for them to talk about personal matters in such way.

'Don't ever marry someone unless you love him,' he suddenly said. She wanted to cry, knowing he had married Buvana on the demand of others in the family. She was weeping also because she knew he was the only person in the family who understood her.

The moon was shining beautifully. Under the mango tree they talked. 'Rajah is madly in love with you,' he said. She thought Ragu was in a strange mood. The children were enjoying a radio programme in the hall. Grandma was cooking a vegetable curry for the swami. Dad and Mum had gone to visit a neighbour who was ill.

'Did you hear what I said?' He was waiting for her reply.

'Well, you didn't ask me a question, but you told me that Rajah is madly in love with me. What am I supposed to do if someone is in love with me?' she asked him.

Ragu looked at her kindly, the moonlight reflecting in her eyes, which welled up with tears.

'Make up your mind, and be decisive. If you want to stay in the village, it would be better to go along with the system rather than go with your feelings. But if you want to be yourself...please be careful, you might marry a stranger. You could end up like Kamala,' he said sadly.

Was he still thinking about her? She would be finishing her

nursing course soon. Then she could leave Jaffna and perhaps get a job in Batticaloa. She had been on vacation many times but had never visited Kolavil. Gowri knew the reason.

'My dear grandson, can't you hear what the village is saying? Please think it over and go back to Buvana.' Grandma came to sit next to them.

'I won't go.'

'Think about Buvana,' Grandma begged him.

'If she thought about me, she would have come with me. I'm still waiting.'

Gowri knew Buvana would never go back to him. She would follow the village tradition and stay in her parents' house.

The next day, Gowri got ready to go to Batticaloa with Vasantha and other students. It was about seven o'clock in the morning when the radio announced important news about the historic peaceful protest. The Ceylon government had declared it illegal for the protest to continue. Tamil leaders had been arrested and some placed under house arrest. What was happening?

Many hundreds of non-violent protesters had been attacked and beaten by soldiers. 'Why didn't you all hit back?' Sangar asked angrily, when he saw a man bleeding badly.

'What are you talking about? They're the army, with guns and bullets. We're peace-loving Tamils,' the bleeding man sobbed.

'Bullshit! You all want to be like Jesus Christ? If someone hits you, you should hit them back. There's no need for Tamils to act like slaves to Sinhalese chauvinism.' Sangar was furious.

The villagers were frightened. They were afraid of a repeat of the army atrocities of a few years earlier. The elders urged Rajah to go away for a while, as they were scared the army would come again in search of Tamil boys.

The schoolmaster was angry with people who encouraged the students to get involved with the *Satyagraha* without considering the government's reaction.

'Look what's happening now. The protest brought the army to the village. Who is going to suffer now? Innocent women and children and naïve students,' he said. With most of the boys in hiding, the classroom was nearly empty.

'Sir, the army is the tool the government uses to oppress us. We have to show our anger against the system,' Gowri retorted bitterly.

'Your cousin Rajah is making you talk like this, isn't he?'

'Nobody has to make me talk like this,' she snapped. She understood that he was desperate to protect his students and to teach them the politics behind the communal issue, but he failed to grasp that villagers like those in Kolavil were controlled by religion, caste, the clan system and traditional beliefs.

'If the teacher's really concerned about the villagers,' she thought, 'he should talk to people like Rajah.' She reflected on how politics affected ordinary people who were in no way powerful, yet who – according to the fundamental principle of democracy – held power.

She had read much literature that Nathan had given her, but still refused to accept his view that all struggles over nationalism were based on economics. If the Sinhalese government was out to oppress purely on an economic basis, why had it made the estate Tamil workers stateless? Those Tamil people who since the mid-nineteenth century had transformed the Ceylon jungle into profitable tea and rubber plantations and still dwelt in slums and barrack-like 'line houses' and had no civil or political rights?

She took part in peaceful protests as an ordinary Tamil girl who did not like state racialism. The teacher continued to attack Tamil leaders who arrived in foreign cars, wearing sunglasses, and told the Tamils in English that it was important to fight for Tamil rights such as the Tamil language.

Because of the protests which had lasted for months in Tamil areas, the GCE exam results came much later than usual. Gowri had been waiting to find out what possibilities were open to her, while Grandma had been indirectly nagging her parents to think about her future.

The villagers were busy involving themselves in the April New Year celebrations. People were still talking about the forthcoming Ragu-Buvana court case and also the local election, which was to be held soon. Auntie Sathya came to Gowri's house and told them that Mailar was planning to stand as a candidate.

'What's the matter with your husband? He's a power-hungry beast. Look at what's happened in his son's life. He's not worried about his own son. Because others are standing at the election, he thinks he can do that, too.' Grandma was furious with Mailar for not understanding the pain Ragu was going through.

'It's my fate to suffer with him.' Poor Auntie Sathya had not done much recently but cry and be miserable. Her unlucky son Ragu, her awful husband Mailar and her selfish and stubborn daughter Saratha, all were the reasons for her being so upset.

Some kind-hearted people were trying to do something good for Ragu and Buvana, but each attempt failed. Kasi was furious with Mailar's family for humiliating his daughter in such a way. He argued that, according to village tradition, the bridegroom should move in with the bride, and he detested Mailar for trying to change things to suit his own desires, manipulating two innocent young people, who could have been one of the nicest couples in the village.

Mailar did not give a damn what others thought. He wanted to be the chairman of the village council – and he had formed a plan. He had forced his son to marry Kasi's daughter in order to gain power within the co-operative, but this had not worked. So, now he had another idea. He thought of all his relatives, including his brother's children, as being under his control. Since Saratha's wedding, he had now and then talked about Gowri's marriage as a thoughtful uncle might do. But when the village council election nominations were about to be made, she began to understand his interest in her future.

Palipody came to her one day, wearing a broad grin.

'What's the matter?' Gowri asked him while shelling prawns.

The old man cackled in his usual way.

'Are you drunk?' she asked.

'No, I'm going to be very happy and get very drunk.' His high-pitched giggle was like that of an old woman. He was one of the one of the few people in the locality who found almost everything funny. 'Hey, little princess, when are you going to get married?'

'What?' She stopped cleaning the prawns.

'Well...girls shouldn't wait too long before getting married; otherwise, people will begin to talk about them the way they do about Vasantha.'

'What's wrong with Vasantha?'

'She flirts with boys.' He giggled.

'Why don't you talk and giggle about the boys who flirt with her?' She looked at him angrily.

'Gowri, my darling, girls should careful. They must keep their good name and virtue.'

She was really angry. Now, Palipody was preaching about womanhood and virtue.

It was then that Gowri realised that there was more to what her great-uncle was saying. Mailar was planning to make Gowri marry Rajah in order to win the support of the village for his candidacy. Mailar would then be a close relative of Rajah, whose father was also hoping to become a councillor. The villagers might then dissuade Rajah's father Nayagam from trying for the position of chairman, since they would disapprove of conflict within the family, and in any case, they would not know for whom to cast their votes.

Chapter 35

owri could hardly believe that she was in such a situation. For years, Grandma had nagged her to marry Rajah, thinking that this would be a good match and that she would become the richest wife in the village. The poor old woman's dream for her granddaughter was as genuine as that of any other grandmother. Grandma was a sincere woman who loved her kith and kin. She had old-fashioned values and practices regarding women and their duties to family and society, but had no intention of using a woman as a pawn in a political power game.

But Mailar was planning to use her to further his own ambition. Gowri really hated her uncle for his ruthlessness, selfishness and most of all his plan to trade her off in exchange for more political power. She had never liked him, because of his obnoxious manners, rude and loud mouth and the way he treated his wife and children. Now, he has trying to manipulate her life so that his own dream would come true. She stopped cleaning the prawns.

When old Palipody spoke, he had no intention to hurt her. But she was boiling with anger. However, there was nobody whom she could tell about her wicked uncle's awful plan. Mentioning Rajah to Grandma would not be wise. Gowri could not talk to Ragu; he had become completely silent as the court case approached, and the swami spent most of his time at the temple educating boys on religious matters. Dad was not a man who forced or pressured others into doing what was upsetting, but she could not openly discuss her innermost feelings with him.

Grandma was very bitter towards Gowri, saying that the whole village expected her to marry Rajah and she should agree. 'After all, you are the one he wants to marry...' Grandma was indirectly telling her that Rajah's flirtation with Vasantha was nothing. Gowri was the one he would choose.

'I don't want to get married.'

'Why not?'

'Shall I say that I won't marry Rajah because I'm not going to be happy with him, or tell her that he'll place me in his little prison with silk sarees and jewellery as a pretty show piece in his collection? And continue to use and throw away as many women as he has the power, money and good looks to do?' she wondered.

'I don't want to get married,' Gowri shouted.

'But why not?'

'I want to be a teacher.'

'How long will it take you to become a teacher? After all, we don't see many unmarried teachers in our school.'

'Become a teacher? Maybe...maybe twenty years,' Gowri lied in her anger.

'What?' Poor Grandma did not realise that this was untrue. 'Did anyone hear that? She intends to be single for twenty years,' Grandmother cried angrily.

'Grandma, please try to understand. The world has changed. I don't want to be like you, I want to do something different.' Gowri had wanted to avoid upsetting Grandma, but that was exactly what she was doing. Grandma was in tears.

307

Gowri knew that Grandma did not understand her. There were nearly sixty years between them, a conflict between the old and modern world. 'Whatever you say, Grandma, I'm not going to get married now.' Gowri was crying with her grandmother.

Ragu came in halfway through their conversation, then went into the hall without Grandma noticing him and listened to both of them.

'Why don't you tell her the truth?' Ragu asked Gowri.

'What is the truth?'

'Instead of telling her that you don't want to get married, you should explain that you don't want to marry Rajah,' he suggested bluntly.

She did not say much, indeed, she did want to say anything. She could not discuss the war going on within her mind. Only she knew what she was going through. She was no longer a thirteen-year-old girl. She was nearly seventeen, and most of the girls in the village had married already; her mother had Gowri when she was only sixteen years of age. She could not play little girls' games with Grandma, who had very little knowledge about the outside world and Gowri's ambition for the future.

The GCE exam results arrived. Ramanathan was the happiest teacher in the school, for he had spent the most time preparing his pupils to do well in the exam. Gowri had passed with excellent results. She came home very happy, though Grandma did not share her joy.

'Tell your father that you want to do A-levels and go to university,' the teacher had advised her.

'That's not what I want to do – I'd rather go to teacher

training college and become a teacher,' she had said to him.

'Why don't you go to university?' Dad asked. He was very pleased for her. He knew the battle she had been through to go to school.

Gowri went to Saratha to share the news. She was making preparations to join Shiva in town. She was looking more radiant than ever. She giggled and said that she had not had a period for two months; she thought she was pregnant. She stroked her stomach as tenderly as if the baby inside had been growing for nine months.

'I'm really glad for you,' Gowri said.

'But Dad isn't happy for me, as I'm going to Batticaloa.'

'Why is he against it?' Gowri inquired.

'He says I shouldn't go to strange places, but I think he just doesn't want me to go with Shiva.'

'What?'

'Dad says why can't Shiva come every weekend and visit me? But I want to be with my husband.'

Gowri knew how stubborn Saratha could be. She was not like Ragu, soft and confused. Saratha was not like Buvana, ever ready to listen to her parents, but firm and determined. So, Saratha was ready to battle with her father for the right to follow her husband.

Gowri had not seen Buvana for some time. The case was due to come to court soon. Gowri could not believe that Buvana and Ragu were about to discuss their relationship in a court of law in front of strangers. 'Why could Buvana not be more like Saratha?' Gowri asked herself.

Gowri reluctantly went to visit Buvana, as seeing Rajah along the way was an unpleasant prospect. He might or might not have got the message that Gowri did not want to marry him, but she had no wish to face him. She did not feel strong enough to argue with him; she just wanted to be left alone in peace to get on with her life.

When she arrived, Buvana was at the sewing machine, making a dress. She looked thin and unhappy. Her eyes were dull and sore, as if she had been crying. Auntie Indira and Poorani were in the garden. Gowri could see the new well. It had been dug very recently. 'Why had it not been done earlier? It might have prevented the court case,' Gowri thought.

When Buvana saw Gowri, she smiled briefly. It was a sad smile. 'I haven't seen you for a long time.' Buvana cleared a space near her so that Gowri could sit down.

Neither knew what to say.

'The well has been finished.' Gowri started the conversation.

It looked very smart. In the distance, by contrast, the River Thillai seemed shallow. Wild bulls wallowed in the muddy water.

'Come on, we'll go over and have a look at it.'

Gowri got up and walked towards it. The memory of Nathan walking towards Rajah's well, and of the aftermath, flashed through Gowri's mind. She sat down on the cement floor which surrounded the well. Darkness began to spread across the sky; here and there a star seemed to drop.

'It's pity your parents couldn't have built the well a bit earlier,' Gowri commended sadly. Buvana said nothing. She sat near Gowri and closed her eyes, trying to hold back her tears.

'Saratha is moving to Batticaloa.' Gowri fixed her eyes on Buvana, although the moon had not yet risen over the River Thillai to shed enough light to see her expression.

'Do you think Uncle Mailar will let her?' Buvana asked hesitantly.

'Why ever not?' Gowri asked Buvana.

'Well...'

'Well, what? Saratha loves her husband and will follow him, even if she has to go to the ends of the earth. You know Saratha, she doesn't give a damn about anyone, and she would do anything to get what she wants.'

Buvana said nothing.

'If anyone tries to stop her going to Shiva, she'll fight to her last drop of blood,' Gowri continued.

Buvana remained silent. How could Gowri persuade her that, if men stopped someone from living in dignity as a human being, it was up to her to fight to regain it? Buvana started to cry.

Gowri was quiet for a while. Then she said, 'Buvana, there's no point in crying. I don't like letting people make me cry. They can be selfish, especially men. They create rules and regulations to suit their own needs and desires and keep women under their control. Can't you see what your husband and father-in-law are doing to you?' Gowri exploded with words.

The moon started to peep between the leaves of the coconut palm. The air was cool, the smell of the night fresh and pleasant. They sat there for a long time, with few words.

Buvana looked like a temple statue in the moonlight, but Gowri did not realise that this image of her cousin would never fade from her mind. Gowri had never been able to talk to Buvana in the same way that she did with Saratha and Kamala. Buvana had always seemed difficult to communicate with.

'Why am I suffering in this way?' Buvana asked.

'I don't approve of self-pity,' Gowri said sharply.

Buvana tried the question again: 'Why is my fate like this?'

'Don't be so silly. Nobody lays fate on you. We achieve what we work for.' This was one of Gowri's mottos.

'Up to now, only the villagers have laughed at me. Now I have to go to court and be laughed at by strangers.' Buvana wept uncontrollably.

'Why do you want to go to court?' Gowri asked.

'What do you mean?' Buvana dried her eyes.

'Buvana...' Gowri began softly but firmly. She continued, 'Buvana, do you love your husband?' Buvana sobbed loudly now.

'Buvana, if you love your husband, come with me. If you do that, there won't be any court case to go to.'

Buvana stopped crying immediately at this request. 'I have my self-respect, you know,' Buvana nearly shouted to Gowri.

'I'm glad to hear it.' Gowri's tone was a shade sarcastic.

'How can you expect me to do that?'

'It's not such a big deal. It's your husband you'd be going to. He respects you.'

'Does he?' Buvana was staring at the sky.

Gowri felt deeply sorry for her and felt angry with the system which had placed her in this situation. Gowri also felt angry with Buvana's parents, who had been so stubborn and arrogant. She was furious with Mailar, who sought to

312

manipulate everything regardless of Buvana's and Ragu's agony, and also with Rajah, who had persuaded Uncle Kasi to go to court to humiliate Ragu. Why did all these people have to play games with the lives of innocent Buvana and Ragu? Was Rajah angry with Ragu for bringing Nathan closer to Gowri? Gowri was fed up with everything and everyone.

'It's all over now; my life is finished,' Buvana remarked bitterly.

'Oh, no, they won't think like that. They're going to make you happy and do lots of things.'

'Who's going to do that?'

'Your parents and friends.' Gowri did not want to spell out who these 'friends' were.

'What are they going to do to me?'

'Make you get married again to make you happy.'

'What?' Buvana screamed angrily.

'Buvana, think carefully. You're only seventeen. Do you think your parents are going to let you stay at home forever? Why should you, anyway? They'll find someone sooner or later.'

'Make me get married, again?' Buvana asked, huddling close to Gowri and holding her hand very tightly.

'What's wrong with marrying someone who can make you happy?'

'Don't be silly, Gowri.'

'I'm not being silly. You must show people that you can do better and can be happy, too.'

'I'm a Hindu Tamil woman.'

'So? You're also a human being, too, with feelings and expectations.'

'Listen, Gowri, I'm not going let it happen. I married your cousin and lived with him for two months. If that's all the gods allowed me, that's my fate. But I'm not going to get pushed into another relationship just because my parents want me to. That'll never happen,' Buvana exploded.

'Why not?'

'I'd rather die.' Buvana said those words slowly and clearly.

Gowri had a low opinion of cowards who died because they did not have the courage to face life. She stayed quiet for a while.

'What are you thinking?' Buvana asked, as she knew that Gowri hated negative talk about suicide and running away from problems.

'Well, if people finish themselves off because they can't handle the world, there wouldn't be any humans left. There's nobody in the world who's free of problems. Maybe the kind of problem varies from one person to another, but that doesn't mean that one suffers less than the other.'

'Oh yeah, you can talk philosophy. You read a lot, like your cousin Ragu,' Buvana said sarcastically.

'What else should I do? Cry about everything I see and face?' Gowri asked.

Buvana continued to weep softly for a short while. Then suddenly she asked Gowri, 'Is your cousin's friend still talking to you?'

'Do you mean Nathan?'

'Yes. Are you talking to him?'

Gowri had not been anticipating this question. 'Yes. I talk to him just as I talk to other people we know.'

'You and Saratha are determined characters.'

'Well, Buvana, we think for ourselves; we don't let others think for us or make plans for us.'

'I see...' Buvana mumbled something inaudible.

'No, Buvana, you don't see things the way we see them. It's okay for us to listen to and obey our parents. But when it comes to our own lives, it's better for us to make major decisions ourselves. Life is so short; life is beautiful. We can't let others spoil it or plan it for us. Self-respect is more important than respecting traditions that upset us.'

'In that case...I don't want anyone to plan my life.'

'Well, you're going to court on your parents' instructions.'

'Oh, no, I'm going because my husband has forced me to,' Buvana said bitterly.

'Buvana, you love your husband, and you should have gone to him.'

'I would have, if he had come and asked me.'

'I don't understand you, Buvana. You seem to be waiting for others to do things for you. You'll have to decide what's best for you.' Gowri wondered if she had spoken too strongly.

'I haven't had the chance yet.'

'You make your own chances,' Gowri said in a tone of frustration.

'When am I ever going to be happy?' Buvana wept.

'I don't know. It's up to you to decide when and where and how to be happy.'

What was the meaning of happiness? Was it the feeling some situations and people gave you, Gowri wondered, or was it a result of mind over matter? She sometimes enjoyed arguing with Grandma and was happy discussing many things with Ragu, and it was a pleasant feeling when Nathan gave her a lovely smile. She was absolutely over the moon when she passed her exam. Did happiness sometimes just mean the satisfaction of ego? Whatever it was, Gowri had no intention of searching for it. If it came her way, she would be happy; otherwise, she would get on with her life.

'You're deep in thought.' Buvana got up as her mother was calling her, still holding Gowri's hand.

'I'm not thinking that deeply, but today you talked a lot. Some of the things you mentioned made me think a bit – but I'm always getting lost in thought,' Gowri said, laughing.

'I didn't say anything that others haven't said at some time. Whatever I said has been said many times before by people thinking about love, loneliness and self-pity.' Buvana proved that she was not as dull as others reckoned.

They could hear a bicycle in the lane. Gowri feared that Rajah was approaching, but it was Sangar, who had come to look for Gowri at Grandma's behest.

'I passed my O-levels,' Gowri told Buvana as they reached the lane.

'I know. Are you going to be a teacher like Nathan?'

'Yes, a teacher like Punitha.'

Gowri followed Sangar along the lane. There was much noise coming from Rajah's house, which was full of people. Maybe preparations for the local election had begun.

'They're buying votes from poor people,' Sangar said.

'Your father could buy votes, too.'

'We don't have that much money anymore,' Sangar said sadly.

'Well, your father could sell a plot of land,' Gowri said bitterly.

Chapter 36

A few weeks later, the day of Ragu's and Buvana's court case arrived.

For several days, nobody in Gowri's household had been happy. They had never been to court in their lives. Ragu avoided talking to people, and Gowri did not want to discuss the case with anyone. Everyone seemed to be biased. Some were against Ragu, others against Buvana. How many of them knew what was going on in the minds of the two young people who had become the showpieces of the village?

Gowri grew increasingly angry with Ragu. After Gowri's conversation with Buvana, Gowri felt that Ragu should have gone to Buvana if he had really wanted to make the marriage work. But he had not done so. Why not? She did not know the answer, but she thought that he was no different from other men in the village, who did not care about or understand the pain they caused to women, while they massaged their own egos.

What was the difference between Mailar and Ragu? Mailar was old-fashioned and nasty. Ragu might be more receptive to new ideas, but he did not have the courage to challenge the system or make up his own mind. If he had been a reasonable person, he would have gone to Buvana, led her away from her house and started a new life. Why had he not done so?

Was he a coward? He could have openly declared that he was in love with Kamala and refused to marry Buvana, when his father tried to manipulate him. When he was in trouble, he had not made plans to sort out his problems.

Ragu was not like most men regarding money, power and women. But he was a weak person in not standing up against his father.

Ragu was the opposite of Rajah, who had money, power and women who would do anything for him, such as Vasantha. He was behind the misery of Ragu and Buvana. Why were some men's egos based on getting satisfaction out of controlling and constructing things to gain prominence in society, regardless of who got hurt in the process?

Ragu did not want to live with Buvana because of his lack of personal strength in standing up to challenges, although she loved him. Rajah wanted to be with Gowri because he thought he had the power, know-how and strategy to get his way even though she did not love him. He had been waiting and watching for the right moment to get his prize.

Gowri was not enough of a fool to get caught in such a trap. 'Buvana is the victim of Mailar's, Nayagam's and Rajah's power games, but I'll never give them the pleasure of having me under their control,' Gowri promised herself.

On the day of the divorce hearing, Gowri woke up to the sound of Mailar's voice next door. He was shouting at the barber, who had not come in time to give him a shave.

Until recently, barbers had visited houses to shave the rich men in the village. Nowadays, however, young barbers opened salons and expected the villagers to come to them if they wanted anything done with their hair. Mailar had made a big fuss when they opened salons. He never liked change and preferred tradition to be upheld. The *dhobies* opened laundries, too.

The barber was at Mailar's house, trimming his big moustache. 'I want to look smart,' he was demanding.

'What is he on about? He's not going to a wedding,' Gowri murmured to herself.

Ragu came to the well to wash. Gowri was nearly ready to say her prayers. The swami was already in yoga trance.

She looked at Ragu, who was about to face Buvana. Of what would they accuse each other? Would Buvana say, 'Ragu has been cruel to me?' How could they behave like strangers? Ragu was twenty-two and Buvana only seventeen, their lives barely begun. Gowri was deep in thought.

'What's the matter?' he asked his cousin.

'Men are selfish.' She was upset to think that her beloved Ragu and Buvana were going to be legally separated in a few hours' time.

'Did Buvana say I was selfish?' Ragu asked Gowri.

'Nobody had to say it. Men – most men are selfish.'

He looked at her promptly, and said, 'She would have come to me if she wanted us to be together.' He was almost talking to himself. He stared at the sky. The rising sun was making fantastically coloured patterns in the sky. He gave a big sigh and closed his eyes as if he did not want to see the reality unfolding in front of him. He looked so sad that Gowri felt sorry for him and wanted to hug him and cry with him. She also wanted to scream at him and tell him to please go to Buvana.

Although it was early in the morning, the children were already making a racket. Some were making silly noises imitating cuckoos perched on the mango trees. When a bird piped 'cuckoo', they imitated the call. This annoyed Grandma.

She came out and gave Ragu a sympathetic look. 'My darling, I'm so sorry for you.' Her voice was cracking.

'Grandma, it's better to see the end of...' He had not completed his sentence when, they heard extremely loud shrieking coming from Buvana's house.

Gowri felt shocked. Her look expressed a fear which sent Ragu running towards the house. She followed him, and people nearby who had heard the shriek hurried after them.

Auntie Indira was screaming, 'Buvana has fallen into the well!' The stone was hard in that area, so dynamite had been used to shatter the rock beneath the soil.

Ragu clambered down in a hurry. The new well had not been completely cleared yet. It was filled with rocks and stones, on which Buvana had hit her head. The water level was not high, since the well was new, and the hole had not been fully opened. The villagers gathered there within a few minutes. Everyone was talking at the same time, trying to find a reason for the accident.

Gowri remembered that Buvana had told her, 'It's better to die than live with terrible pain in your heart.' Was this really an accident?

'Someone has done a *sooniyam* (malevolent spell) on her,' Grandma was yelling, wailing.

'There is no need for anyone to be doing anything to harm this family, we have enough malevolent people among us,' Gowri wanted to tell Grandma.

Mailar arrived in his new clothes, which he had put on to go to court, and his trimmed moustache. Rajah's family were there, too. Shiva and Saratha came running. Ragu carried Buvana out of the well. She was not breathing or moving.

'Go and fetch a doctor,' Uncle Kasi was shouting.

'Please do something,' Auntie Indira was crying loudly.

Ragu had laid Buvana on her stomach to get the water out. Her head was bleeding. Someone bandaged her wound.

'Take her to hospital,' Rajah ordered authoritatively.

It was a stupid thing to say; there was no car in the village to take her to hospital. Gowri was angry with Rajah's suggestion.

'Mind your own stupid business,' Ragu yelled at him.

'Hah, he never bothered with her when she was alive.' Rajah implied cruelly that Buvana was dead.

'Shut up, you worm, and get lost!' Sangar was shouting at Rajah now.

Buvana's bleeding did not stop. By the time the doctor arrived, she appeared pale and lifeless. Auntie Indira understood the situation. She wailed hysterically, and other women joined her; it was chaos.

Gowri could hear Buvana's words. 'I don't want anyone to touch me anymore. I loved Ragu and lived with him for a short period and had a baby with him, but I lost both of them. Those are enough memories until I die.'

Ragu held her body in his arms for a long time. He was crying. Not only the women but also almost all the men there wept, too. Ragu and Buvana would no longer face strangers to discuss their personal lives in a divorce case. Uncle Kasi cried like a child to watch his elder daughter die. The daughter, who could not leave the house without his permission, was no longer there.

By this time, the sun had fully risen, and all the villagers were there. With them, they had brought the whole system of tradition, the beliefs and practices for which Buvana had died. Now, they would blame each other for what had happened.

'Am I part of the reason for her death?' Gowri asked herself. 'Rajah wouldn't have insulted Nathan if he hadn't thought that Nathan was attracted to me, would he?'

It was too late for blame; it would be pointless. Buvana was dead and gone. Ragu's tears covered Buvana's face. He wept, and the whole village witnessed his pain, which no-one had understood up to now.

That evening, Nathan came to comfort his friend. But words could not easily heal the pain. Society, Gowri felt, was responsible for Buvana's death. The old ideas, values and beliefs had taken the lives of many women, and Buvana was one of them. Who could rage against this injustice?

The very people who had brought about her death carried her body to the cemetery. They cried and talked about her sudden death. No-one had anticipated this. They had thought that, after the court case, Mailar would shout and scream, and Kasi would have the support of the village. Nobody thought about Buvana, who was only seventeen years old, having to go through this horrendous and humiliating experience.

Auntie Indira was nearly mad with grief and loss. She was in shock and would not eat or talk to anyone. She cried most of the time and slept very little. Grandma was still lamenting about witchcraft and black magic and telling people that an 'evil power' had snatched her granddaughter from the world.

The first eight days of mourning were completed and all the rituals observed. Most villagers blamed Mailar for his selfishness in forcing two people together who were not ready to take on the responsibility of married life, ending in tragedy. Some mothers asked their daughters if they were in love. Nobody wanted anyone else to die because of their parents' arrogance and expectations. Those in Gowri's house dared not open their mouths to her about marriage.

Ragu seemed almost to have lost the power of speech. Normally he spoke little, but now he hardly said anything. The only person to whom he would say a few words was Nathan, who came to the village regularly to see him. After the thirty-first day after the funeral ceremony, Gowri got up early to pray, and she saw Ragu was having a wash.

'Don't sacrifice your life for anyone, not even for your husband,' he said to her. She could feel his distress. 'Gowri, the world is cruel. You have to be careful, otherwise, it will destroy you in no time. People who are greedy, selfish and powerful control the world nowadays. Be cautious around them. Don't let yourself be a victim of the system.'

She listened to him silently. The morning sun was rising, the River Thillai glittering in its rays. The river seemed to be watching the village and its chaos and changes.

He returned to the house, a towel on his shoulder. Gowri never saw him again. He left the village that morning. She was the last person with whom he talked.

It was rumoured that, after a period of time, he became a swami and went to India.

Chapter 37

1962

The years went by. After striving for three years, Gowri was accepted at a teacher training college. She was very pleased, indeed. Grandma was not.

Rajah had married someone from another village. Since Gowri refused him, he then announced that he would marry someone many times better than her. He found a rich wife, whom he brought home with him; contrary to village tradition, he did not move into the bride's house.

Within a week, that girl had gone back to her parent's home in tears. Nobody knew exactly what had happened, but some said that he had been cursed because of his role in destroying Ragu's marriage. However, others knew that his affair with Vasantha was still going on and said that was the reason for his short-lived marriage.

Poorani had grown into one of the most beautiful women in the village. She would sing and dance in school art events. Sangar was nineteen and had written a love letter to her. He had been caught by Mailar and beaten badly. Sangar had threatened to commit suicide unless he was allowed to marry Poorani, and Mailar could not say a word against him after that.

Saratha left the village to move to Batticaloa town with her husband, where she went to the cinema as often as she could and went around singing songs from the films to her children rather than singing traditional folk songs.

Grandma was nearly eighty years old and had been weakened by successive illnesses. Her eyesight as well as her memory had deteriorated, and she could not see anything clearly. She often got confused. She would say that the dog Amuthavalli was smiling at her, and the lazy cat was trying to steal her gold necklace.

She had seen many traditional doctors, who had no success in treating her eyes. So Gowri took her to Batticaloa Hospital. On the way to the eye department, they saw Kamala, who was working there as a nurse. She invited them to her living quarters, as Grandma wanted to use the toilet.

When they reached Kamala's quarters, Nathan was there. The love affair between Nathan and Kamala had been openly known in the village. 'They may get married soon,' Gowri had been told by Saratha.

Seeing Nathan, Gowri felt a sharp pain in her heart. Their eyes met and locked for a few seconds. Both were shocked to meet in this way, and she tried very hard to hold back her tears.

Kamala said she would make some tea and went into the kitchen, and Grandma went to the toilet. Gowri and Nathan were alone.

She picked up a paper to read. He started to speak. She said, 'Ssh, there is no need to say anything.'

They looked at each other with no one else around; both wanted to hold onto that moment, and each other's images, eternally in their hearts.

He had not changed during the last three years. He was

very handsome, indeed. She could not prevent the tears falling. She bent down to read the paper and wiped her tears away.

'It's not my fault...' He mumbled something else as well in a soft voice.

She 'shushed' him again to stop him talking further. He obeyed but looked at her for a long time. She did not want that to stop. At the same time, she liked Kamala whole-heartedly and did not want her to have any suspicions about her future husband.

Kamala brought tea and biscuits, while Grandma returned from the toilet. They talked about village matters in general. Gowri was careful not to mention Ragu to Kamala. They finished drinking tea, and Gowri took Grandma to the eye clinic.

It had been three years since she last saw Nathan. The last time they had met, she had told him that she did not want to see him again. It was a lie, and she knew it. What else could she do? She could not have achieved what she wanted if she had revealed her true feelings.

She remembered the day she had first met him. It had been at the celebration of Saratha's puberty. Gowri had been only thirteen then. He had been friendly, witty, handsome, politically aware and a stranger in her life, the brother of the schoolmaster and a friend of Ragu.

When Ragu left the village, Nathan had offered much-needed support and comfort to Auntie Sathya. He visited Kolavil more often than ever before; since his training had finished, he had plenty of spare time. He had helped to fill the gap left by Ragu. He had brought many books and had talked to Gowri about politics, cinema and literature. She had known that Grandma well as others in the family, were watching her. She had tried hard to be a 'good girl'.

When Buvana died, the schoolmaster had been angry with the villagers for upholding the old-fashioned values that had made her a victim. 'Tamils are never going to think scientifically as long they're imprisoned by their stupid old values and customs which keep the vulnerable under control,' he said.

Gowri replied, 'There are many things in any culture which offer guidelines for social interaction and tolerance of diversity and new thinking; otherwise, humankind couldn't have changed for the better to the extent that it has. But in a society like Kolavil, innocent people are manipulated by those with more power.'

Her teacher was amazed to hear Gowri talking like a grown woman. In those days, she spent most of her time at his house since the people nearest and dearest to her – Ragu, Saratha and Buvana – were no longer there. Without the people she loved, the loneliness was hard to bear.

So, she came to the teacher's house to learn more styles in knitting and dressmaking from his wife Parmes. Those visits inevitably gave her the opportunity to meet Nathan more frequently. As usual, he brought her interesting books. Some were foreign novels in translation. She also learned through Parames, the teacher's wife, that Nathan had published a few poems in national papers.

'Is he going to make you a writer, too, Gowri?' she joked.

'Oh no,' Gowri smiled. 'He wanted me to understand the meaning of culture, tradition, language and religion to understand where oppression began. By reading, I could question poverty, caste, and women's oppression and think about various other issues.' In those books she identified many characters who oppressed other people for their own benefit, like certain people in her village such as Nayagam and her Uncle Mailar.

'When you start fighting oppression, you have to be honest and determined,' the teacher Ramanathan advised his favourite student.

Nathan was kind and understanding when she cried about Buvana. Gowri no longer blamed him for starting the split between the couple by going to wash his dirty feet in Rajah's well. Nathan was a stranger who could not have been expected completely to understand the mind of the village, where Rajah had set his mind to making Gowri his property and would not tolerate even a tiny glance from an outsider like Nathan.

In her innocence, she continued to blame herself for annoying Rajah by talking to Nathan. She would cry alone about the destruction of Ragu's and Buvana's lives. She could not talk to anyone in her family about this. A firm bond between her and Nathan formed, through exchanging books and talking about many subjects.

'Gowri, when you want to assist others who need your help and advice, please don't think that you have an answer for everything. Life is a vast university; our experiences give us more knowledge so we can better understand the world.' He told her that frequently when she questioned why Buvana had to kill herself. It was a question he couldn't answer, but he believed that experience might give her clearer insight.

'I wish I could understand your pain, but I want you to understand what goes on inside in your own mind. Please don't assume you understand yourself because others tell you who or what you are. It takes us all a long time to know what we want out of life and how to get it. Until then, don't mess up your life by thinking too much about complex issues.'

Nathan seemed wonderful. She admired his thoughts and beliefs and, most of all, his genuine love for her.

He had left with his brother, who had transferred to an estate school. The teacher had always wanted to go back to teach the children and help send one or two to university. He was sad to leave Kolavil, which had given him so much heartache with its old traditions and practices, but also so much pleasure in working for improvements with Gowri's father Nadesan, Uncle Kasi and Ragu, especially creating a library. Ramanathan had earned great respect from everyone for an especially important development – he had made ongoing education for women possible in Kolavil. With his hard work and Gowri's determination, there were now many girls seeking to study even further than Gowri, with plans to go to university.

As the teacher was moving away from Kolavil, and Nathan had obtained a teaching post in Trincomalee, he had no reason to visit any more. Nadesan invited them for a farewell meal in their house. At the time, Gowri's refusal to marry Rajah was not yet openly discussed in the village.

At dinner they talked about many things, including Buvana's death. The teacher hinted that Gowri should not be forced to get married. 'No, I'll never do that – if she wants to do something different, I'll support her,' Gowri's father had promised him.

Gowri was helping Grandma in the kitchen; they both heard what Dad was saying. Grandma did not look at her.

After the meal, the men had chatted over a bottle of fine liquor which Palipody had brought. Gowri took her little brother to the swing to tell him a story before he went to sleep. The full moon was shining brilliantly and a cool breeze blended with the fragrance of jasmine to give an incredibly sweet smell.

'I brought you some books.' She turned. Nathan had been standing near her under the big jak tree. Although the entire family could see them, they could not be heard as the radio was playing film songs at full volume, and the children were playing hide and seek behind the pineapple bushes, mango and orange trees.

'Thank you.' She had taken the books.

'Will you miss me?' he asked her.

What a stupid question, Gowri thought. Would anyone ask the sky whether it was going to miss the clouds? Could anyone ask the stars whether they were going to miss the moon? Could anyone ask the trees whether they were going to miss the touch of the breeze? Could anyone ask dog Amuthavalli to stop barking? She did not answer him.

'Gowri, there is a letter inside the book.'

'What?' She had not expected that.

'Please read the letter.'

She had not known what to say. For the last few months, they had become close. They had no other friends in the village. They spent much time together, indirectly helping each other to grieve for Buvana and talking about Ragu and

330

Saratha, who were no longer there.

The teacher was talking about prime minister Srimavo Banadaranaike's pact with the Indian prime minister Shastri concerning the 'Indian' plantation Tamils. Some would lose any chance of citizenship and be sent to India, the teacher was saying. Gowri's father was criticising the privileging of Sinhala in schools, the government's plan to dismiss Tamil workers who did not pass a Sinhala language exam and the colonisation of the Gal Oya and Trincomalee area by Sinhalese people. 'Tamils are going to have a hell of a time in Ceylon,' Dad was saying.

'What you thinking?' Nathan inquired after waiting for her reply.

'I'm listening to the political discussion,' she answered.

'There'll be a hard time for all of us,' he remarked.

'I know,' she said with double meaning.

'Will you answer my letter?' he asked softly, his words touching her like the cool night breeze.

She just looked at him. Her brother got out of her lap and ran to join the other children. They were making a lot of noise behind the trees.

'Gowri.'

'Mm?'

'Gowri...Gowri, I love you.'

She did not reply.

'Gowri.'

'Please, please,' she was crying.

'Gowri, you have to be honest with yourself. You know perfectly what I'm talking about. I love you, Gowri.'

'Please don't.'

'Why not?'

'It's not worth it.'

'What isn't?'

'Loving me.'

'Why not? Explain to me, Gowri, please.'

'I-I-I don't want to give trouble to anyone.' She was trembling with emotion. She always knew that one day he was going to be open about his feelings towards to her. Hearing his declaration of love frightened her.

'Gowri, you're not going to give trouble to anyone. Please.'

'I-I'm not prepared to love...anyone.'

'What?' His voice sounded as shaky as she felt. It was if they were both on fire.

'I'm so scared of that word.'

'Gowri, I know you're too young to understand a lot of things, including love.'

'I'm not that young, I'm nearly seventeen years old.'

'Okay, old lady, please read my letter,' he said, half-joking. There was silence from Gowri.

She looked at him for a few seconds, tears falling down her cheek. She had returned his letter back to him and said, 'No, thank you.'

'Gowri.' He was begging.

'Please don't see me again.' She ran away crying.

She thought that maybe he would wait a year or two, but in the following years she had not changed her mind. However, Gowri now realised that her separation from Nathan was the most painful thing she had ever experienced. She had not previously realised how special their relationship had been.

She was brought back to the present when Grandma told her that they could go home now. She had finished with the eye doctor. They both walked to the bus stop. There was Nathan, waiting in front of the hospital. Grandma laughed suddenly.

'Why are you laughing?' Gowri asked her Grandma. The old woman looked at him and Gowri and carried on laughing. Gowri did not know what had amused the old woman.

'I'm on my way to the bus stop, too,' he said to Gowri, indicating that he wanted to talk to her.

'I'm not going to Saratha's.' Gowri knew that he was staying there.

'I know. We're going in opposite directions.'

She looked directly into his eyes, as if she wanted to see into his heart to know what he meant. They walked silently.

Grandma continued to giggle. These days she got so muddled that sometimes it was not easy to understand what she was saying.

Batticaloa town centre was crowded with people, full of hustle and bustle. It was a pleasant evening. Grandma loved walking, as did Gowri. But she was not walking alone. Her mind was filled with recollections of the past.

He walked alongside, like a shadow. Both knew that they had much to say but few words. Maybe he wanted to ask why she had refused his love. If he asked that question, she would have been unable to answer. She did not want to reply because she might lie, which could hurt him. He and the memories of him were the most precious things she held in her mind.

'How is the village?'

'Same as ever,' she said. He smiled, she too.

During the past three years, there had been changes. When Rajah's wife left him after two weeks of marriage, the villagers mocked Rajah as a two weeks' groom, just like Rajah had taunted Ragu as a two months' groom.

Sadly, Rajah's wife had died of snakebite after a few months of separation. People in the village said, 'That's the curse of Ragu.' However, Gowri knew that her cousin would never curse anyone. Rajah was still friendly with Vasantha. Sangar's and Poorani's love affair was well-known in the village. The swami was building a wedding hall near the temple.

They reached the stop. The bus had not arrived. Grandma sat down on a bench to wait for the bus. Suddenly she laughed loudly and said, 'Gowri, you and Kamala poured yellow water on Nathan at Saratha's celebration.'

Gowri looked at Nathan, recalling the incident. That had been his first day in the village, when Kamala and Gowri poured perfumed turmeric water onto the stranger who had just walked into their village and their lives. Did he know the traditional belief that if a young woman poured yellow water on a young man during her puberty ceremony, it meant that she wanted tell the world that she loved him and they would end up marrying each other?

She did not explain to him the background of Grandma's statement about the past, and they both felt uncomfortable in the silence. The lagoon was filled with silver, the reflection of the sun.

'Gowri,' he called to her softly. She turned to him. Nothing in the world could stop her crying in front of him; she forgot that they were at a public bus stop under the gaze of Grandma.

'I'm so sorry if I'm the reason for your crying,' he said.

She turned her face again to the lagoon, as she did not want Grandma to see her crying in front of Nathan. 'You were always the reason for my happiness,' she said, coming closer to him.

'What?' He was confused.

She did not want to repeat it.

'Gowri, will you tell me why you…?'

She interrupted him. 'Please stop asking me these questions. I have nothing to tell you.'

How could she explain to him that the villagers would never have allowed her to marry a stranger while she was being connected in their conversations with a powerful person like Rajah? If she had gone against the whole village and left with Nathan, what would people have said about her? They'd say, all her life she claimed that she wanted to be a teacher and educate the children in the village, and then she goes off with an outsider?

She loved and respected her village more than almost anything else. She respected Nathan, too, and adored him ever more. But she knew that she could not have been happy in her personal life if she had married Nathan rather than Rajah; he would have taken revenge on them in various ways and made them unhappy. She had loved Nathan deeply and wanted him to be happy.

'Kamala is very nice,' she said.

'I know.'

'She'll make you very happy.'

Grandma got up as the bus pulled up.

'I wish you all the happiness in the world, Gowri,' he said.

She got into the bus and looked at him through the window. She could not see him clearly as her eyes were welling up with tears.

He said, 'Goodbye, Gowri.'

The bus moved off. One day, before she died, she wanted to tell him what she had felt for him and why she could not marry him when he asked her to read his love letter, under the moonlight near the jak tree, when she was just seventeen.

THE END